THE
HIGHEST
TIDE

a novel

JIM LYNCH

BLOOMSBURY

First published in Great Britain 2005

Excerpts from *The Edge of the Sea* by Rachel Carson. Copyright © 1955 by Rachel L. Carson, renewed 1983 by Roger Christie. Reprinted by permission of Houghton Mifflin Company. All rights reserved

Bloomsbury Publishing Plc, 36 Soho Square, London W1D 3QY

A CIP catalogue record for this book is available from the British Library

ISBN 0 7475 7844 3
9780747578444

10 9 8 7 6 5 4 3 2 1

Typeset by Hewer Text UK Ltd, Edinburgh

Printed in the United States of America by Quebecor World Fairfield

All papers used by Bloomsbury Publishing are natural, recyclable products made from wood grown in well-managed forests. The manufacturing processes conform to the environmental regulations of the country of origin

www.bloomsbury.com/jimlynch

For Denise

CHAPTER 1

I LEARNED EARLY ON that if you tell people what you see at low tide they'll think you're exaggerating or lying when you're actually just explaining strange and wonderful things as clearly as you can. Most of the time I understated what I saw because I couldn't find words powerful enough, but that's the nature of marine life and the inland bays I grew up on. You'd have to be a scientist, a poet and a comedian to hope to describe it all accurately, and even then you'd often fall short. The truth is I sometimes lied about where or when I saw things, but take that little misdirection away and I saw everything I said I saw and more.

Most people realize the sea covers two thirds of the planet, but few take the time to understand even a gallon of it. Watch what happens when you try to explain something as basic as the tides, that the suction of the moon and the sun creates a bulge across the ocean that turns into a slow and sneaky yet massive wave that covers our salty beaches twice a day. People look at you as if you're making it up as you go. Plus, tides aren't *news*. They don't crash like floods or exit like rivers. They operate beyond the fringe of most attention spans. Anyone can tell you where the sun is, but ask where the tides are, and only fishermen, oystermen and deep-keeled sailors will know without looking. I grew up hearing seemingly intelligent grown-ups say "what a beautiful lake," no matter how many times we politely educated them it was a *bay*, a briny backwater connected to the world's largest ocean. We'd point to charts that showed the Strait of Juan de Fuca inhaling the Pacific all the way down to our shallow, muddy bays at the southern end of Puget Sound. It still wouldn't stick. It was the same way with beach scavengers. There was no way to make them understand they were tromping across the roofs of clam condos. Most people don't want to invest a moment contemplating something like that unless they happen to stroll low tide alone at night with a flashlight and watch life bubble, skitter and spit in the shallows. Then they'll have a hard time not thinking about the beginnings of life itself and of an earth without pavement, plastic or Man.

People usually take decades to sort out their view of the universe, if they bother to sort at all. I did my sorting during one freakish summer in which I was ambushed by science, fame and suggestions of the divine. You may recall hearing pieces of it, or seeing that photo of me looking like some bloodshot orphan on the mudflats. Maybe you remember the ridiculous headline *USA Today* pinned on me after that crazy cult took an interest: KID MESSIAH? You could have seen the same article recycled in the London *Times* or the *Bangkok Post*. Then again, you might have been among the hundreds of rubber-neckers who traveled to our bay to see things for yourself.

Part of the fuss had to be my appearance. I was a pink-skinned, four-foot-eight, seventy-eight-pound soprano. I came off as an innocent nine-year-old even though I was an increasingly horny, speed-reading thirteen-year-old insomniac. Blame Rachel Carson for the insomnia. She was long dead by the time I arrived but I couldn't resist reading her books over and over. I even read *The Sea Around Us* aloud to make it stick.

"There is no drop of water in the ocean, not even in the deepest parts of the abyss, that does not know and respond to the mysterious forces that create the tide."

How do you read that sentence, yawn and turn out the lights?

My family lived in a tiny, metal-roofed house on the soggy, fog-draped bottom of the Sound where the Pacific Ocean came to relax. Farther north, glassy dream homes loomed on rocky bluffs above the splash, but once you reached Olympia's bays the rocks crumbled to gravel, the beige bluffs flattened to green fields and the shoreside mansions turned into remodeled summer cabins.

The front half of our house stood on stout pilings that got soaked during the few extreme tides each year. Behind the house was a detached garage, over which I lived in a makeshift storage room with a closet toilet like you'd find in a sailboat. The best thing about my room was that its low, slanted ceilings kept the adults away, and its back stairway allowed me to step unnoticed into nights like the one that set the summer of my life into motion.

I loaded up my kayak with a short shovel, a backpack and Ziploc sacks and paddled north out of Skookumchuck Bay around Penrose Point into Chatham Cove, a shallow, cedar-ringed half-circle of gravelly flats that sprawled before me like an enormous glistening disc. It was two-fifteen A.M., an hour before the lowest night tide of the summer with an albino moon so close and bright it seemed to give off heat. There was no wind, no voices, nothing but the occasional whir of wings, the squirts of clams and the faint hiss of retreating water draining through gravel. Mostly there were odors—the fishy composting reek of living, dead and dying kelp, sea lettuce, clams, crabs, sand dollars and starfish.

It was my first summer collecting marine specimens for money. I sold stars, snails, hermit crabs, and other tidal creatures to public aquariums. I also sold clams to an Olympia restaurant and assorted sea life to a private aquarium dealer who made my throat tighten every time he pulled up in his baby-blue El Camino. Almost everything had a market, I was discovering, and collecting under a bright moon was when I often made my best haul, which worsened my insomnia and complicated my stories because I wasn't allowed on the flats after dusk. The other part of it was that you see *less* and *more* at night. You also see things that turn out not to be real.

I walked the glimmering edge, headlamp bouncing, picking my way to avoid crushing sand dollars and clam shells facing the sky like tiny satellite dishes. I saw a purple ochre sea star, then fifteen more strewn higher on the beach, their five legs similarly cocked, pinwheeling in slow motion back toward the water. None of them were striking or unusual enough to sell to the aquariums. They wanted head-turners and exotics. Like anything else, people wanted to see beauties or freaks.

As I crossed the line where gravel yielded to sand and mud, I saw a massive moon snail, the great clam-killer himself, his undersized shell riding high on his body like the cab of a bulldozer, below which his mound of oozing flesh prowled the flats for any clam unlucky enough to be hiding in its path. Moon snails were often hard to find because they burrow deeply, feeding on clams, their tiny jagged tongues drilling peepholes right above the hinge that holds clams together. Then they inject a muscle relaxant that liquefies the clam to the point where it can be sucked out through the hole like a milkshake, which explains the sudden troves of empty shells with perfectly round holes in the exact same spot, as if someone had tried to string a necklace underground, or as if you'd stumbled onto a crime scene in which an entire clam family had been executed gangland style.

A feisty entourage of purple shore crabs scurried alongside the snail, their oversized pinchers drawn like Uzis. I thought about grabbing the moon snail, but I knew that even after it squeezed inside its shell like some contortionist stunt, it would still hog too much room in my pack. So I noted where it was and moved on until I saw the blue flash. It wasn't truly flashing, but with moonlight bouncing off it that was the effect. I steadied my headlamp and closed in on a starfish that radiated blue, as if it had just been pulled from a kiln. But it wasn't just the color that jarred me. Its two lower legs clung strangely together in line with its top leg and perpendicular to its two side legs, making it stand out in the black mud like a blue crucifix.

Mottled sea stars were common, but I'd examined thousands of stars and had never seen this same color or pose. I picked it up. Its underside was as pale as a black man's palm, and its two bottom legs appeared fused. I wondered how it moved well enough to hunt, but it looked healthy, its hundreds of tiny suction-cup feet apparently fully operable. I stuck it in a sack with some water and slipped it into my backpack. I then waded up to my calves toward the mid-sized oyster farm belonging to Judge Stegner.

That was my alibi if I was caught out there, that I was tending the judge's oysters. He paid me twenty dollars a month to help maintain them, though not at night, of course. Still, it was nice to have an answer if someone asked what I was doing out there at that hour. I had the words *Judge Stegner* on my side, and I knew how everyone felt about him. My father tucked his shirt in whenever he came around. And when the judge spoke in his deep, easy rumble, nobody interrupted.

Near the oyster farm something happened that never failed to spook me in the dark. I saw a few dozen shore crabs scrambling near the rectangular, foot-high mesh fence around the judge's oyster beds. Crabs amused me in small crowds. It's when they clustered at night that they unhinged me, especially when they were in water where they moved twice as fast as on land. It was obvious there were more crabs—and bigger crabs—than usual, so I tried not to expand my range of vision too fast. It was no use. I saw hundreds, maybe thousands, assembling like tank battalions. I stepped back and felt their shells crunch beneath my feet and the wind pop out of me. Once I steadied, I flashed my headlamp on the oyster fence that three red rock crabs were aggressively scaling. It looked like a jail break with the biggest ringleaders leading the escape. I suddenly heard their clicking pinchers clasping holds in the fence, jimmying their armored bodies higher. How had I missed that sound? The judge's oysters were under siege, but I couldn't bring myself to interfere. It felt like none of my business.

I picked my steps, knowing if I slipped and tumbled I'd feel them skittering around me as cool water filled my boots. I rounded the oyster beds, to the far side, relieved to find it relatively crab free. It was low tide by then, and I saw the water hesitating at its apex, neither leaving nor returning, patiently waiting for the gravitational gears to shift. Dozens of anxious clams started squirting in unison like they did whenever vibrating grains of sand warned them predators were approaching. I stopped and waited with them, to actually see the moment when the tide started returning with its invisible buffet of plankton for the clams, oysters, mussels and other filter feeders. It was right then, ankle deep in the Sound, feet numbing, eyes relaxed, that I saw the nudibranch.

In all my time on the flats I'd never seen one before. I'd read about them, sure. I'd handled them at aquariums but never in the wild, and I'd never even seen a photo of one this stunning.

It was just three inches long but with dozens of fluorescent, orange-tipped hornlike plumes jutting from the back of its see-through body that appeared to be lit from within.

Nudibranchs are often called the butterflies of the sea, but even that understates their dazzle. Almost everything else in the northern Pacific is dressed to blend with pale surroundings. Nudibranchs don't bother, in part because they taste so lousy they don't need camouflage to survive. But also, I decided right then, because their beauty is so startling it earns them a free pass, the same way everyday life brakes for peacocks, parade floats and supermodels.

I bagged that sea slug—it weighed nothing—and set it in my backpack next to the Jesus star. Then I gave the crabs a wide berth, found the moon snail, poked him in the belly until he contracted, bagged him and paddled south toward home beneath the almost-full moon.

And that's where it happened.

The dark mudflats loomed like wet, flattened dunes stretching deep into Skookumchuck Bay in front of our house. From a distance, they looked too barren to support sea life. Up close, they still did, unless you knew where to find the hearty clams, worms and tiny creatures that flourish in mud so fine that at least two Evergreen State College grads get stuck every June during their naked graduation prance across the bay's shallowest neck. I'm not sure why I decided to take a look. It was still an hour before sunrise, and I knew exactly what the bars looked like in the moonlight, but for some reason, I couldn't resist.

I heard it long before I saw it. It was an exhale, a release of sorts, and I instantly wondered if a whale was stranded again. We had a young minke stuck out there two summers prior, and it made similar noises until the tide rose high enough for rescuers to help free it. You would have thought the whole city had a baby, the pride people showed in guiding that little whale to deeper water. I looked for a hulking silhouette but couldn't find one. I waited, but there were no more sounds. Still, I went toward what I thought I'd heard, avoiding stepping into the mud until I had to. I knew the flats well enough to know I could get stuck just about anywhere. The general rule was you didn't venture out past the shells and gravel with an incoming tide. I sank up to my knees twice, and numbing water filled my boots.

South Sound is the warm end of the fjord because most of its bays are no deeper than forty feet and Skookumchuck is shallower still, but even in August the water rarely climbs much above fifty-five degrees and it can still take your breath. I kept stepping toward the one sound I'd heard, a growing part of me hoping I'd find nothing at all.

When I stopped to rest and yank up my socks, my headlamp crossed it. My first thought? A giant octopus.

Puget Sound has some of the biggest octopi in the world. They often balloon to a hundred pounds. Even the great Jacques Cousteau himself came to study them. But when I saw the long tubular shape of its upper body and the tangle of tentacles below it, I knew it was more than an octopus. I came closer, within fifty feet, close enough to see its large cylindrical siphon quiver. I couldn't tell if it was making any sounds at that point because it was impossible to hear anything over the blood in my ears. My mother once told me that she had an oversized heart. I took her literally and assumed I was similarly designed because there were moments when mine sounded way too loud for a boy my size.

The creature's body came to a triangular point above narrow fins that lay flat on the mud like wings, but it was hard to be sure exactly where it all began or ended, or how long its tentacles truly were because I was afraid to pry my eyes off its jumble of arms for more than half a second. I didn't know whether I was within reach, and its arms were as big around as my ankle and lined with suckers the size of half dollars. If they even twitched I would have run. So, I was looking at it and not looking at it while my heart spangled my vision. I saw fragments, pieces, and tried to fuse them in my mind but couldn't be certain of the whole. I knew what it had to be, but I wouldn't allow myself to even think the two words. Then I gradually realized the dark shiny disc in the middle of the rubbery mass was too perfectly round to be mud or a reflection.

It was too late to smother my scream. Its eye was the size of a hubcap.

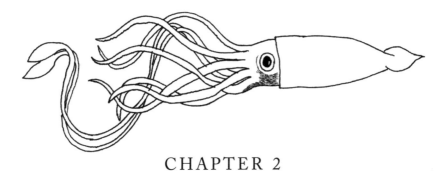

CHAPTER 2

O NCE PROFESSOR KRAMER'S home answering machine clicked on, I couldn't control my voice, and my mother shuffled out in a long MARINERS shirt, a finger on her lips, as if the most important thing at that moment was not waking my father. I fended her off with one hand and ignored her teeth-clenched cussing after she spotted the growing puddle beneath me on the kitchen floor. She stormed into the laundry room just as I finished my frantic message and the professor himself picked up for real. I told him the same stuff, only louder, then heard myself yell, "It's a giant squid!"

Not *I think it is a giant squid*, or *It might be a giant squid*. I stated it as fact in the cool dawn and my mother suspended her furious mopping to squint at me through puffy, nearsighted eyes as if her son were speaking in tongues.

I'd read enough about giant squid to know the most remarkable thing about this one wasn't its size, but its location. They didn't show up just anywhere, especially not in shallow, dead-end inlets within a few hundred yards of a tavern and a couple miles from a bowling alley, a golf course and a state capitol dome. Not *rarely*. Never. Most giant squid were found, if they were found at all, in the bellies of sperm whales or sprawled on the beaches of New Zealand, Norway and Newfoundland.

Another thing about them: They were always dead. That is unless you bought those old seafaring tales of two-hundred-foot squid attacking ships and wrestling whales. I knew most people preferred myths to science, especially when it came to sea monsters. It helped justify their fear of open water. I never wanted any part of that nonsense. Upon coming eyeball to eyeball with that animal on the flats, my impulse was to run from it, but my goal, before I'd reached shore, was to save it.

By the time Professor Kramer arrived, the mud glistened in the dawn, and the incoming tide created a boulevard of suds-and-algae-twirled water that sloshed through the gentle dark dunes but still fell several feet shy of the stranded squid. The professor didn't come alone. He was tailed by the local whale rescue crew: three women and two ponytailed men who scrambled from their van onto the mud with towels, buckets and cameras.

They treated me like some irrelevant runaway until the professor explained that I was the one who'd called about "the creature." He still called it a creature, which I took personally at the time, but understood in hindsight, and was flattered that he trusted me enough to not only come running himself but to roust the local rescue squad too. Plus, he hadn't even seen it yet.

Professor Kramer was my favorite adult. When he took Mrs. Halverson's class on a field trip, I asked so many questions he invited me to his lab. That's where he showed me all the plants and animals that live in a thimble of seawater, creatures the size of pepper flakes feeding on even tinier plants. And I was hooked. He also taught me how to collect specimens, gave me a microscope, a twenty-gallon aquarium and, ultimately, the names and numbers of people who would buy whatever I gathered. He wasn't a god like

Rachel Carson, but someone with the right information in his head, which looked normal enough except for his kinky hair, which rose straight up from his scalp then flowered like the heads of those red tube worms that cling to dock pilings.

Once the professor arrived, I lost control of everything. The night I'd had to myself had surrendered to a bright morning that exposed the entire hourglass bay, pinched at its waist by the nearby Spencer Spit, which kept the Mud Bay Tavern, six rental cabins and the eastern end of the Heron Street Bridge just above the high water mark. And my discovery was definitely no longer *mine*.

Even in daylight, the squid didn't look real. It came off like a unicorn or a jackalope or some other fantasy creature—an oversized octopus mixed with the back end of a porpoise or some other torpedo-shaped mammal. But what I couldn't get over was how powerful and durable it looked. Its blotchy-purple skin reminded me of the thick rubber used for wet suits, and I noticed how the suckers along the inside of its ten arms shrank to the size of dimes near the tips.

"Jesus, Mary and Joseph," Professor Kramer muttered after he'd walked around it twice. Most of the rescuers were unwilling to get very close. They winced and cussed as if it stank, which it didn't. We all watched the professor examine and measure its head, its siphon, its arms and its nine-and-a-half-inch eyes, mumbling technical terms into a tiny recorder. What was clear to me was he didn't have the slightest idea how to check its vitals or keep it alive. Finally, I couldn't resist asking the obvious.

He replied, without looking up: "It's as dead as it's gonna get, Miles."

Still, the rescuers continued pouring buckets of water on it, as if putting out a fire. "Who said it was still breathing?" one of them demanded.

The professor one-eyed me. "What did draw you out here in the dark, Miles?"

"I heard it."

"What'd you hear?"

"Breathing." I knew they were all staring at me now, but all I could see were tall silhouettes and the oversized sun flickering behind them. I looked away to where cedars and firs cascaded to the beach like long summer dresses.

"You woke up and came out here because you heard something *breathing*?" the pushy rescuer asked.

"Well, it squealed or something. It made some loud noise, and I put on my boots and came out here."

It was one of those moments when your face can't back up your mouth. I hoped none of them knew enough about beached squid to know whether they could squeal or make noises that could wake up a kid a few hundred yards away. What had I heard? A snort or a sigh? Did I imagine it altogether? Would an autopsy prove I was a liar, that it had been dead for seven hours?

Luckily, everyone forgot about me as a KING 5 van rolled onto the Heron bridge with its crew popping out military style. The rescuers resumed dumping buckets of seawater on the squid. At least they had a role. I didn't even know where to stand as the television team splashed across the mud, and a short lady with hair that wind couldn't rustle slipped to her knee and let loose a gasp topped only by the noise she made when she got close enough to see the squid's huge cloudy-black eye. That's when she turned around and puked on the mud. Four young mallards suddenly flapped in single file overhead, laughing at us. A grouchy blue heron glided by to give us hell too.

Time hopped around on me, but soon almost everyone was on the mud, including my parents, whom I'd never seen that far out on the flats before. My mother stayed as far away from the squid as possible without standing in water. My father kept checking his watch to make sure he wasn't late for his early shift at the brewery. From a distance they looked alike, short and rounded in identical sweat jackets, but they stood paces apart, like neighbors who didn't get along.

A cheerful Judge Stegner arrived with two hot thermoses, as if it were a scheduled event he'd agreed to host. He also brought a flotilla of inflatable rafts and canoes, thinking ahead as usual, considering the flats we'd all crossed were sinking.

Another van arrived, then another and still another. The entire bridge filled with shiny white news vans, their satellite dishes telescoping into the new sky. The judge greeted and shuttled them to our shrinking island of mud. I'd never seen so many people who looked like mannequins before, or so many so afraid of a dead animal. Soon they competed to see who could ask Professor Kramer the loudest question. Finally, he asked them to be quiet and just listen to him for a few minutes.

"It's too soon to be certain," he said, "but it appears that this squid is too big to be a *Moroteuthis robusta*, the large Pacific squid that occasionally washes up on Washington beaches. No, this indeed appears to be an *Architeuthis*, better known as simply the giant squid." He spelled *Architeuthis* for them, then said, "Unofficially, this one measures out at thirty-seven feet from the top of its mantle to the end of its longest tentacle. That would not only make it a bona fide *Architeuthis* but perhaps the biggest one ever found in the Pacific and one of the largest found *anywhere* in years."

The professor's voice always changed slightly when he lectured, but this was different. This was the sound of bottled excitement, as if he were struggling to resist shouting. "What astonishes me at this point is that the giant squid is a deep-ocean creature," he continued. "How this one wound up down here in shallow South Sound in such amazingly good condition is . . ." He hesitated, searching for the perfect words. "A mystery of colossal proportions."

The air pressure changed after he said all that. Granted, this revelation involved a beached squid, not a moon landing or a Kennedy assassination, but anyone who was on the mud that morning when the professor put that marooned creature into perspective felt as if they were witnessing a moment that mattered.

He then explained that the giant squid is the world's largest invertebrate with the biggest eyes of any earthling. "Little is known about the giant squid because it has never been studied in its own habitat. We don't even know what colors it comes in, although it can probably change hues on a whim." He took a breath before predicting that scientists from across the nation would likely rush to study this specimen.

One of the ponytailed rescuers filled the lull that followed with a rant about pollutants endangering mammals in the Sound, which I suspected had little to do with this wrong-way squid. The judge then spontaneously interjected the history and geology of the bay with the authority of someone describing how he built his house. I tired of listening to everybody and was trying to figure out how to get a ride to shore without my parents when I heard the question resurface as to who found the squid.

Professor Kramer said my name, somehow spotted me and smiled warmly, as if the squid were my gift to him. Cameras swiveled toward me.

"What did you see, Miles?" asked the mannequin who'd puked earlier.

"The same thing you're seeing," I said, "except that I think it was breathing."

"Please speak up, Miles," she said in a voice so designed to relax me it alarmed me. "So, it was alive, Miles?"

"It made a noise." I wished people would stop saying my name. I turned to Professor Kramer, hoping he would take over, but his eyes were on the squid.

"Did you have any idea what it was?" she asked.

I squinted. "Well, I could tell it was a cephalopod, and as soon as I saw the eye, I was sure it was a squid and probably a giant."

More people and equipment crowded me, blocking the low sun. I could see the urgency and excitement in their faces, which scared me all the more.

"You called it a 'sifla-what'?" she asked.

I could already discuss phyla, hydroids, mollusks and crustaceans as easily as most kids chatted about bands and movies. The catch was nobody my age was interested in hearing any of it. Neither were my parents. So it churned inside me like a secret language and whenever it slipped out, people bug-eyed me like I'd shifted into Portuguese. "A *cephalopod*," I corrected, "which basically means its arms spring from its head."

"Was it dark when you came out here?" she asked.

"The moon was bright and I had a headlamp."

This struck them as astounding. People kneeled in front of me. Four microphones crowded my chin.

"Did it actually wake you up, Miles?"

See how people put you in a position where you have to lie or get in trouble? I tried to find my mother's puffy eyes. "I was kinda already awake."

"So you heard it and came out to see what it was?"

"Uh-huh."

"All by yourself?"

That's the sort of crap you hear when you're tiny for your age. I didn't respond, hoping the cameras and the microphones would go to someone else.

"How old are you, Miles?"

"Almost fourteen." I heard people murmuring, repeating the number.

"Why do you think this deep-ocean creature, this 'giant squid,' as Professor Kramer calls it, ended up in this little bay by your house?"

That's when I said what I said. It was a throwaway line, the sort of thing I'd heard fancy-smart people say on television when asked impossible questions. I could blame it on exhaustion, but there was a part of me that believed it. All of that doesn't much matter, though, because I said it: "Maybe the earth is trying to tell us something."

They liked that a lot. A kid says something like that, and people go *ahhh*. Offer a plausible scientific explanation and they yawn. Dip into the mystical, especially if you appear to be an unsullied, clearheaded child, and they want to write a song about you.

CHAPTER 3

ANGIE STEGNER ALMOST slept through it all. By the time she rose, all she saw was the squid sprawled on bright silver tarps on a flat trailer above the boat ramp next to the tavern. She moseyed around it once and laughed at the sky, as if the squid were a joke from above, then sauntered back across the bridge toward our side of the bay with me at her hip.

My parents had rushed to work after giving me more looks that assured me I had some explaining ahead of me. I didn't care about that or anything. I was dizzy with sleepiness, and Angie had her arm around me, bracing me, as if she could tell I might collapse. I milked it, walking as slowly as I could, trying to fix in my mind the leafy smell of her hair and the weight and warmth of her long tanned arm draped across my shoulders. I considered asking her if we should try to get old Florence out to see the squid before it got hauled to the lab, but I knew what an ordeal that would entail and didn't want to share Angie with anyone.

I think my fixation with Angie started when she read *Goodnight Moon* to me, back before I stored much in my head beyond emotion.

She babysat me so much in the early years she smelled like family, but it was hard to keep up with her moods and changes. When she turned eighteen she cut her hair to chin length and had a black rose tattooed to her stomach. She also pierced her eyebrow with a silver hoop, which made her look as if some fisherman had hooked her once but she got away. She chewed her nails, rarely washed her hair and wore baggy cargo pants, trying everything imaginable to hide her beauty. It didn't fool me. I found it difficult to think around her. Even breathing got complicated.

Angie sang in a band called "L.O.C.O." You couldn't call it "Loco" for some reason. I'd seen her perform just once, at an outdoor concert in Sylvester Park. She wore a horizontally striped red and pink dress that fell to the middle of her thighs, and she sang—whispered and screamed, actually—some song about charming devils and two-faced angels. It went on and on as if she were afraid to stop. It was just her and this drummer with too much hair and thick, crablike forearms. She played bass and howled, bobbing her head just enough to swing her hair while her frantic drummer turned into a sweat sprinkler. The music spooked me but literally moved others. People didn't dance so much as vibrate to it, shaking across the grass as if it were an involuntary act. And Angie was getting famous, in part because she occasionally fainted during shows, which provided rich gossip for those of us huddled around the bay. I overheard my mother asking her friends what it would mean for the judge now that his only daughter had "gone public" with her craziness. When I heard about Angie's faintings I had just one thought: I wanted to figure out how to catch her the next time.

Angie asked better questions than the others had, and I didn't mind telling her everything I knew and a few things I made up. When I finally pried my eyes off her, I noticed the tide climbing all the way back up, which somehow always relieved me, especially when it came up higher than usual, mirrored the sky and slowed time.

After I finished telling Angie everything, I started over again with the moment that interested her the most—when it was just me, the moon and the squid—hoping she wouldn't leave me while I climbed inside a huge hammock my mother brought back from Mexico long before I was born.

Angie not only didn't leave, she swung the hammock by nudging her stomach into my hip. I looked up into her green eyes and her connect-the-dot freckles. I was close enough to hear her stomach gurgle. Offered a moment to be stuck in, I might have chosen that one. Against my will, I drifted. Sleep was like that with me. It only came uninvited.

I missed her first few words, then caught the ones that said boys try too hard to please her. When she paused over that, I said, "That's real common." I told her how the three-spined stickleback, a homely rockfish, dances wildly to try to attract a mate. "It's way over the top," I said. "You wouldn't believe it. The male toadfish is even more ridiculous. When he wants to mate he vibrates his bladder muscles so fast they make a humming sound that's so loud it can annoy people on houseboats."

She showed me her teeth. Who knows if I would have become so obsessed with marine life if what I'd learned and found hadn't made Angie Stegner smile.

I drifted again until her black rose bumped my hip and she volunteered that she still hadn't met a boy—or man—who sought love that lasted more than one night. I had no idea what she meant, but I didn't want to sound naïve so I offered the first insight that popped to mind even though it was nothing more than a bumper-sticker slogan I'd puzzled over.

"Eat oysters," I whispered. "Love longer."

Her giggle was the last thing I recall from that morning.

CHAPTER 4

THE NEWS CHANNELS all had something on the squid. Most of them played it as yet another quirky news flash out of Olympia. They obviously didn't know what to make of it, other than to repeat its dimensions—thirty-seven feet and 923 pounds—then shift into phony chitchat about whether the squid was placed there by Republicans or Democrats and whether it would make people queasy about swimming in the Sound. Their footage of the squid itself was brief, as if they worried it might haunt people.

Channel 7 was the only one that went beyond snippets.

I'd never seen anyone I knew on television other than Judge Stegner, so I was surprised by how little Professor Kramer resembled himself. He looked pale, almost criminal, his collar askew, his hair reckless. Then the camera panned to some kid who came up to the professor's bicep and looked a whole lot like me, staring at the squid, orange hair fluttering, the high camera angle reducing me to one of Charlie Brown's big-headed side-kicks.

Suddenly my peeling nose was bigger than life in front of me. I looked into the camera the way a baby does, as if I didn't realize it was really on *me*, which was the truth.

"Little Miles O'Malley says the squid was *alive* when he happened upon it in the dark early this morning," the TV said. *"If so, this would be among the first and only times anyone has seen a giant squid alive. Repeated efforts by marine scientists to study the elusive creatures in the wild have failed."*

Then I stared straight out of our TV at myself. "It was breathing," I said, as if describing my run-in with an alien. The camera zoomed in on one of the squid's eyes before fading to the studio where a cheerful lady gushed, "Wow! Miles will never forget that!"

The weatherman, who'd mastered the ability to simultaneously smile and speak, promised his forecast was next, then stranded me with a commercial that left me with the confusing impression that waterskiing was somehow safer and more fun with Tampax. I waited for the phone to bark, the door to collapse, the house to be surrounded by hecklers. But nothing happened.

Once my pulse slowed, I felt relieved that they hadn't shown me saying the earth was trying to "tell us something." Then it hit me: *I was on television!* So what if I looked like a mumbling dwarf! Then I panicked again, dwelling on their choice of words. *If so* . . . In other words, this Miles O'Malley is an unreliable child who *claims* he saw the squid alive. *If so* was code for *we all know this kid was lying or imagining things.* I wondered again if I'd really heard it breathing at all. The evidence would be there in Professor Kramer's report, wouldn't it? Then what would happen? I'd be sent to a reformatory school for liars—that's what.

My parents didn't see the five o'clock news, but they heard about it and huddled around the television at five before eleven with their late dinner of leftover tuna loaf and brass-colored cocktails.

They were so startled by the attention their boy was getting that they didn't even question my lie that the squid's death moans pulled me from bed. Dad, however, made sure I understood—while showing me a mouthful of ground tuna—how easy it was to get stuck in the mud, something he knew nothing about. That's what parenting looked like to me then, tuning in just often enough to warn your kids about things that they knew more about than you did. Mom scolded me for wearing the same green army shorts *every damn day*, then cut me a half-smile the way she did right before she'd say she had no idea where I came from, which always left me wondering, if not from you, then who?

They didn't ask a single question about the squid. They simply couldn't get past their amazement that I was on the same segment with the judge, as if there'd been some sort of mistaken-identity screwup.

As expected, my father eventually dwelled on how tiny I looked on TV. It was obvious where he was headed, seeing how, unfortunately, it was the first of July. He asked me to slip off my shoes and stand in front of the broom closet. As usual, I started to sweat. Most kids were measured a few times a year. For me, it was the first of every month.

My father was obsessed with height. He was five five and wished he were six one, preferably six four. He was so height-oriented he respected people just for being tall, as if their elevation were some refinement or survival skill he lacked. It wasn't just the crap that women crave tall men. He was convinced people listen more carefully if you're tall, that tall men get better jobs, better pay and loom over crowds like gods. Plus, tall men dunk basketballs, and what could possibly top that?

You need to understand this about me: I loved being small and *unchanged*. (My fifth-, sixth- and seventh-grade pictures were nearly identical.) Tall kids stepped into rooms and people expected them to deliver speeches. I could hide in daylight, and there were advantages to having my brain so close to my feet. I could scramble up trees and jump off low roofs. I was so small there was little that could go wrong. The only catch was I felt guilty for stunting my own growth after reading that kids grow the most in their sleep.

I fluffed my hair and stood so straight I felt vertebrae separating. I lifted my chin and snuck undetectable air beneath my heels. If my father could scratch a pencil line a quarter-inch above the last one it spun him into such a great mood that the house throbbed with his goodwill; the tuna was awesome, my mother was gorgeous and I was the perfect kid. But on this night he argued gently with my mother over whether the hardback balancing on my skull was level, then darkened the pencil line from the prior month, leading to a final wince and bourbon-tuna exhale. I'd grown just a third of an inch during the prior thirteen months. I was stuck at four eight and seven-sixteenths.

I later overheard them debating which side of the family deserved credit for my brains, singling out smart uncles, cousins and grandmas. At one point, Dad observed, "He's always been really smart for his *size*." Then my mother reminded him for the second time that week that she'd been on her way to med school before she'd *inexplicably* hitched up with him.

I'd seen it building inside her, this troubling investigation into the sequence of events that stranded her in a tiny, stilted house with an unambitious baseball fanatic who still barhopped with his high school pals—the three Dons—and cried during Academy Awards speeches. (My mother had little use for sentimentality. Our family photos stayed in shoe boxes, and Santa, the Easter Bunny and the Tooth Fairy stopped showing up once I turned seven.) Maybe, I thought, her *pathetic* job at the state personnel department was what disappointed her most.

Or maybe it was me.

My father treated her increasingly frequent rants as comical interludes. And she could be funny in a breathless, sarcastic way, but it was easy to sort the humor from the anger. She talked faster and her lips paled whenever she was furious.

The truth is my father saw what he wanted to see, and if he could find a way around a showdown he'd take it. I rarely heard him state an opinion or suggestion that led to an argument. There was a hesitancy about him that snowballed around my mother. He started watching Mariners games with the sound off so they wouldn't annoy her. He'd stand behind the couch, with an aluminum bat in his hands, sizing up the pitcher. Then he'd swing as the tiny ball darted across our twenty-one-inch screen, or rather he'd check-swing or half-swing, unsure to the end whether to commit.

The tide was all the way out again, and the flats stunk in a way that always made me uneasy. My mother hated our house; the winter mold, the fall spiders and, worst of all, the summer stink of the flats whenever sun-rotted seaweed drummed up too much hydrogen sulfide, which probably explained my nightmares in which the tide stayed out for days until every living creature on the flats baked, died and stank in the heat, driving my mother to scream that we needed to move.

Eventually, I overheard my father circle back to how tiny I looked on television. "He's *still* not growing," he whined. "It's getting embarrassing."

CHAPTER 5

TWO DAYS LATER, the low tide was a minus-three, and when the water dropped a yard lower than usual in Chatham Cove additional football fields of mud, gravel and sea life unfurled, tripling our chances of seeing something unusual or finding large clams.

See, Professor Kramer had helped me get a specimen collector's agreement and a commercial clamming license from the state. So if I found marketable clams I sold them to the owner of the Saigon Secret. And when it came to digging up the largest, most deeply burrowed clams around, I usually called on the long arms of Kenny Phelps.

Phelps was a month younger and a head taller than me with a lazy swagger and long brown bangs that hid his right eye whenever he looked down. "Fuck-you bangs" is what he called them. His favorite pastime was air guitar, but unlike the rest of us, he took it seriously. When he mimicked Hendrix, for example, he'd flip over his imaginary guitar and play it upside down and left-handed. Another thing about him: He was a slacker. His philosophy was that the best jobs involved the least amount of work. His favorite scam? Going door to door offering to clean roofs and gutters in the fall. The beauty of it, he explained, was that homeowners couldn't watch him work. If he said it took two hours then it took two hours, even if one and a half were spent huddled near the chimney puffing Kent Menthol 100s he stole from his mother. And Phelps was clever with a cigarette. He loved to pop off large smoke rings, then squeeze three little ones right through them whenever he had an audience. The only thing screwing up his bad-boy act was his long, friendly smile that came so easily he could've held it for those old, slow cameras and still looked natural.

Phelps wanted me to pay him by the hour, including a half-hour lunch and two fifteen-minute smoke breaks every three hours. His stepdad was big in the electricians' union, and Phelps liked to throw union standards and slogans at me. I offered him half of whatever we earned, which was nothing some days, days he likened to slavery. Why'd I put up with him? I wasn't superchummy with anyone my age. My best friend was old Florence, and she never left her cabin and was getting sicker by the week. Phelps was convenient. He was the closest kid to the bay, so summers tossed us together. Plus, his gangly arms and long, strong fingers were built for clamming.

We started out studying the little chimney holes in the mud through which clams siphoned and spat seawater, hunting for the telltale signs of the mighty geoduck. Most of those huge clams— pronounced *gooey-duck* for some reason—lived farther out in the bay, but there were still plenty of exposed burrows if the tide fell low enough and you knew where to look.

As usual, we were the only ones out there. Most clammers and beachcombers headed north to rockier shores where tidal life was supposedly more abundant even though our southern bays endured the biggest tidal swings in the West, with water levels fluctuating as much as twenty feet in six hours. Still, South Sound had a reputation for mass-producing sand dollars and little else. The people behind those theories apparently never spent any time on Chatham Cove. The assumption was the Squaxins owned it, but actually just a slice of the flats belonged to the tribe, which was pointed out to me by Judge Stegner, who owned a slice himself. The state owned the rest, and from what I could tell, Chatham and the shoals north of it gathered new species of stars, snails, crabs, worms or jellies on a weekly basis—not that Phelps noticed.

While we searched for figure-eight depressions, he updated me on Wendy Pratto's breasts. He'd seen her in Safeway and swore her hooters were already a size bigger than they were the last day of school. "I'm guessing they're thirty-four Cs, now," he said authoritatively.

He stooped, pinched loose a tip of root-beer-colored kelp, chewed it to shreds then spat it out. He'd initially tried to con me into paying him to taste beach life, then did it to amuse himself. It became a habit. He nibbled on sea lettuce and eel grass. He ate baby shrimp and manilas straight from the shell. I saw him corner and catch a baby sculpin in a tide pool and swallow that one-inch fish whole. He gave me the latest on Christy Decker's chest too, claiming he'd seen it rise from the YMCA pool with nipples he could've hung his bathrobe on.

It wasn't that I didn't notice the same girls, but to me they were as remote and two-dimensional as movie stars. If I couldn't talk to them, they didn't enter my fantasies. I could talk to Angie Stegner—even if I didn't always make sense.

The pale two-thirds moon still hung in the sky, and for some reason I chose that moment to inform Phelps that Rachel Carson believed the moon was originally a glob of earth that ripped loose from the bottom of the Pacific and spun into the sky while the planet was still cooling.

"She also said the gravitational pull from the moon causes friction that is gradually slowing the earth's spin. So while it now takes twenty-four hours for it to rotate, it will eventually take fifty times that long. You imagine living in a world that has the equivalent of fifty straight days of light followed by fifty days of darkness?"

Phelps glared up at me from our clam ditch through those fuck-you bangs. "You're a freak," he said. "Why don't you use all your homo-reading to study something of value to us?"

"Like what?"

"Like the G-spot."

"The what?"

"The G-spot, Squid Boy." Phelps popped out a Kent, clutched it between the least dirty of his fingers and lit it. "It's the button inside women that drives them wild." He mumbled around his cigarette like a gangster. "Once we find out where it's at, we're *in*."

I was baffled. I'd never heard about any secret control panel inside women.

"Let's see your fingers," Phelps said.

I reluctantly stuck out my hand. He frowned. "I think they're too short."

"For what?"

"To reach the button. My brother says you need a finger that's at least two and a half inches long. Either that or you've gotta get your pecker to bend upwards."

I thought about my pecker. If anything it bent slightly to the left. "How're you supposed to do that?"

He glared at me as if I were his slowest student. "Concentration," he said knowingly.

"You're full of crap," I said. "Your brother is messing with you again."

"Whatever you say, Squid Boy."

"I say, keep digging."

The G-spot? It definitely hadn't come up in sex ed. In fact, there was nothing sexy about sex ed. All I got from it was the unsettling understanding that my life was a ridiculous long shot. First, my mother had to be flattered by my father while waiting impatiently for meatball subs at Meconi's. Then one particular sperm cell of his eighteen zillion sperm cells had to elude whatever *goalie*—my father's term—they were using. (I'd overheard my mother call me "an accident" at least seven times.) Then that blind, microscopic sperm of his had to find and crack that one particular moody egg of hers during that vague window of time it was available without later getting aborted by some bald, distracted doctor who was thinking about the Mariners' bullpen at the time. What were the odds? I was a fluke in a classroom full of flukes on a planet overpopulated by flukes.

A while later, I caught Phelps glancing at the moon, the closest thing to a cloud up there. "When did Rachel Carson write all that stuff?" he asked.

"Early nineteen-fifties."

"How old was she?"

"Her late forties."

"When'd she die?"

"Nineteen sixty-four."

"What of?"

"Breast cancer."

"How many books she write?"

"Four. All best sellers. She was the one who warned us that if we keep spraying poisons on fields we'll stop hearing birds in the spring."

"How many kids she have?"

"None. Never married."

"You know everything about her, don't you?"

I didn't say anything for a couple beats. "I know she was brave and brilliant."

"Know what I know?" Phelps couldn't control his smile. "I know you're in love with a spinster who's been dead for decades."

"Keep digging."

Phelps eventually dug up a seven-pound geoduck that would convert into three and a half bucks for each of us. If you haven't seen a geoduck before you'd be astonished. They're not the clams you know. Their shells are ridiculously undersized. Even when contracted, their necks hang way out. Think of bodybuilders in Speedos, or as Professor Kramer himself put it, there's no getting around their resemblance to horse dicks.

When I helped the professor explain the tidal flats to third-graders it was always hard to get them past the giggles to make them understand that as silly as geoducks look, they possess one of the most durable designs on earth. They bury themselves two feet deep in sand, then shove their oversized necks up through the sea floor where they can comfortably inhale plankton and spit out waste for a century or more. By the time I'd tell them that the biggest ones swell to twenty pounds and live up to 150 years without ever having to move, I'd be talking to myself.

The tide was returning quicker than I'd expected, sneaking up on me the way it did when my mind drifted. So instead of digging flooding burrows, I waded, hunting for anything the big aquariums might want, wishing I'd started searching earlier instead of wasting time trying to educate someone as thickheaded as Phelps.

I told him to help me turn rocks before they submerged, hoping to find baby octopus, reminding him to put the rocks back exactly the way he found them. A few minutes later, I saw five toothpick-legged sandpipers scissor-stepping across the flats in such choreographed precision I half-expected them to start twirling canes and whistling in unison. Then I heard Phelps shriek.

By the time I looked his way, he was already tripping backward onto compact sand. That part wasn't unusual. Phelps rarely went a day without hurting himself. Who else broke his collarbone bowling or sprained his neck sneezing? But this time he was reeling and screeching, as if chased. "It snapped at me!"

I knew what he'd seen before I got to the rock he'd flipped.

Midshipmen rank among the Sound's creepiest bottom fish. Their bodies are mostly heads, and their heads are mostly eyes and teeth. And for whatever reason, the females rise up from the dark canyons to drop their eggs beneath rocks in the shallows. The males then guard the eggs until they hatch, and if you startle them they'll show you their piranhalike teeth. After this daddy showed me his, I saw tiny eggs adhered to the underside of the upturned rock and the baby midshipmen spinning inside them, their metallic stripes creating a sparkling light show. I waved Phelps over.

He stood hesitantly behind me as the flashing babies popped from their eggs and splashed into two inches of water where they huddled against their father's belly. Then the tumult passed and they all became so still, the babies seemingly disappearing, the father blending into the rocks.

"Now *that*," Phelps whispered, "is amazing."

"Look around." I held out my hands, as if catching rain.

CHAPTER 6

W HEN WE GOT back to my house with one geoduck, thirty-
two manila and eight butter clams, we heard voices, laughter
and music echoing from the Stegner house.

The Stegners technically lived next door, but their house loomed
on a knoll a quarter mile away and was unlike any other home on
the bay. Nothing about its design hinted that it began as a
Methodist church, but something about its posture, the way it
faced sunrise and occupied the highest bump of lowlands ringing
the west flank of the bay, made it easy to see how some people
might pick it as a place to chat with God. Yet it was hard to imagine
that it had ever belonged to anyone but the Stegners. It fit their
stature and high expectations, at least it had when the judge was still
married and Angie's three older Eagle Scout brothers were still
around. Still, both times my mother stepped inside she swore she
heard a Methodist choir.

We found Angie beneath the willow near our property line
sharing a cigarette with Frankie Marx. Frankie was always friendly
to me, but I hated him anyway. He was obnoxiously handsome, and

I didn't trust anyone who made looking cool seem that easy. So, of course, I was determined to save Angie from him, but I couldn't resist Lizzy, his hyper chocolate Lab, who got up, tongue dangling, to greet us.

Angie whistled Lizzy back into the grass, then stroked her belly. I'd never seen her touch phony Frankie, but I saw her cuddle with that dog often enough to envy it. I asked her about the party.

"It's the big old oyster feed for Dad's richest contributors," she said, without looking up. Her eyelids were so heavy it looked as if she were hiding.

I nodded, but I didn't know what she meant other than that being a state supreme court judge was something like being a mayor or a governor. After an awkward lull, it occurred to Phelps that she was the same Angie his brother raved about. "I hear you play an awesome bass," he said.

"Yeah?" She grinned.

"Cool," Phelps told her.

"You think so?" She blew a cone of smoke at the sky. "Wouldn't it be cooler if I played lead guitar?"

"Yeah, but bass is cool too."

She looked to see if I was enjoying this. She'd definitely been crying. I glared at Frankie, and he smiled warmly back. He was such an effortless Marlboro man he made me feel like a circus midget.

"You play?" she asked politely.

"A little," Phelps said.

"Air guitar," I clarified, mimicking his lip scowl and frantic fingering.

"Fuck yourself, Miles. My brother has a Gibson," he bragged. "An electric."

"He lets you play it?" she asked.

"Not when he's around." Phelps smiled so broadly Angie laughed.

"Help yourselves to the food," she told us, "before the old folks gobble it all up."

I saw a crowd in sun hats, flowered dresses and slacks the color of Easter eggs. "I don't think we're dressed right."

She glanced at our mud-splattered shorts. "You're perfect. It's summertime." She went back to rubbing Lizzy until the dog's foot twitched like an outboard engine about to turn over.

We strolled off, and when I looked back I caught Angie crying, which reminded me of what my mother had called her a month earlier when Angie waded bare-legged in front of our house. I was the only one who could see her tears, but before I could point them out my mother asked my father if he didn't have anything better to do than ogle that crazy *dundula*. It was a word my Croatian grandmother passed down. I didn't ask what it meant and I didn't say anything to anyone a week later when I saw Angie pacing the crown of the Stegner roof, which was so steep slipping meant dying.

I led Phelps toward the long white food table where people huddled around Judge Norman Stegner as if he were passing out money.

"It's my oyster man!" he announced once he spotted me.

Gray heads spun—I heard gristle pop in some old neck—their eyes flailing above mine, then dropping to find me. Oyster *man? The judge is such a kidder.*

I recognized one of them from the newspaper or television as the judge thrust his clean, strong hand at me.

There was nothing imposing about Judge Stegner other than his voice. He was chinless and bird-chested with dull forgettable eyes and thin, seagull-white hair, but his voice made everyone else's sound like a squeaky clarinet they were still learning how to play. I looked for Phelps, but he'd already abandoned me for food. The judge introduced me by my full name—just in case there were any Irish genealogy buffs in the mix—and explained that I oversaw the very oyster farm from which they were feasting.

They hummed on cue, but that was just the setup for wherever he was headed. The judge was like that. He never rushed, but he was always going somewhere. "This is the young *man* who found the giant squid. Tell them, Miles."

I pointed to where it beached. "I heard it," I said softly, "and went to see what it was."

"*Speak up*, Miles," the judge boomed. "Just *talk* about it."

There was no quick way out. I widened my stance in the grass. "Well, I expected to find a sick whale or sea lion or something else stuck high on the mud."

One of the ladies blurted out that she'd seen me on television. It killed me to watch a deviled egg go in and out of her tiny mouth while she shared that.

"It's not as if things don't get stranded down here," I continued. "A minke and even a gray whale got confused once. The tide leaves pretty fast and goes all the way out. And to tell you the truth, I still wasn't sure what it was when I got as close as I was willing to get, but then I saw the long tentacles with those big suckers and then that huge eye and I knew."

Goose bumps covered me—some stories tighten their hold on me the more I tell them—and the grown-ups leaned in, just in case this was all building to something remarkable they could share with their most interesting friends. I watched them clean their teeth with their tongues, their eyes on me as if I were an exotic discovery myself. A lady with a heavy gold necklace winced as though the subject burned her belly, but the judge beamed as if I were riding a unicycle. "You're looking at the next Jacques Cousteau." It sounded as irrefutable as any court order, and everyone marveled at the notion. Grown-ups are always more fascinated by what you might become than what you are.

"How big was the eye?" inquired a tall, crooked man, guiding a cracker between yellow teeth.

"As big as your face," I said.

The man stopped chewing. Someone laughed, a lady tittered, then the judge described the morning media crush and his role as water taxi, historian and waiter, milking riotous laughter out of every inflated detail. I left the instant their eyes lost me, and found Phelps cross-legged in the grass with greasy lips, slogging through a mound of chicken wings.

I grabbed some sourdough and four grilled oysters and handed Phelps a napkin, so I could stomach looking at him, then led him to the edge of the bay.

"That Frankie Marx seems cool," he said, watching me.

"He's a moron." I shoved bread into my mouth. "There's nothing real about him."

"Uh-huh."

His tone assured me I'd already blown my secret. I'd never wanted him to know the first thing about Angie. And I didn't know what I'd do if he started boasting about how many bathrobes he could hang on *her* rack.

I eyed the meandering line of flotsam left high on the sand from the last high tide. Professor Kramer knew people who studied tidal lines to forecast changes in ocean currents and sea life. I just saw it as the Sound's equivalent of a lint catcher. From forty feet, I made out a spindled collection of seaweed, kelp, broken shells, seagull feathers, crab pinchers and salmon bones.

I was finishing my third oyster when I saw Lizzy loose, sniffing along the waterfront on my folks' property, which I assumed meant that Angie and Frankie were making out so dang hard they'd lost track of their dog. I figured Lizzy would go no farther than the city-owned blackberry tangle on the far side of our land. Not even cats ventured into that barbed jungle. The prickly vines were as fat as lamp poles and growing at a horror-movie pace. If I hadn't kept snipping them back, they would've already overwhelmed the garage and barred my windows. I heard Lizzy bark, then saw her chase a truck on the stubby two-lane bridge the news vans clogged that morning when the squid showed up. The truck was hauling a white tool trailer that Lizzy apparently hadn't noticed because after she quit chasing, she veered behind the truck just enough for the trailer to thump, spin and flip her over the low railing.

I rose and sprinted across our property and slogged through driftwood slop in front of the blackberries before I heard Angie and Frankie yelling, *Lizzy!* I kept my eyes on her splash, but didn't see any movement beyond the initial ripples. It was mid-tide, which meant there was five feet of water beneath the middle of the bridge—enough to dive if I had to.

When I got halfway across the bridge, I saw that she was actually only a few feet from shore, yet she wasn't on the surface or the bottom, but rather suspended sideways, as if cast in ice. I wheezed across the bridge, splashed knee-deep into mud and kelp and pulled her ashore with one hand on her collar and the other around her chest until I could drag her high enough in the mud to keep her head above water. She didn't respond to back slaps. I fanned her snout and felt no air, so I cupped her nose in my hands and blew three strong puffs into her. Nothing happened. I panted, then tried again, sealing her snout with my lips this time, and puffed hard. Still nothing. I could hear Phelps's breathing by then and Angie's hollers and the distant clatter and drone of the Stegner party. I forced air into Lizzy once more and felt her resist. She then shook herself from my lap, wobbled, fell down, puked water, panted and whimpered before getting back up, shaking herself again, whining some more and lying on her stomach, chest heaving, tongue dangling.

I felt queasy and wiped my mouth. It didn't taste great. My throat burned with oyster burps. I splashed my face, but it still took a few moments before I wanted to stand. Then Angie and phony Frankie were there with wild eyes, shuttling between Lizzy and me, Phelps telling, retelling and exaggerating everything. "Thank you, thank you, thank you," Frankie kept moaning. I saw the Stegner party crowd the waterfront to eyeball us too, piecing together what they'd seen and hadn't seen. Listen to people at times like these, and it's amazing police get accurate accounts of anything.

I couldn't tell if Angie was proud of me or feared me. I shrugged an instant before she hugged me so that she pinned my shoulders to my ears and squeezed. It apparently didn't matter to her that I was soaked and muddy with dog slobber on my face. Frankie interrupted the hug to thank me again. "You're welcome," I said faintly, "but I didn't do it for you." I avoided Angie's eyes as she let go, and soon it was just me and Phelps wringing out my shirt.

"I'm starting to understand you, Miles."

"Yeah?" I rubbed my mouth with the back of my hand until my lips numbed. I watched a heron glide over the bay and felt as if I were doing the exact same thing. I looked down to improve my bearings. Sea lettuce never looked so brilliant. I picked up the first peach-colored scallop shell I ever saw and watched a massive red jellyfish pulse on by like a bloody heart dragging four-foot tentacles.

"You love dead spinsters," Phelps said, "and truck-chasing dogs."

Words couldn't dent my mood. I'd stopped something bad from *happening*. What else could I accomplish if I just paid attention? A long eel or worm undulated under the bridge, then vanished.

The material was too rich for Phelps to let it go. "I can't even get you to engage in a healthy discussion about Christy Decker's rack." He found a baby shrimp burrowed in the mud next to his foot, rinsed it and tossed it back like a vitamin. "Then the next thing I know you're making out with a chocolate Lab."

I shrugged and looked around for a soft place to lie down.

CHAPTER 7

I COULDN'T SLEEP. What terrific sleepers never understand is that sleeping isn't optional or something you talk yourself into. You can either do it or you can't. So I stayed up skimming a book called *The Erotic Ocean* in which some scientist kept noticing, with Phelps-like single-mindedness, all the mating going on in the shallows, including these incredibly horny sea urchins who decorated moonlit water with red eggs and white sperm. This was the same night that I overheard my parents discussing divorce, or rather my mother discussing it and my father grunting.

It would have been easier if it had been the sort of soon-to-be-regretted shouting match grown-ups have when they just want to win an argument and don't care if they're right or wrong and apologize later for being jerks. What I overheard during my aborted midnight peanut butter run was my mother's practical assessment of the pros and cons of it, as if she were debating whether to fly to Las Vegas or remodel the kitchen.

Instead of waiting for the birds to whistle me to sleep, I slipped out just before sunrise beneath a copper sky. You may wonder how I came and went so easily. Part of it was that I lived above the garage. The other part was that my folks never really wanted to be parents. I overheard that too. It's not that there wasn't love. There just wasn't supervision.

The bay was as calm as a waiting bath, which always startled me because I'd witnessed its bullying winds and violent waves to the point where it seemed miraculous to find trees and houses still standing some mornings. But by July it was hard to remember the bay's tantrums, with the water liquid silver, just V-wakes of ducks and crescents of kelp dimpling its surface. And when the tide brimmed a foot higher than normal, as it did that windless morning, the water hovered above its borders the way a perfect milkshake hovers above the rim of your glass.

I knew there probably wouldn't be anything to collect, but there might be something to see. If you watched the bay often enough you eventually saw the inexplicable. I once saw a healthy eagle with a five-foot wingspan dive for fish and never resurface. I saw a winter duck—a red-breasted merganser—ride on the head of a seal for a full minute. I watched a snapping shrimp swing a claw at a sculpin twice its size and knock it unconscious. And more than once I watched surface water bulge and ripple, as if pushed by whales, yet with nothing behind or beneath it, with the water so clear and empty I could see the bottom. It took me a long time to learn to keep such moments to myself. Nobody has anywhere to file them, including me.

I paddled through high water into the first direct sunlight as two pigeon guillemots blundered across the bay like a comedy team looking for fish, flapping furiously, the two of them barely able to keep their crayon-red feet aloft. A western gull whirled past too, followed by a hummingbird that defied physics with its helicopter-like gift for hovering.

Skookumchuck Bay taught me distance and direction. A mile across at its widest and exactly two miles long, the bay sat north-south lengthwise, turning deeper and sandier the farther north you paddled to Penrose Point. Across from Penrose was the old oyster-packing plant that died long before I was born, yet remained as a time capsule for the inlet's early days because nobody ever bothered to tear it down or haul away the discarded oyster shells piled up like mountains of poker chips taller than me. Another half mile farther south was the old Mud Bay Tavern and the rickety cabins facing the fat bottom of the bay where steep forests had always covered its eastern flank, and cattle and horses had always browsed the broad, flat fields behind the eleven houses strewn along its western shore. As the judge liked to say, the bay hadn't changed in sixty years, which was probably why everyone was so astonished when they heard about the plans to construct a gated neighborhood of million-dollar mansions along its southeastern rim. I'd heard the whining chain saws and the rumbling cement mixers since spring, but until this clear morning I hadn't paddled close enough to make out the new, swimming-pool-sized foundations or the fake fountain centerpiece of Sunset Estates.

I turned and paddled hard to the north, trying to feel the way I thought I should feel about overhearing my parents' divorce chat. When I was six, my mother challenged me, in front of my cousins, to go one whole day without crying. I'd rarely cried since. Maybe that was part of it. The other part was it was hard for me to feel fear or sadness at dawn on that bay, especially when I knew the sun wouldn't set for another fifteen hours and thirty-two minutes, and the water was so clear I could see coon-stripe shrimp in the eelgrass near the tavern and the bottomless bed of white clam shells pooled across the sunken tip of Penrose Point.

Those shells, as unique and timeless as bones, helped me realize that we all die young, that in the life of the earth, we are houseflies, here for one flash of light.

"You were put here to do great things," Florence assured me after I dropped into her rocker and faced her later that morning.

It was a typical Florence line that I assumed she tossed to all of

45

her friends the way others say "have a great day." But she hit me with it after a week in which I'd found a giant squid and brought a dog back from the dead. It wasn't that I was starting to feel that I actually had some higher calling, it's that I'd begun to feel as though I'd received a bigger role than I'd auditioned for.

Florence lived on the other side of the Stegners in a steel-roofed summer cabin similar to ours, but smaller. And while half of ours stood on stilts, hers rested entirely on six-by-sixes, and the ten highest tides of the year washed completely beneath her, leaving about two feet of air between her floorboards and the suds, kelp and jellyfish. When the stink of low tide blew inside her drafty cabin it overpowered the musty odor of old hardbacks and, more recently, the faint whiff of urine.

Florence had lived alone since her sister died a decade earlier, and she'd been on the bay since 1938, which made her its senior resident, not counting some of the clams who might've been there twice as long. Angie once told me Florence used to babysit the judge, and he'd recently turned sixty-eight, so that tells you how old she was even if she wouldn't give out a number.

On this day, I found her with an inch-long forehead gash like boxers get along the seams of their eyebrows. I knew she had some cruel variation of Parkinson's. She'd shown me the paperwork, but I was slow to understand what it was doing to her. I just knew that she seemed stiffer almost every time I saw her, and at some point she'd started shuffling instead of walking. She'd rock her shoulders to loosen her feet, then she'd baby-step toward the kitchen as if crossing a wet log. And when you shuffle, I learned, you eventually fall.

Her old friend Yvonne shopped for her, so she didn't need to go out, but even her stairless cabin had turned treacherous. This was the second time within a month that I'd found her trying to mend a head wound with butterfly Band-Aids. She downplayed it, as usual, but I insisted she ice it, and she finally agreed once I pointed out that the swelling drew attention to an otherwise perfectly disguised wound.

I'd visited Florence at least weekly for the past three years, in part because she increasingly seemed like the person most like me. She was almost as short and skinny but with huge bottom-fish eyes, as if she were designed to read in the dark, which suited her seeing how her gloomy home overflowed with books to the point stacks had to be moved to offer seats to more than one visitor. The clutter also added to the assumption that she was nuts. Most people didn't know what else to call someone who called herself a psychic. My mother did. She called Florence a crazy witch.

She used to have a tiny upstairs office off Franklin Street, where her sign—PALM READINGS, TAROT READINGS AND OTHER PSYCHIC PREDICTIONS—always struck me as far more irresistible than the nearby insurance, restaurant or clothing storefronts, yet there was never anyone inside but her. The worst part of it was that her reputation was that of a psychic who was always wrong.

At least that was her rep, my mother explained, after Florence began testifying at hearings against housing developments, off-ramps and roundabouts based on her intuitions about safety. She even argued that the proposed Capitale Apartments shouldn't be constructed near Capitol Lake because the building would be vulnerable to a future earthquake. Not surprisingly, it was built anyway and had endured thirteen years and a few regional quakes without so much as a ceiling crack.

None of that made me doubt her. All I had to do was watch her eyes, which reflected light from so many angles it was impossible to tell whether she was looking at you, past you or *into* you. Plus, she read me better than anyone. I made a point of not thinking too loudly around Florence.

"This is your summer, Miles. This is the summer that defines you."

That was the sort of thing she'd been saying ever since school got out, as if she were preparing me for something she knew was over my head. She also kept insisting that she didn't want to burden me.

It really didn't strike me as a burden—at first—to wait on her and save her trips to the medicine cabinet. And in exchange, she increasingly gave me what she thought I needed, including lessons on how to meditate, how to "dream while awake" and how to see auras.

I tried. I practiced kicking thoughts from my head until it was empty, but instead of leading to meditation it led to even crazier thoughts. And trying to dream while I was wide awake did nothing but make me feel psycho. As for auras, I stared at imaginary dots in the middle of people's foreheads until my vision blurred, but during a whole week of that I still saw nothing more than confused people looking at me like I had something in my eye. Florence swore I had one of the brightest yellow auras she'd ever seen. I took it as a compliment, but I couldn't see it no matter how many times I snuck up on myself in mirrors.

"What did Norman say about it?" She often asked about the judge.

"About what?"

"About you rescuing that dog."

"He said, 'That's my oyster man!'"

Florence grinned. "He adores you. You know that?"

Sweat lathered my neck like it usually did when I sat in that rocker. Florence kept the thermostat at seventy-nine, and always said things that heated me up.

"Are you sleeping at all?" She was the only one who knew much about my insomnia.

"A little," I explained. "Usually from three in the morning until around seven or eight. Didn't sleep at all last night though."

"You staying up to read or explore?"

"Both," I said. "I've been reading about how scientists disagree like crazy when it comes to giant squid. Some think they're probably among the fastest swimmers in the sea, that they're these great sprinters who dart along at more than thirty miles an hour with their siphons giving them jet propulsion and their two hearts pumping like mad. Can you imagine having *two* hearts racing inside you? But see, nobody's actually ever seen them swim, so other scientists insist they're probably slow and weak for their size, that they just hover in deep water, then wait and watch with those huge eyes until something swims within their grasp. Then they pull their catch to their mouth, which is like a parrot's beak, but ten times as big, and strong enough to break steel cables. The one thing we know for sure is that sperm whales swallow 'em whole even though their arms are filled with ammonium chloride, which makes them buoyant, but also probably makes them taste like bleach. Yuck, huh?"

I told her how Professor Kramer had called the day before to update me on what little they'd learned from studying the giant I'd found. "They were all excited to see what was in her belly because they still don't know exactly what they eat. Guess what they found: nothing. Maybe she'd been fasting because she'd just spawned. Who knows? Squid were originally called 'kraken,' which means 'uprooted tree,' which makes perfect sense if you picture one."

Florence listened so intently she pulled words out of me, then digested them without those space fillers most grown-ups leaned on—*I see . . . anyway . . . at any rate . . . all right then*—or those hums, grunts and sighs that don't mean anything other than perhaps that they weren't listening at all. Finally, she sat up with a wince and told me to trust my intuition, then half-closed her bottomfish eyes and informed me that something big was going to happen during the next two weeks, something right there in the bay.

"Bigger than the squid?" I asked, trying to sound captivated.

"Different."

"What?"

She hated to be pressed. "There also will be a freak tide this fall."

"When's that?"

"September eighth," she confided. "It'll come up higher than anyone expects."

I looked away. Maybe Florence used to be a bit psychic, I thought, at least as psychic as people usually ever get. But her gift had apparently exited without saying good-bye. There was no reason for me to think quietly around her anymore. Vague predictions were one thing, but once she crossed into Rachel Carson's precise world of science she'd left her realm.

Tide tables were remarkably accurate. Tides were no more likely to blindside us than the sun would rise an hour earlier than expected. Plus, September was known for mild tides.

"Even science goes haywire sometimes, Miles."

I blushed, wishing she'd at least lower her eyelids.

She caught me looking at her wound again. "Thanks for not telling anyone about this little cut."

That was pure Florence. Instead of asking you to keep a secret, she thanked you in advance for preserving it. She flattered instead of burdened.

"If the state people learn that I occasionally have these little falls," she said, "they'll want to move me into a *home*."

I couldn't tell if she was making a prediction or sharing a fact, but I knew her well enough to see fear.

The odd thing was it scared me too. Not just because I couldn't imagine losing her, but because it fit into my growing sensation that everything was shifting beneath me. It wasn't just my folks' divorce chitchat. There was the likelihood that Angie would go away to college in September, and maybe the judge would decide that he didn't need such a big house anymore. Even the bay itself was seemingly shifting into something else—a trophy view for people rich enough to build houses in Sunset Estates.

I didn't have any terrific idea how to accomplish it, but my goal for the rest of the summer was to stop things from changing, to keep my bay, as I knew it, intact.

Maybe Florence heard me thinking, or maybe she was confronting her own ghosts, because her eyes reddened and her swollen knuckles waved me toward her until I was close enough for her to kiss my forehead without getting up.

CHAPTER 8

AFTER SLEEPING HARD for a few hours I woke to an empty house and a note: "Dad's going to the M's game with the 3 Dons and I'm meeting Aunt Janet at a play in Seattle. Be home late. Leftover tuna loaf in fridge, ramen in cupboard. Love, Mom."

What read like a routine night out suddenly sounded ominous. The three Dons were no longer just my father's festive buddies who called me their main man. They were three old *divorced* bachelors my mother called permanent teenagers. And Aunt Janet wasn't just my mother's wealthy sister anymore, but someone who never seemed to like my father, something he'd occasionally point out hours after she left with some glancing comment that my mother usually ignored. I ate two bowls of Cheerios staring at my parents' wedding photo. It looked like a different couple. Time had erased their cheekbones and dulled their eyes and skin the way ocean surf rounds and fades rocks until they all look the same.

I emptied and loaded the dishwasher before finding my mother's to-do list atop an avalanche of unopened mail. The dusting and vacuuming was easy enough, as was weeding the roses. I tried cleaning the oven with dishwashing soap, but that was hopeless, and I couldn't find the toilet scrubber so I poured a ton of Comet in the bowl and flushed. Then I turned the bathroom scale back three pounds and headed out to Chatham Cove feeling hopeful about everything.

When I hooked up with Phelps, I could tell right off that something was different.

He kept asking in his roundabout way about tidal life. I'd seen it creeping up on him. You can only keep your curiosity down for so long out there. Eventually you want to know.

So I started at the top of the beach amid the jumble of logs, rocks and root wads. "This is the roughest part of Tidal Town," I said. "Basically only barnacles and mussels are tough enough to handle the waves, weather and birds. Mussels can hack it because they spin anchor lines that attach to *anything*. Barnacles are even tougher. Their conical shape fends off waves, and they secrete a natural glue that permanently fixes them to wherever they land as babies." Phelps was obviously fading so I asked him how he figured they reproduce.

"By getting girl barnacles drunk?"

"Think about it," I urged. "They can't move. They're stuck for life wherever they land. So how do they get pregnant?"

He shrugged. "Immaculate conception?"

"Nope. Their penises are rolled up like fire hoses inside their shells. When the time is right, they unfurl them and feel around outside their shells for willing mates to shoot their sperm inside."

Phelps laughed. "Come on. Fire hoses?"

"That's right. A barnacle's penis can be four times as long as the diameter of its base. So, yeah, those four-inch-wide giant barnacles you see along the coast are packing sixteen-inch penises."

Phelps pointed at a log half-crusted with tiny barnacles. "These guys are the studs of the beach?"

I showed him a hermit crab shopping for a larger shell, its antennae-ball eyes looking both ways before it dashed from its undersized shell into one left behind by a mudflat snail. The crab tried it on, but found it too heavy and hurried back into its old shell. "They've got little suction cups on their butts," I said, "that help them secure themselves in there."

Phelps yawned.

I pointed out striped, quarter-sized limpets that looked like Chinese coolie hats. I told him Aristotle himself marveled at their homing instinct that allows them to slide snail-like around the beach, scraping up food, before returning to the exact same spot. It struck me right then that I needed to alert somebody that old Florence was already a limpet and on her way to becoming as stuck as a barnacle.

As we neared the tidal line I reminded Phelps that sea stars can regrow lost legs, and that severed legs can grow new mouths and bodies as well. Then I explained that there were millions of microscopic critters living on top of the water and in between grains of sand, and that someone recently counted two hundred different species in one square yard of gravel, sand and mud off Whiskey Point.

I turned over rocks and found longer worms and more crabs than I expected, to the point I thought maybe it was time to coax Professor Kramer out on the flats to ask him about the changes. I showed Phelps how sand dollars travel by moving one grain of sand at a time with their tiny, glistening Velcro-like feet. "And do you realize that all sand comes from rock, and eventually all rock breaks down to sand and falls into the sea, which makes the ocean saltier?"

Phelps groaned. "Except for that stuff about the barnacle peckers that was some of the boringest shit I've heard since school got out."

I couldn't even look at him.

"Cheer up," he said. "I brought some real entertainment." He pulled a brittle copy of *The Godfather* from his backpack and started reading some scene that began on page twenty-seven—he knew the sexy page numbers by heart—in which some imaginary woman described how *big* this imaginary Sonny was to her friends, then suddenly Huge Imaginary Sonny was having his way with one of those imaginary friends, fast and rough, with no more romantic conversation than strangers at a Laundromat.

Something about it made me feel defensive, as did most of the crap I heard directly or indirectly about what girls wanted. *Tall, dark and handsome?* I was short, pink and ordinary. My size, I was beginning to fear, put me on the outside of romance, like a frog who couldn't croak loud enough to attract a female.

"How 'bout them apples?" Phelps threw his entire face into a leer.

"You would like that," I muttered. "Bigger is better. Might is right. All that crap. That's *so* you."

His mouth fell open. "Crap? Are you doubting Mario Puzo?"

"You're in love with Mario Puzo," I snapped.

"You're ridiculous."

"Just because you read someone's made-up sex lies doesn't make you an expert on love." I instantly regretted my choice of words.

"*Love?*" Phelps cried. "Who's talking love? What do you think love is anyway, Squid Boy?"

"Love means you'd do almost anything for someone even if you knew you'd get nothing in return." I couldn't stop myself. I'd been thinking about rescuing Angie again, and for some reason I was furious. "You'd even do it anonymously!"

Phelps looked at me as if I'd lost my mind. "*That* is so fucked up."

"Yeah?"

"Yeah. Love isn't charity. Love is doing fun stuff for each other. You bring her flowers and she takes off her shirt. Stuff like that."

"What's the difference," I demanded, "between that and going to Seattle and paying a prostitute to let you feel her up?"

That stopped him. "You'd be paying someone you don't even know," he said finally. "Plus, it would be more expensive and not as fun."

"So, love is affordable, fun sex with someone you know?"

"Exactly."

"You're sick."

"Me? I'm not the one who was caught French-kissing chocolate Labs."

"You're fired," I said, walking away.

He laughed. "On what grounds?"

"Being a jerk," I shouted over my shoulder.

"You know that's not a *fireable offense*."

Phelps followed me into the water, chatting away, trying to reel me back. I wouldn't give him anything, even though I was dying to ask him how much warning he'd had before his parents got divorced, and how long he'd lived in that apartment before his mother married his stepdad, and, most importantly, how much say he'd had in picking his stepdad or their next house.

But I still couldn't even look at him. It's hard to see anything when you're that angry, which is probably why it took a giant sea cucumber lounging in a foot of water to get my attention.

It wasn't fair to the cucumber or Phelps what happened next, but who's any good at defending decisions they make when they're pissed?

"The hell is that?" he asked.

It was at least sixteen inches long and red enough to sell to the aquariums. But I wasn't thinking about money.

I held it evenly and gently at my waist with both hands until Phelps reached for it. I handed it to him gingerly and stepped back.

He studied it intently, trying to patch things up with me. When he turned it lengthwise and looked down into its flowering end it ejected its red, stringy innards with such force they splattered against the right side of his head.

From where I stood it looked like half of Phelps's face had been shot off. He didn't make a sound. He just one-eyed me in total astonishment.

I took the deflated animal from his long fingers and set it back into the bay to recuperate, then yanked off my shirt and handed it to him.

"You knew that would happen." He wiped his face and splashed it repeatedly.

When frightened, sea cucumbers have this strange ability to vomit their organs, then amazingly and quickly regrow them once they're out of danger. I'd never actually seen them do it, but I'd read about it and had my hopes.

He continued splashing his face. As the water settled beneath him I felt relief at the sight of his reflected smile.

Calm open water amplifies voices. Quiet conversations are overheard a hundred yards away. So it's safe to say that you probably could have heard our laughter from a couple miles.

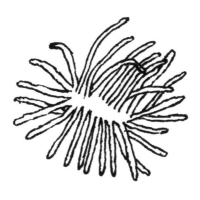

CHAPTER 9

T HE NIGHT OF July seventeenth was attached to one of those forgettable summer days when everyone is so slowed and dazed by heat it seems nothing memorable is capable of happening other than a sunset that turns as purple as the inside of a mussel shell.

Shoreside temperatures along South Sound usually swing between forty and sixty degrees, with summer offering more of the same until it suddenly broils into the eighties and nineties for a few weeks, the aggressive heat feeling like a fabulous mistake, as if tropical weather had been sent to the wrong zip code. When the sun sets, though, the temperature falls with it the way it does in the mountains, but in this case it's the ocean, not the altitude, chilling the air. Any breeze blowing off the north Pacific is refrigerated by cold deep water unless the sun is around to bake it. So T-shirt nights are as novel as blizzards to kids growing up along the Sound. And this was one of those nights, with the added attraction that every paddle stroke lit up the water like a wet torch.

Phosphorescent nights turn paddles into magic wands and

children into wizards. I indulged the fantasy for years until Professor Kramer made it even richer by explaining what was really going on. During certain plankton blooms the bay gets so dense with luminescent plants and animals the size of dust motes and smaller that they slam into each other and light up whenever the water stirs. Such nights often go unnoticed in calm inland waters, but they're hard to miss on the coast when waves light up as they crash ashore. The professor's explanation helped me understand how much denser life is in the sea than the air, as did learning that hundred-foot blue whales survive on rice-sized shrimplike krill, which if you think about it, is like elephants living on gnats.

So the heat wave and the phosphorescence pulled me onto the bay, and I didn't bring bags or a shovel because I wasn't looking for anything beyond my flashing paddle and whatever else flickered in the quietest hours. I sat too low to see much beyond the light I created and the flash of fish darting past like shooting stars, but the luminous thrashing off Penrose Point was dramatic enough to pull me off course.

I assumed it was the work of a playful seal or wrestling birds, yet it seemed too intense for them to sustain. It went on for so long that I had time to paddle a quarter mile to take a look. I slowed as I neared, not wanting to get all the way up on something so frenzied before I knew what it was. When I got as close as I dared, I flicked on my headlamp—the batteries were fading—and felt as if I'd paddled into one of those old seafaring yarns in which captains swore they saw multiarmed monsters writhing on the surface.

I coasted closer without meaning to and the bright tumult—about six feet across—went from looking like a glow-in-the-dark octopus to something that slowly made sense. I'd read how worms occasionally mate in surface swarms, but I never imagined so many, nor worms so large. They were still twenty feet away, but I was close enough to count at least ten, their bodies blue and green and almost two feet long. And that's the last I saw of those horny phosphorescent worms because the thought of one of them wiggling into my kayak inspired a flurry of short, frantic strokes that pulled me toward the unbroken shoreline belonging to Evergreen.

The only hint that there was a college nearby was the nude beach that spilled out beneath a curtain of tall firs. I'd rarely seen more than bearded, tattooed men looking like they'd lost their bathrobes, but the occasional oddly shaped woman was enough to lure me back—even at night. I paddled close enough to make out crumpled jeans and a half-empty pint of something clear. I looked eagerly up the beach, my heart still galloping from the worms, hoping for a moonlit glimpse of naked women playfully drunk at four in the morning.

I glided as high as the tide would allow without risking running aground or slamming into boulders or stumps that had washed up or tumbled down the hillside, my eyes straining, until I saw something rocking along the water's lacy edge.

My first hope, of course, was entangled lovers, but whatever it was looked too long and bulky, even for a large couple. The closer I got the more it resembled a harbor seal, yet it was still too long. So I assumed it was a sea lion, but I knew they weren't fond of muddy South Sound, and it wasn't *that* big. I beached the kayak, stretched my legs, then trudged toward whatever it was.

The lapping tide gave it the illusion of life, but the creature already stunk. It was at least nine feet long, and had the girth, but none of the grace, of a tuna. It had fins, but no scales. It wasn't a seal, porpoise, dolphin, sea lion or baby whale. The more I examined it the more prehistoric it looked, its chocolate-brown skin scarred and lashed as if it had been sideswiped by tugboats or dragged across broken glass. It also had a peculiar arc of circular welts across its side that I realized, with a jolt, were about the same size as the smaller suckers on the arms of that giant squid.

I removed my bow line, wrapped it around the fish's tail and tied the line to a stranded stump that I hoped wouldn't float away at high tide. Then I paddled hard toward home, imagining Angie watching from above as I blazed diagonally across the black bay like a phosphorescent fuse, trying so hard to impress that girl my arms were sore for days.

This time it was just Professor Kramer and a state biologist. At first, I feared I'd called in a nonevent, but the way the two men glanced at that fish and each other told me it wasn't a trivial discovery to either of them.

The professor's first priority, however, was to lecture me on the dangers of boating alone at night. He inspected my ragged life vest, clucked his tongue, then examined my kayak.

My father had made me stack it broadside across our beach for a whole month after a storm magically delivered it to me. That was almost a year ago, but I still wasn't past the fear that at any moment someone might claim it.

"You go everywhere in this?" he asked. I could tell that to him it looked like fourteen feet of cheap, battered plastic.

"It doesn't leak at all," I said defensively. "And it's never flipped. It's perfect . . . for me."

The professor mumbled something that had the word *careful* in it, then rejoined the biologist in examining the fish. I didn't interrupt to rave about the phosphorescent worms or ask about the squid. I simply waited for a moment to point out the welts.

The biologist eyed the fish through thick glasses that magnified his astonishment, then repeatedly glanced at the professor, checking to see if they were seeing the same things. That's the way those guys played it. They didn't share their thoughts aloud until they finished measuring, classifying, sketching and muttering technical terms. *Icosteus aenigmaticus*, in this case, which meant *soft-boned enigma*. I suspected it was a bottom fish. What I didn't know was that, like the giant squid, it was yet another secret from the abyss usually only found in the bellies of sperm whales. And yes, the men slowly, reluctantly acknowledged the obvious, that the grouped circular welts along its flanks sure looked to be of the same size and pattern as the giant squid's suckers.

"Good God," the professor groaned. "What in God's name is this ragfish doing *here*?"

The startling thing about that question was he didn't look at the state guy when he asked it. "Do you think they were fighting all the way down the Sound?" he asked. "Good God, Miles."

I started tingling. His words put the giant squid in motion for me, wielding its tentacles like long sticky whips as it battled this strange bottom fish, the two of them tumbling from the deep into the Sound, dueling toward shallow water, confusion, exhaustion and death.

"Good God," Professor Kramer said again. It was one thing for me to be startled, but the professor had seen and read everything, and *he* was at such a loss he was throwing God into the equation.

That was probably the moment when I started to secretly wonder whether I was being used as a messenger of sorts. Maybe Florence was right, I thought, about me being put here to do something big.

All that self-grandeur over finding a couple dead animals may sound childish and delusional, but you weren't the thirteen-year-old standing out there on that freakishly warm phosphorescent night with those two overgrown scientists exchanging spooked and excited glances, their flashlights winking off that fish, making it look even more unworldly than it ever would in daylight, as if it were some relic the ocean had spat up to remind us how little we know.

Even the noisy half-dressed college lovers that stumbled upon the three of us couldn't get their minds around that fish well enough to speak.

CHAPTER 10

A REPORTER CALLED the next day to ask if she could talk to me about the *unusual* fish that had been hauled away that morning to the same university lab where Professor Kramer and other scientists were still examining that dang squid.

When I opened the door, a tall angular lady with a camera strapped diagonally between her breasts looked down and asked me if Miles O'Malley was home. She couldn't hide her delight when I told her she was looking at him. It fell out in a half-laugh.

"You were the one who found the ratfish?"

"*Rag*fish."

"*You* also found that giant squid?"

"Uh-huh."

I thought she was going to squeal. She had one of those faces that would be perfect to hang out with if you were deaf. She wanted to know where my parents were and seemed even more delighted when I told her they were at work. Her eyes ransacked the house. Then I took her outside and showed her my room. She kneeled to scribble Rachel Carson titles and the names of the marine books stacked next to my bed. From my angle, I could see down her unbuttoned shirt to her lacy bra and the upper bulge of mid-sized boobs. I felt obliged to look, knowing Phelps would have swallowed three jellyfish for the view. I showed her my aquarium and talked about my collection business. Her head bopped as if listening to her favorite song.

I assumed this all fascinated her the way it consumed me, that I'd found someone who—on impact—shared the obsession. After struggling to enlighten Phelps, I was thrilled to find a pretty lady who not only seemed to understand my excitement but even *took notes* on what I said. She urged me to continue yakking as we strolled toward the bay, then snapped pictures of me, her camera clicking madly as if she'd confused me with some jeans model.

"Act like you're collecting stuff," she directed from behind the lens.

I glanced around. "At high tide?"

"Don't you collect stuff at high tide too?"

"Not really."

"Well, just look like you are."

Some kids are terrific pretenders. I wasn't wired that way, but if you saw the photo you know I squatted and picked up your basic heart cockle shell and puzzled over it as if it were a riddle.

"What's that, Miles?" she asked, while the clicking continued.

"A clam shell," I said.

"*Really?* What kind of clam?"

She squatted with the camera to her face and her blouse sagging open. I resisted looking again and glanced nervously about to make sure there wasn't someone kneeling behind me so that I'd trip onto my back at the slightest tap to my chest. Phelps, it won't surprise you, loved that gag. But there was nobody out there but us. And as my eyes swept across the bay she caught the image that landed in the newspaper of me holding that stupid cockle, gazing out on the water as if I were about to spot another ragfish, giant squid or perhaps a few dozen blue whales.

64

The truth is I thought all this would roll into a paragraph deep inside the newspaper somewhere, but then she abruptly demanded Professor Kramer's and my parents' work numbers. She also informed me that she intended to talk to Judge Stegner and even Phelps.

"What for?" The incoming current was delivering a kelp or trash wad behind her.

She frowned impatiently. "If I'm gonna write a story about you, I need to talk to people who know you, right?"

"I thought the story was about the ragfish."

She laughed. This lady showed every card. "It's just a little story about the boy who keeps finding cool stuff in the Sound."

"What kind of a story?"

"A good one. A good little one."

I nodded, but I was confused. She put her camera away and glanced toward her car.

"The next good low is at eleven-eighteen tomorrow," I said desperately, "if you want me to show you around." I felt like I was losing a friend.

"I'd love to," she said, though her face told me that wasn't close to true. "But I doubt I'll be able to make that." She eyed her tiny wristwatch. "Are you considered small for your age, Miles?"

"Are you considered rude for yours?" It just popped out.

She stepped back as if I'd fired a spitball at her forehead, then laughed a one-note laugh, a comic-strip *ha!* "Touché," she said.

Suddenly she was thanking me and pumping my hand in her long hot fingers as if I'd agreed to weed her garden for free.

She then ran-walked to her tiny car and drove off, her tires spitting gravel.

I waded to my hips to see what had drifted in behind her. Tiny barnacles had claimed almost every inch of it so it wasn't until I twirled it around that I realized it was a hockey glove.

A baseball glove would have made a lot more sense. I didn't know anyone who played hockey. Plus, the glove was stiff as wood and amazingly heavy. I studied it for a long while, wondering if it meant something.

My mother's hands shook as she read the paper.

Sometimes her pulse alone could do that, shaking her bones with each beat. My father never shook, but he usually stunk. If it wasn't Old Spice it was Mennen's or Scope. And if it wasn't those it was BO, tuna breath, Crown Royal or a mixture of the above. This morning his breath smelled like an aquarium that hadn't been cleaned in a month. He was reading over Mom's shoulder, telling her to *wait, wait, wait* before she turned the page.

I'd already read the story twice, once at the mailbox and once on the way back to the house. That newspaper lady cast me as the local Tom Sawyer who spent his summers finding beach treasures with his buddy Huck Phelps. Professor Kramer called me a gifted child with an "insatiable interest in marine life" and called the squid and the ragfish two of South Sound's biggest finds ever. Then Judge Stegner called me the most knowledgeable and reliable youngster he'd ever hired to oversee his oyster farm. And my loyal pal Phelps had this to say about me: "He's a freak. He's a decent enough guy, but he's a total freak when it comes to sea life."

There also were things I said, or that the lady claimed I said, that left me thirsty and dizzy, imagining the little article yellowing over time, lining people's drawers like some cold historical document. I pictured all that before reluctantly handing the paper to my mother, feeling the way you feel when you have too many blankets on your bed and your fever turns from cold to hot. I knew bad things would come of that story, but on that morning I couldn't get past the opening line. It was such a daring lie it left me mute.

"The beach talks to Miles O'Malley."

I didn't tell her that! I spoke to her for almost two hours and never said anything about any beach saying boo to me! Where'd she get that? Kids already thought of me as the science dork. I needed them to think I conversed with sand?

I waited for my parents to question me about it, to ask whether I was psycho, but they somehow read right over it. What pissed Mom off was the description of our house as "a modest old cabin that looks like it's about to collapse into the bay."

"She's saying we're poor, Sean!"

"Where does she say *that*?" Dad's eyes were bloodshot. It took him forever to read the sentence. Maybe he read it a few times. "Sounds 'bout right," he said, then returned to where he was in the story until Mom leaned away from his breath again and tried to rile him by repeating the line that said, "Miles's father, Sean O'Malley, works at the brewery." "She doesn't mention that you're a shift manager, does she?"

My father grunted, then shrugged. When people asked him what he did, he'd say he made beer, leaving my mother to boast about the twenty-six people beneath him. He plodded to the end of the story and looked at me, not with pride or shame, but wonder. "You got all these books beside your bed, and you've read most of them at least twice?"

He kept saying, *wow*, which didn't help me gauge much until the phone chirped repeatedly, and they heard from four thrilled friends. Suddenly my mother was poaching eggs the way I liked them and calling me "our boy genius." I liked the *our* part. How finding some ugly fish could help keep my parents together didn't make sense, but I hadn't seen my mother so happy since Judge Stegner told her she was one of the most informed citizens he knew. My father, though, looked as if he'd bonked his head. He tailed me into the garage for the first time in months and stared at my writhing, half-full aquarium, his bulging eyes lingering on that orange nudibranch.

After my folks left for work the next wave of calls hit. Reporters for the *Tacoma News Tribune*, the *Seattle Times* and three other newspapers tried to coax me into inviting them out to *just talk*. I had nothing to say. I called that reporter from the *Olympian* who'd left her little card on our table. She answered before it completed one full ring.

"This is Miles."

"Front-page Miles? What's up?"

"I never said the beach talks to me."

She laughed a short *ha!* "*I* said that. You didn't say that. That was my way, you know, of getting across how well you understand the beach."

"Makes me sound crazy. I mean I hear the clams squirt, which tells me maybe they're nervous, and I hear the tide drain through gravel, which tells me it's going out instead of sloshing in, and there's the sound of crabs skittering and barnacles clicking their shells shut, but the beach isn't saying, 'Hey Miles, what's happenin'?'"

She laughed another hurried *ha!* as if there were no time for full laughs anymore. "It makes you sound smart, not crazy. Everyone who reads newspapers knows that only the sentences I put quote marks around are things people actually said. The rest is what *I'm* saying, Miles, based on what I observed."

She was obviously trying to weasel out of it, but I didn't feel right trying to make her feel guilty either. Some people won't admit they screwed up no matter how many chances you give them. "Low tide is in two hours," I said, "if you really want to see what's out there."

"What?" She sounded like a different person. "Sorry. Gotta go. Call ya later."

She didn't call back, of course, until her cutesy fable about little Miles O'Malley took a more dramatic turn.

CHAPTER 11

"SO WHAT'S THE beach saying to you right now?" Phelps asked, straight-faced as a priest.

"Shut up." I'd been blushing for hours. "You're the *freak*. You're a tit freak. You know that?"

"Who's denying that? You're upset about me telling that lady you're a *freak*? That's why you're all Mr. Moody? You should be proud of being a freak, Miles. Look at the attention it's getting ya."

"Oh yeah. It's terrific."

"Shhhh!" Phelps said. "I think the beach just said something. Shhh."

"Quit it."

"Shush. There . . . It said it again." His voice lowered and he did a convincing job of not moving his lips: "*I can't wait for the goddamn motherfucking tide to come back in.*'"

He laughed until he lost his balance and his breath, which made him look so pathetic I almost joined him.

We were on Chatham Cove again, with a minus-two to ourselves, the sun frying me the way July did even when it was cloudy.

Phelps had no such problems, being, as he put it, tall, dark and irresistible. Whenever I'd start to think I was actually tanning he'd stick his mahogany arm alongside mine and whistle—further proof I'd be chickless long after he scored.

When we broke for lunch, I worried about Florence. I'd made her lunch six of the past eight days. Just tuna sandwiches and grapes, but from what I could tell if I didn't make it, she went without it. I thought of her waiting in her chair for me, and it struck me that in the span of a week I'd gone from feeling proud when I made her lunch to feeling guilty when I didn't.

Phelps interrupted my guilt to tell me that he'd brought another educational treat for me. I braced for another *Godfather* reading that would make me feel like a hopeless dwarf, but this time it was a magazine called *Variations* that was no bigger than a *TV Guide*. The woman on the cover showed me her tongue and breasts.

"Where'd you get that?" I asked, without breaking eye contact with her.

"Behind my brother's *Car & Driver*s."

"Is she a singer?"

Phelps laughed. "What's it matter?"

"I just wondered if she's an actress or a singer or someone we might know. I just like to know who I'm looking at is all."

"Yeah?" He laughed again. "Then check this babe out. Maybe you'll recognize her." He flipped quickly through pages. It was mostly words, but there were plenty of little pictures too. He opened to some girl in a pair of cutoffs that had fallen to her knees somehow. She displayed her breasts in her hands as if selling apples. Above the photo were the words: GIRL NEXT-DOOR.

"Recognize her?" Phelps baited.

My mind scrambled. *"No."*

"She's the girl next-door." He winked.

"Next-door to who?" I started sweating.

"To *somebody*. You think beautiful naked women don't have neighbors?"

I didn't know what to say to that. She looked as if her breasts felt so good she couldn't keep her own hands off them. Phelps explained that she no doubt benefited from airbrushing, some photographic trickery his brother told him about that covered up zits, mosquito bites and birthmarks. "They can even change lips, smiles, eye colors and nipple sizes," he said authoritatively.

"I know," I said, tired of feeling ignorant.

He flipped, fingers twitching, through the pages for something else. Suddenly there were tiny pictures of women showing me their privates and coaxing me to have my way with them. At least that's what the captions shouted. Their phone numbers were right there too. I couldn't believe it. You could apparently call them right up if you had the guts.

I backed up, overwhelmed. I'd seen *Playboy* foldouts. I'd studied every photo in *Sports Illustrated*'s bikini issue, but I'd never seen women's privates laid out right next to their phone numbers before.

Phelps laughed. "What's up? You don't like looking at naked women?"

"I'm not their doctor," I said. It was one of the stupidest things I could have said to someone like Phelps.

He laughed himself sideways, then said, "Bet you'd like to be Angie's doctor."

My slap caught him mid-blink, rocking on his heels, and knocked him back over his knobby knees onto the beach with his brother's sicko magazine clutched above his chest so—God forbid—it wouldn't get wet.

It all happened too fast to even explain it to myself, and before Phelps could call me a "fuckin' freak" for a second time I heard the cameraman and saw the lady who'd asked me all those questions about the squid the morning I found it.

They talked loudly as they stumbled over the barnacled rocks toward us, oblivious to how far their voices carried.

"Ah crap," I said. "It's television people."

"Good." Phelps climbed onto his feet. "They can film me kicking the shit out of you." But it was obvious he didn't have it in him. Who wants to be caught on TV whupping someone half their size?

The lady shouted my name and waved hello as if we were cousins.

"She's cute," Phelps declared, from fifty yards.

When she got close enough she extended her hand toward me. I tried to shake it, but got caught between a real shake and a fingers-only lady shake. She checked her hand for mud and found some. "You remember me, Miles?"

The puking mannequin, I thought, and nodded. My goal was to say nothing, but what if that didn't matter? What if she started speaking for me the way the newspaper lady had?

She wasn't as foxy as Phelps claimed either. Her eyes were so far apart she looked like a hammerhead shark. She said a whole bunch of crap I missed until she mentioned that during the squid morning, I'd said that perhaps the earth was trying to tell us something.

Phelps smothered a laugh.

"I shouldn't have said that," I mumbled.

"Why not? We all thought it was so provocative at the time, in a smart way. And now, in light of the ratfish you found, well—"

"*Rag*fish. I don't have any proof of that."

"Of what?"

"Of the earth trying to tell us anything." I resumed my effort to not appear to be listening to the beach, the water, the sky or anything but her.

"Well, how do you explain it then, Miles?"

"I don't. I just see what I see."

"Great. Great! Could we follow you around out here, seeing what you see?"

I looked around self-consciously, then down at her brand-new rubber boots. "We're just digging clams and looking for things."

"Excellent!" She finally introduced the camera guy. He grunted hello, the camera braced on his shoulder, flexing his knees as if preparing to fart or throw a shot put.

I hadn't noticed that I'd agreed to anything, that I'd said anything at all, but she and the cameraman followed us out toward the tideline where Phelps spontaneously transformed into the most inspired and informed clammer I'd ever seen.

"See the keyhole shape?" He pointed to a tiny hole in the mud. "A butter clam will be about eight inches down right here." He zeroed in with his shovel, digging near the clam in a few dramatic strokes, then scraping gently with the shovel's edge until he spotted the fat gray mollusk. He popped the clam onto the shovel and dropped it triumphantly into the bucket without ever touching it with his hands. The TV people gawked at the clam, its pale meat bulging between its shells, then at Phelps. He winked the only eye they could see.

I wandered along the receding tidal line, hearing Phelps blabber on, hoping they would get sick of listening to him and leave. When I found a geoduck siphon, though, I reluctantly called him over. He was really the hero this time. He shoveled valiantly, sweat bubbling across his forehead, as the hole backfilled with water. When he sprawled chest down in the mud and long-armed that geoduck out, the lady laughed in odd throaty bursts. I knew Phelps would do it, but I didn't want to see it so I turned and stomped off. A few seconds later I heard him whinny like a stallion.

They lost track of me then, which I liked, because I saw more when nobody else was around. But soon she was at my side again, asking what I was looking for. "Sea stars mostly," I said, "but anything unusual."

I wished she'd leave, but I couldn't resist pointing out the barnacles waving nets in the shallows like Southern women fanning themselves. "They're catching tiny plants and animals, then pulling them inside their shells to eat. See?"

She mumbled something about them being hard "to shoot," then walked so close to me her perfume made it hard to concentrate. Some perfume pushes you away or makes you sneeze. This stuff made me feel flattered to be near it.

"Even barnacles interest you?" she asked.

"If it wasn't for them, we probably wouldn't exist," I told her.

Her mouth popped open, but no words fell out. I kept walking, drawing her into ankle-deep water. I pointed out the differences between the black-clawed mud crab, the flat porcelain crab and the green shore crab. She asked me to pick one up, but the cameraman was shadowing us, and I didn't want another phony image of me holding something I didn't collect.

"You hear that crunching sound?" I asked.

"Yeah."

"You're killing sand dollars."

She winced.

"Walk over here," I said.

Mildly embarrassed, she followed gingerly. The cameraman grunted, then yawned.

"What do you think that is?" I asked.

She followed my pointing finger. "Part of a rubber tire?"

"Nope."

"An old toilet plunger?"

"Nope. A few thousand moon snail eggs." I explained how moon snails mix eggs with sand and mucus and spin the casings off their large round bodies and discard them along the beach in such haphazard fashion that well-intentioned beachcombers often bag them as litter.

While boring her with that, I suddenly saw what looked like a live, creeping, multitentacled rendition of the sun.

It was almost the size of a manhole cover and crawling back toward the water as fast as any sea star could possibly move, inching over the sand, a reddish-brown shimmering mass with all twenty-two legs engaged. The TV lady gasped. The cameraman swore.

"What's it doing here?" she asked, as Phelps came over and blurted a couple *fuck*s.

"Feasting on clams," I speculated. "Divers are the only ones who usually see sunflower stars, especially big ones like this, but apparently this guy was too busy eating and lost track of time or didn't think the water would go this far out."

I reached down with both hands and gingerly flipped it over, its thousands of tiny, suction-cup feet glimmering. I set it back upright and pointed out the light-sensitive eyes on the tips of each of its legs. "Sunflowers are the world's biggest sea stars. So it's quite possible we're looking at one of the largest stars on the planet." I explained that sunflowers are the grizzlies of the tidal flats. "Other sea life freaks when they smell them coming. Sea cucumbers inch-worm out of their way, cockles start hopping and sand dollars bury themselves way faster than usual." I measured the star, studied its colors, ran a finger across its spiny back.

"Why do you think *you* found it, Miles?" she asked.

I started to answer, then caught myself.

"Why is it that you always seem to find amazing things in these bays?" she persisted. I noticed the silver microphone in her hand and looked past her into the camera.

"Because I'm always looking," I said, "and there are so many things to see."

"But you keep seeing things that people shouldn't normally be able to see, right?"

"The unusual becomes routine if you spend enough time out here." I couldn't stop myself. "Like those new crabs with the hairy pinchers at Whiskey Point: I never saw them until about five weeks ago. Now they're everywhere out there. There's also this new seaweed that's taken over Flapjack Bay to the point that it's hard to find almost anything else out there anymore."

I told her more about all that as a large eagle dove behind her toward the water before aborting its attack and gliding across the beach. Eagles have a way of making all other birds look underdressed.

"So, maybe," she said tentatively, "like you said the other day when you found that squid, maybe the earth *is* trying to tell us something. And if so, what do you think it's saying?"

I hesitated. "It's probably saying, 'Pay attention.'"

"Is that a problem, Miles, that people don't pay attention?"

I stopped myself, and heard Phelps mutter, "Here you go again."

"I didn't say there was a *problem*. Rachel Carson said the more people learn about the ocean the less likely they are to harm it."

"Who's Rachel Carson?"

Phelps giggled behind me. "She's a genius," I said.

"A dead one," Phelps added.

She tried to keep me talking, but I was done. I said I was tired, which was true, but it was more than that. I wanted all this to stop.

"What do you think needs to be done, Miles?"

I took a long breath, then said, "I think I need to get this big star into my aquarium already. Could you maybe give us a lift?"

Of course she could. She put her arm around me the way Angie had, but there wasn't anything about it worth storing. Her perfume suddenly smelled like it was trying too hard, its odor so out of place on the mud it frightened me.

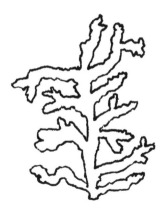

CHAPTER 12

LUCKILY THERE WAS nobody waiting for me at home, so I slept. It was more like a coma.

Griping gulls and squawking herons couldn't stir me, neither could the sporadic Heron bridge traffic or the distant kazoo of Highway 101. Even the buzz and rumble of saws, hammers and trucks in Sunset Estates wasn't up to it. I slept until I'd had enough, then woke gradually, absently studying a dust swirl that reminded me of the fish mobile that rotated above my crib. My first word, according to my mother, was *fish*. Make of that what you will. I closed my eyes and images swirled. The strongest ones involved Angie and that Girl Next-Door. I merged the two and it worked temporarily while I began having my way with my bedsheets, but then the television mannequin's face hopped onto Next-Door's body and jarred me almost completely awake. No matter how hard I tried, I couldn't keep Angie's face in the mix, felt guilty for involving it in the first place and unfaithful as hell for attaching it to some other body. I also didn't feel terrific about using Florence's dreaming-while-awake trick for such sick purposes.

So I was more confused than aroused when I heard the musical knock on my door, which was so loose at the latch it rattled with each tap.

Why hadn't I heard someone climb the steps? My mother was the only one who ventured up, but it was too early for her, wasn't it? Everything borderline sexy about the prior moment was long gone. I yanked on shorts and prayed that whoever it was—God help me if it was Phelps—hadn't peeked through the window.

I opened the door and there stood half-lidded Angie Stegner, her lips sliding into an exhausted smile. "There's my media darling," she said, glancing down at my naked chest.

It was the first time Angie had come to my room when she wasn't babysitting, which meant it had been at least three years. She laughed at the heaps of books and socks and underpants, then swaggered in, smelling like cigarettes and soap, and sat on my rumpled bed with her knees apart.

"Congratulations," she said, glancing again at my blushing torso.

"For what?" I asked. "I was just doing some push-ups and leg lifts. Getting in shape for wrestling next year. I might turn out, you know, if I feel like it. I mean, they want me to, but I don't know. The coach is kind of a freak and I've got lots of other options."

I read somewhere that people unconsciously hold their breath when they lie, which explains why I felt so dizzy. If I'd kept talking I might have passed out.

She studied me with squinting eyes and a cockeyed grin, then lifted her butt and straightened the sheets beneath her. "So, how'd you turn your latest discovery into a front-page story, Smarty-pants?"

"I didn't want that."

"No?"

"It's embarrassing." My mouth dried to the point my lips stuck to each other. "I don't hear the beach talking to me, okay?"

She giggled. "All's I know is newspapers always tell us how shitty everything is. Then all of a sudden there's this sweet story about my Miles."

I considered telling her about Channel 7, and how I feared I'd told them too much too, but her head was rocking from ear to ear on my pillow, and her jeaned knees wobbled back and forth until I noticed the dark patch up higher, where she came together.

"Miles."

"Yeah?"

"Can I smoke in here?"

"I do it all the time."

"Why? It's one of the stupidest things you could do." She tapped one out.

"I agree," I said. "I don't do it often."

That cracked her up, but even when she laughed *at me* there was still no place I'd rather be.

When I recall Angie's babysitting, I see her jumping herself in checkers, or barking so convincingly that the Ericksons' spaniels flip out. Or I see us crawling across her lawn, pretending we're rock climbing, with me yelling, *On belay?*—the only lingo I know—until she loses it. We used to roam along the flats where Angie was the first to spend more than impatient moments with me. She taught me which birds passed through when, showed me how to estimate the age of clams by counting the rings on their shells, and during one autumn explained the boomerang life cycle of salmon. She was skinny as a ballerina back then, with a face overrun by freckles and a shiny tangle of hair that had never been cut. I was a first-grader, strapped into an adult life vest in the bow of her canoe, watching her paddle us toward the acrobatic salmon that had invaded our bay. She said they were jumping like crazy to loosen their egg sacks. Then she told me that the same big fish had all left McKenzie Creek three years ago as pinky-sized babies, and had toured the ocean until it occurred to them it was time to swim all the way home to spawn and die in the exact same creek they were hatched. "How do you think they found their way back without a map, Miles?" I was speechless and overwhelmed. The closer we drifted to the leaping salmon the more battered and scary they looked, scarred and discolored, skin sluffing off their sides. Two landed close enough to make Angie swear. Then another broke the surface, surged toward the middle of our canoe, leaped again and rammed into fiberglass. I clutched the shuddering rails. "Watch where you're going!" she shouted at the fish, then laughed so hard my ears rang.

Angie watched her smoke curl into my ceiling. "Tell me something, Miles: What do you think of my songs?"

The question was so unexpected my mind jammed. "I love them," I said. The truth was she sang so hard it worried me. Her voice reminded me of a siren. "I think the words are very cool," I added.

She coughed out another cloud. "Don't try to please me, Miles. Please don't ever just try to please me. My world is over-fucking-loaded with people who try to please me."

I didn't know what to say next.

"Okay," she said. "Let's hear your favorite lyric."

"I like the sound of your voice," I said. "The words are kind of hard for me to make out."

"Now there's my honest Miles. The words aren't about sweet boys like you anyway. I write about bad men and gullible women. I write about revenge and disillusionment, about people who see death as an option."

That froze me. "I can't understand that," I said. "I mean, what's the hurry?"

"Hey!" She brightened. "Now there's a line. That's as good of a reason to stick around as any. 'What's the hurry?' Let's write *that* song, Miles."

It sounded like a lousy idea to me, but she laughed so hard her head snapped back, her cigarette cherry grazing and blackening the slanted ceiling. I didn't care if she burned down the neighborhood as long as she didn't leave.

"I'm sorry," she said after clearing her throat three times. "I'm really quite stoned right now."

I nodded knowingly, as if I were about to roll a few joints myself.

"You're inspiring, Miles." She watched smoke gather along the ceiling. "You don't lose focus. Stay that way, okay? My life is a wreck. I made more bad decisions last night than most people make in a year."

"I doubt it."

"Really? Well, I drank half a bottle of Jose, jumped off the Fremont Bridge, then took some Ecstasy and had sloppy sex with some couple I hope like hell I never see again. After all that, I spent almost a night's pay on a cab ride home, and the poor guy had to pull over twice for me to puke." Her eyes were greener and glassier than usual. She held her head back so they wouldn't overflow. "I'm a wreck."

"No you're not," I mumbled, scrambling to reassemble what she'd just told me.

She tried to laugh, but nothing came out. "That wasn't very convincing, Miles, but thanks for trying." She lay back, thighs wiggling, one boot on the floor, the other on my bed, sloughing dirt onto my comforter. "The hell with talking about me. Fuck me. I came to congratulate you. So tell me some of the cool stuff you've learned lately."

I considered showing her the sunflower star in the aquarium, but didn't want her to move. *Fuck me?* I could look right between her legs without her noticing, which didn't feel fair to her or me. It was hard to hold a decent thought in my head.

I wanted to tell her that my parents were acting like strangers again, and ask her why her mother left and how long it took to get used to that. Most of all I wanted to tell her how sick Florence was—it was getting harder for her to feed herself—without breaking promises. But this is what I said: "You know how most sea life tries to blend in with the scenery? Well, the decorator crabs go so far as to attach kelp, sea lettuce and eel grass to the pointy parts of their shells. I've seen them do it. They're like kids dressing up for an imaginary ball." I couldn't tell if she was listening. She tapped her foot on the floor, as if waiting for her turn to sing. "Some sea horses look so much like floating plants you would never think they were animals at all," I added, "unless you spotted their eyes or noticed their tiny fins suspending them like hummingbird wings." I forced myself to look away from her breasts, cradled like water balloons near her collar. "But the best blender of all," I said, "might be the peacock flounder." She stretched both arms over her head until her T-shirt rode up her belly and the black rose sprang into view, the stem disappearing down the front of beltless Levi's. "It looks pretty much like any other flounder, but I saw this show where they placed a chessboard on the bottom of an aquarium, then dropped a peacock flounder onto it. Its eyes popped up like periscopes and checked out the board colors. Then, in a few seconds, you could see its body start to change. See, its eyes told its skin cells which pigments to produce, and they did it just like that." I snapped my fingers. "Well, it wasn't right away, and it wasn't a perfect match, but this beige bottom fish turned into a black-and-white checkered flounder right before my eyes."

Her eyes closed and she yawned long enough for me to count three fillings on her bottom molars. There was no way she was still listening. Her upright knee swung in and out. To music in her head? She stopped wiggling and her breathing amplified. "Octopuses change colors when they mate," I whispered. "Their colors change with their emotions. So"—I ad-libbed this part— "the more intense the lovemaking the more spectacular their color changes." Her lips fell apart. She was definitely asleep. "And nobody takes much notice of barnacles," I added, "but you should see them mate. They've got these amazingly long penises that they unroll and arc out of their shells in search of willing mates."

She lifted her head and eyed me over her water balloons. "You hitting on me, Miles?" She followed that with a noisy laugh.

I wished she wouldn't have found it quite so hilarious, and I hoped what tickled her wasn't the notion that I'd have to be built like a barnacle to have a chance with her. But I was so happy to be laughing with her in my very own room that it didn't matter what she was thinking.

An instant later she looked sad again, as if her laughter and sorrow were separated by a week of trouble. "I was accepted at the University of North Carolina's music program," she said suddenly. "I picked it because it was so far away, but I don't know if that's such a great idea anymore."

"Fire ants," I said, desperately. "There are tons of fire ants in the Carolinas. They climb your legs and bite the hell out of you. And the jellyfish all sting. Every one of them. They blind people all the time."

She sniffled, stood and pinch-pulled her jeans toward her knees. "What's the hurry?" she sang, then grazed my forearm with surprisingly callused fingertips. The grin she left me with was sisterly and sympathetic, but my mind found a way to make it provocative.

I had my way with the bedsheet and comforter, the pillows and the mattress, all of which smelled of her soap and smoke. The first time I was rough, the second time gentle and sweet before breaking that effort off and feeling like the biggest fool in the history of fools as I headed into a shower that lasted so long I had plenty of time to contemplate how to save Angie Stegner's life.

CHAPTER 13

P ANSING SHOWED UP first. He had arms the color of old
pennies and a smile so quick it was easy to miss. He studied the
geoduck from three angles and carefully set it in an iced cooler, then
jammed thirty-two manilas and nine butter clams in there with it.

He rarely talked or made eye contact. He'd study my paperwork
that detailed where and when I found the shellfish, then cross-
check all that with the state's water-quality log for the Chatham
Cove area. Then he'd roll and smoke a cigarette on the beach, which
for some reason always relaxed me.

Until this afternoon I'd puzzled over why Pansing bothered to do
business with me. It felt like a favor. Talcott Seafoods could deliver
far more clams and oysters than Secret Saigon could ever serve.
Plus, Pansing owned and managed his restaurant, yet came personally and swiftly every time I called—even for just one geoduck.

On this day he smoked two cigarettes, apparently so he'd have
enough time to tell me how his family had walked from the
southeast corner of Cambodia all the way to Thailand.

"We walk at night, in line, very straight line." He chopped

invisible vegetables with his cigarette to show me how straight the line was. "Always my mother lead, so if we hit land mine we *just* lose a woman." He shook his head. "Crazy."

I tried to picture marching through a dark forest with my mother guiding us through mine fields. It was beyond crazy.

Pansing said the home he left behind was within a mile of a large bay where he fished with his father. "Much bigger than yours, but sometimes calm like this too." Then he explained how hard it had been for him to understand, as a boy, why they had to leave that beautiful bay to live in a stinking refugee camp where his mother died of something that sounded like dung fever. "It's still hard to think about."

"My parents are getting divorced," I said. It was the first time I'd said the words aloud so I didn't realize they'd sting. "I heard them talking."

Pansing said he was sorry, but he didn't mean it the way most people would. He was apologizing for telling me too much, for getting so personal he'd cut me open too. But what caught my breath wasn't that my parents were splitting, but rather the realization that the chances were good that I would have to say good-bye to my bay too.

He smashed his second cigarette before its time, then winced or smiled, it was impossible to tell which, and handed me a perfect twenty and a crisp ten and told me to keep the change.

An hour later, a baby-blue El Camino clattered down our driveway with its muffler rattling, and I braced for B.J., mumbling my tough-guy lines as he wheeled up.

I'd called the big aquariums, but they couldn't send anyone for days. I feared the nudibranch wouldn't last, and the tank was way too small to hold the sunflower any longer, so I'd reluctantly left a message on B.J.'s machine.

I didn't get his name from Professor Kramer. B.J. found me. All he ever said about it was that he had friends in the market for saltwater exotics and knew the Tacoma aquarium folks too. I didn't even know his real name. Just B.J.

He unfolded from his smoking car with bushy sideburns and pillow-creased cheeks. He called himself a drywaller once, but I doubted he worked at all, though he had huge hands that looked like worn-out canvas gloves.

B.J. was the opposite of Pansing. He always talked me down in price, but I'd promised myself that I would hold the line this time or refuse to sell anything. I told him to wait outside the garage while I grabbed what I had to sell.

He followed me in anyway.

The garage was so crammed with tools, spare box springs, bicycles, sleds and leftover lumber it was hard for the two of us to stand next to the aquarium at the same time. I smelled his salami breath as he leaned over me. "Let me get a look here," he demanded.

I tried to back up without touching him and tripped over my mother's bike that she never rode, cutting my forearm on its gear teeth as it crashed to the concrete with me.

B.J. didn't look back. "The slug's been in that bag too long."

"It's fine," I said, dabbing at blood. "I change the water all the time. Check my records."

B.J. never asked to see records. I'd told his answering machine that I had a nudibranch for ten dollars, a sunflower star for fifteen and an unusual mottled star for five. I told him the prices were final.

"The sunflower's too big for anyone to want that thing," he insisted. "It's a monster."

"Fine." I knew he was bluffing. "So do you want the nudibranch or the blue star?" I tried to sound disinterested.

"Can't you see I'm thinking? What's the rush, Squirt?"

"Going fishing with my father," I lied. "He's inside, getting ready."

B.J. snorted. "I'll do you a favor here. I'll take all three of them off your hands."

I bagged the stars and carried them out with the nudibranch. He stacked them in the bed of his El Camino as if they were sacks of nails.

"Got something to put them in?" I asked. "It's pretty hot out."

He dangled a twenty in front of me like a dog treat.

"It's thirty," I said, and left the twenty fluttering between us, above his heavy belt buckle, wishing like hell I'd demanded the money up front like I'd practiced. "The price is—"

"That slug's fading," he interrupted, "and you know it. If it dies right away in some asshole's tank I gotta give him his bills back. And I don't know who the hell will want that blue star anyway. And, like I said, the sunflower's too big for my customers so I'll probably get stuck with that monster if the aquariums don't need him. Twenty is plenty. That's a shitload of bubble gum, Little Man."

I hoped he couldn't see my neck muscles twitching. "It's thirty," I said. I wanted to say more, but didn't want to risk squeaking.

"You're a stubborn little shit. Has anyone told you that? Tell you what, just so you don't start blubbering here, we'll split it. Twenty-five work for you?" He handed me the twenty so he could jam fingers inside a front pocket.

By the time I took the bill he was patting the last of his pockets and grinning sheepishly. "Guess I owe you five. Cool?"

It sickened me to watch B.J. the Drywaller roll away with some of my favorite tidal life, but my teeth stopped grinding once I realized I wouldn't have to see him again.

For almost a week, summer resumed its regularly scheduled programming. I even talked my parents into playing Trivial Pursuit, thinking maybe board games kept families together, but it just made my father feel stupid and pissed off my mother when I got such easy questions that I won. Florence, meanwhile, kept trying to teach me ridiculous things like how to read tarot cards. Talk about confusing. Every card could mean almost anything. The devil could mean enlightenment or bondage or self-punishment or divorce or about six other possibilities. If I thought about it too hard my mind jammed.

One day Florence was so stiff I had to help her out of her chair twice, but I didn't dwell on that or anything other than Angie Stegner who hijacked my thoughts to the point it was getting hard to read.

I snuck out one night to spy on her window. I studied a corner of her bedroom ceiling for at least twenty minutes before realizing she'd probably left the light on and wasn't home. What would Judge Stegner have said if he'd caught his *oyster man*—the next great Cousteau himself—hoping to glimpse his daughter naked?

I saw a photo of one of the homelier guys you ever want to see in the newspaper the next morning. His name was right there for anyone to mumble, along with a couple sentences that told you nothing about him other than that he was a Level 3 sex offender. How many levels were there? And what level was bedroom peeping? It was easy to imagine a lousy picture of me next to a warning that Miles O'Malley was a Level 9 sex offender who peeped in windows and at weak moments mismatched butts, boobs and faces in reckless fantasies he couldn't finish. And then, of course, the ominous closer: *O'Malley is likely to reoffend.*

Yet aside from the Angie distraction, it was starting to feel like the summers before it, with long, anonymous, and forgettable, but nearly perfect days away from stuffy classrooms, sloppy joes and the puke in the halls that the janitors covered with maroon sand that stunk even worse than puke.

It wasn't easy talking Phelps into his first night run. His stepdad slept so lightly not even his brother risked sneaking out, but there was skinny Kenny Phelps waiting for me on Chatham Cove, shivering next to his bucket with an already dimming flashlight.

He had none of his daylight swagger. In fact, he looked spooked. The night beach can do that to anyone who isn't drunk or oblivious. Instead of the comforting banter of bickering gulls and scavenging crows there is the whoosh of bats and the screech of owls. Even the subtle scraping of a mid-sized hermit crab dragging its shell across grains of sand can sound menacing. I once crouched on Chatham Cove for fifteen minutes after spotting a huge Doberman just above the high tide line. It still scared me long after I figured out it was driftwood.

Phelps didn't regain any of his cockiness until he'd plucked a dozen butter clams from the dark sand and I'd granted him his union-mandated smoke break. I joined him, and he was feeling so good by then he didn't razz me about not inhaling. He even indulged my futile effort to get him to see the bullfight I saw in the moon.

"So when's that Channel Seven babe airing her thing on us?" he asked.

"Hard to tell with these things." I was suddenly a media expert. "Hopefully never."

"Fuck that! I was awesome that day." Phelps's teeth were the color of the moon.

I was thrilled Channel 7 hadn't run anything, which I considered the result of my erasing their three phone messages. The thought of talking to the mannequin again turned my belly into needles, especially after the call I got from Professor Kramer. He asked what I knew about the new crabs at Whiskey Point and the seaweed in Flapjack Bay that she'd questioned him about. After I told him, he'd sighed and said, "Well, do you see how you kind of made me and the state look foolish, Miles?"

My heart took off. "Didn't think it was that big of a deal," I squeaked.

"Well, Miles, you certainly know about invasives and the havoc they can cause."

I really didn't, and after I stammered a response I could tell he felt guilty for cornering me. He then explained what Chinese mitten crabs can do to cliffs and what that same strange seaweed did to the Mediterranean. His long explanation was designed to let me know everything was okay between us but it rattled me even more, and I cowered until he updated me on the squid and said a doctor named Stanley Glover was flying out from the Smithsonian to help study it. "We need a working name for her, and seeing how you found it, we thought—"

"Rachel," I said instantly. "Call her Rachel."

We found another cluster of butter clams in the dark and tossed in a few hefty horse clams, which work in chowders and eventually don't taste like rubber bands if they're shredded and boiled long enough with onions and potatoes. Once our buckets were two-thirds full, I rewarded Phelps with another smoke break and a news flash: "I checked out a book on the G-spot."

"From the library?"

"Yeah."

He laughed. "You got balls for a pipsqueak. You tell 'em it was for your mother?"

"Nope. Mixed it in with books on mollusks and cephalopods."

Phelps snorted. "So what's the title?"

The G-Spot.

"Clever. How many pages?"

"One hundred and eighty-five."

"Well?"

"Read it last night."

"You read it in one night?"

"Uh-huh."

"So it was good?"

"It was strange."

"Yeah?"

"It's about women who go through life without ever getting that one spot rubbed just right or any number of other complicated things that go wrong."

Phelps digested that. "So where's the spot?"

I told him.

He nodded knowingly. "What else?"

"Well, it kind of grossed me out."

He laughed. "How could any of that gross out anyone but a homo?"

I let that go. "It was kind of like reading about how to fix a dream car that you don't have yet. Know what I mean? You don't really want to know how complicated and difficult it is to keep it running before you're even old enough to drive."

He smiled. "Speak for yourself."

"Well, it's kinda intimidating and kinda gross is all I'm saying."

"What's gross about it?"

"Well, the long discussion about women ejaculating, for one."

"Cool! I didn't know they could."

"It's a whole lot like peeing."

"*No.*"

"I don't particularly want some girl peeing on me, or thinking she's peeing on me, or worrying that I'm thinking that she's peeing on me. Or—"

"Gross."

"Told ya."

"Weren't there good parts?"

"There were a whole lot of parts about women, who only had first names for some reason, blabbing about how their lives changed when they finally discovered their *spot*. Kinda like those before-and-after commercials when some lady squeezes into tight pants and says, 'I used to be a hippo before I started eating nothing but raisins and sunflower seeds.'"

"Any pictures?"

"Nope. Just some diagrams that, to be honest, were confusing. If you don't have a diagram on the wall while you're trying to do all that it sounds like you could get lost in a hurry."

Phelps thought that one over. "Thousands of people are fucking right this very minute without any problem."

"How do you know?"

"There are how many billions of people? Do the math, Miles."

I nodded. "Maybe."

He laughed. "People fuck in the dark all the time without charts or diagrams to guide them, don't you figure?"

I figured he was right about that, but I didn't want to give him credit. He hadn't read anything. "So?" I said.

"So none of this is helping me."

"Don't blame me." I rocked my shoulders, then stretched my back. "Read it yourself if you want, as long as you get it back to me before the twenty-sixth."

Phelps pondered that during an inhale so long I thought he'd absorbed the smoke. "I don't need it," he said, then snuffed his Kent into a rock and stuck the butt into a plastic bag just like I'd trained him.

Ten minutes later he said, "Name any band."

"Zeppelin," I said, reluctantly playing along.

"Jimmy Page," he replied, and performed a dramatic air riff on Page's double-necked guitar.

"Cream."

"Clapton." In the faint light I swear I saw Eric Clapton, his glasses, light beard and everything.

Phelps was a classic-rock freak, and considered himself an aficionado of lead guitarists during "the age of guitar," as his brother called it. We all deferred to Phelps on music and forgot he didn't know how to actually play anything. He didn't sully his musical reputation by struggling to play "Yankee Doodle." He pursued his calling by acting like a rock star, by sleeping in, smoking in public and scowling at adults. It was easy to forget he wasn't already a bandleader.

"Stones," I said.

"The great Keith Richards." Phelps draped a new cigarette from his lower lip, then leaned back with the expression of a man who'd recently enjoyed a terrific blood transfusion.

By then, Phelps was completely himself again. It didn't matter that it was still pretty dark, that his flashlight beam had shrunk to an orange circle the size of a sand dollar, or that his stepfather would ground him for a month if he got caught. He stood on the flats beneath that peephole moon, his skinny, Keith Richards hips cocked to the left, legs splayed, as if posing for an album cover.

We hunted for more clams to top off our buckets, but the only promising signs were too close to the incoming tide. A fundamental rule of clamming: Don't try to dig water.

Phelps waded up to his calves, looking for what I don't know, but I enjoyed watching him explore on his own. Then he was up to his knees. He'd worn chest-high waders, so I didn't worry about him getting wet, but the mud usually softened the farther out you went, and I told him that.

"Thanks Dad," he said, without looking back. I didn't say anything when he dropped past his knees. "Never seen so many starfish," he shouted. "Some of them might be keepers."

"Probably not, unless they're freaks." I reminded him of the fussy touch-tank buyers. "Plus they're probably too deep for you to grab without getting soaked or stuck, so come on back."

Phelps turned to scowl, I think, but I couldn't make out his expression. He bunched his sweater around his biceps and reached down. His sweater got wet, of course, but he came up with a star that was a burnt orange rarely seen in anything but sunsets.

"Nice," I praised. "Let me take a look." I reached out, hoping to reel him back.

"One more." He switched hands with the star, bunched his sleeves higher and dropped into deeper water. From where I stood it looked as if he'd skipped a step on a staircase. Water rose past his thighs.

He called himself a dumbass, then warned me not to say a word. He tried to turn and retreat. He laughed, but my headlamp caught that trapped-animal look on his face. The more he struggled the lower he sank. His waist was almost under.

"Maybe you can reach down and dig your boots free." I forced myself to sound calm, hoping Phelps didn't realize the tide was returning swiftly enough for his hips to cast a tiny wake.

His face contorted with concentration before he lunged downward, soaking himself to the neck. He straightened a few seconds later, gasping and dripping, then growled, "The fuckin' fuckers are fuckin' stuck!"

"Can you wiggle out of your waders?"

"No way." He was starting to whine. "I could barely get them on."

"Then don't move," I said. He'd sunk another few inches. "I'll dig you out. Relax."

I stripped to my underpants, stepped into the water to my knees, took a shallow dive away from him, then circled back, hyperventilating with my head above the water until I dove again and felt his thighs and followed them into mud that felt as loose and light as flour. It was colder than I expected and impossible to see because the water was dirty and the moon only so bright. I dredged blindly then surfaced, spitting, treading, careful not to stick my own feet in the mud. As much time as I spent on water I was still a crappy swimmer. "Try now."

He said he did, but it didn't look like it.

I dove again and dug more aggressively toward his boots. My breath was so shallow I didn't last long. I impatiently pulled up on his left leg, and that's when I felt the mud grab my right foot and panic rip through the length of me.

I'd been temporarily stuck often enough to know that if I used my

95

left foot for leverage to pry my right foot out I might never breathe again. That's when Phelps grabbed my hair and neck and pulled me free as if I were a kitten. I came up choking, paddling toward shore. The water was up to his sternum now, and I realized I'd made things worse.

People rarely got stuck while wading. It usually happened while they were crossing soft exposed mud, with the typical rescue involving wooden planks upon which trapped mudders would lay their torsos and crawl free from the muck. Oystermen did it all the time. So did Evergreen students. This was different. Phelps wasn't only knee-deep in mud, but also sternum-deep in incoming water. And there weren't any planks around.

The tide was swinging almost eighteen feet over six hours that night, which meant it was rising an average of three feet an hour. Another hour and Phelps might be under. When I shared my next idea, he pleaded with me not to leave him, then screamed for help. Like I've said, water amplifies voices, but there still has to be someone to hear them. And nobody lived along the wooded lip of Chatham Cove.

I pulled on my sweatshirt and boots and ran with a shovel toward Judge Stegner's oyster farm, then past it to the geoduck plantings. The judge and I had packed hundreds of fingernail-sized geoducks inside PVC pipes, which were then planted vertically into the flats. I dug up one three-footer, emptied it onto the beach, felt how it fit around my mouth, then sprinted it back to where skinny Phelps broke the surface like a half-submerged totem pole. I rinsed the pipe, waded out as far as I dared and tossed it to him. He raised a trembling hand, but didn't catch it. Was his arm stiffening? In the dim, reflecting light his face looked green and his eyelids were peeled so wide you could see all the way around his pupils. "Grab it!" I insisted. He slowly obeyed, then held up the pipe and looked at me miserably. "Practice fitting it to your mouth," I said, "so you can make a seal."

"Go get help!" he wailed. He wasn't even trying to sound tough anymore.

A silver ribbon of light shimmered on the water top about twenty feet behind Phelps. There was some red in it too, and while I assumed it was luminous plankton we'd stirred up, it seemed too uniform somehow. Sharks visited South Sound, but usually just three-foot mudders, and what I thought I saw was at least eight feet long and narrow. It didn't appear to be alive either, more like a long sheet of metal—except that it suddenly stuck its head up the way a turtle might. Luckily, Phelps didn't see what alarmed me, but he did start yelling when I hurled a rock at it.

"Be back in a flash," I said, though I really didn't know how long it would take to get to that first cabin or whether anyone would be there when I got there or where I would go next. "Practice breathing through it," I yelled. "And don't waste energy."

"Go!" he yelled.

Then I ran and heard his shouts behind me. It was hard to make out the words, and I felt like a jerk for stranding him, especially when I wasn't sure what I'd seen behind him. I fell twice before entering a dark forest that stayed so damp year-round that sweater-thick moss muted my screams for help.

CHAPTER 14

T HE CLOSEST CABIN was less than a mile away, but I'm guessing it took almost ten minutes to get there, running full tilt in rubber boots. It felt like a whole lot longer than that.

The old man who answered the door later told me he thought he was losing his mind when he didn't see anyone on his stoop until he looked down to find a kid in Fruit of the Loom briefs who couldn't breathe well enough to speak.

Mr. Skugstad was one of those solemn, old live-alone Scandinavians with the deep cheek lines of a man who'd been large once but deflated with age. He looked so old I considered running to the next cabin, but after he calmed me enough to fill him in he phoned the sheriff's office, and we jogged toward the mud with a coil of rope and an inflatable raft he dragged behind us. He stopped repeatedly to bend over like a man about to hit a pool ball. His face was as red as a spawning sockeye, and his breath squealed like wind that's trying to rip branches loose. It occurred to me that I might kill two people that night. Once we burst onto the beach, everything was easier to see, which made me worry I'd lost track of time.

It was impossible to tell by the peaceful water or the reassuring hint of a new sun that anything horrific was happening. That's the thing about the earth: It doesn't stop to acknowledge the daily disasters of the living. It just keeps on spinning and sucking. I think that's what drives people toward faith, that unsettling realization that the physical world goes on without them, before them, after them, without recognition or sympathy.

The tide had returned faster than I'd expected. The truth is it rarely comes in evenly. Its initial retreat and final return are so sneaky-slow they fool you. It's usually only after an hour drifting either way—when you're paying the least attention—that it moves with conviction. It must have been hauling ass during the time it took me to get that old loner onto the flats because once we rounded the point and headed onto the beach where Phelps and I had begun clamming, I was in full side-aching panic: There was no break in the surface, no torso, no pipe.

Nothing.

I'd left Phelps alone with a long silvery creature, and now there was nothing but water.

Old man Skugstad looked across the cove, then wildly at me, as if I'd drowned his own son or pulled the cruelest hoax imaginable.

It took me a few swallows to remember that Phelps and I had roamed farther south on the beach, and another sickening moment to spot the narrow PVC pipe sticking up well beyond the shrinking beach line like one of those tall sticks marking old oyster farms.

On a second frantic look there also was the bulge of Phelps's rock-star mop breaking the surface. I gasped, as if I'd been underwater too, then yelled that we were coming, which, of course, he couldn't hear.

When we got close enough, a panting Mr. Skugstad shoved me out in his raft with the end of a rope tied in a loop. As I frantically hand-paddled out to Phelps, I could see his mouth slightly below the surface, his fist clenched around the pipe and his eyes bulging insanely. I followed the old man's instructions and dropped the loop over the pipe and Phelps's shoulders. He slowly grabbed it with his free hand. "Make sure it's around his chest," the old man yelled. I couldn't tell for sure, but I said it was, then got out of the way as he coiled the slack, then turned and marched up the beach with the rope knotted around his hips. At first, Phelps didn't move, then there was a slight pop, and I saw the PVC pipe moving like a fat snorkel, then Phelps himself emerging and coughing in the shallows like some stranded mammal. The old man repeatedly whacked Phelps's back. He coughed violently. Nothing came out but drool.

"He's gonna be fine," Mr. Skugstad said. It didn't look that way to me. Phelps's lips were bruised purple and the skin around his neck was splotched orange as if he'd been hanged. We helped him out of his sweater and waders, then wrapped him in the old man's coat and hugged him until his shivering slowed.

Finally, Phelps looked at me and stammered, "That s-s-sucked."

He was laughing and crying by the time two women built like softball players jogged onto the beach with a stretcher slung between them. As they panted out to us, burrowed clams greeted them with a squirting finale that could have been set to music, and the sun crawled over the tree line and made the water dance.

If you live on the Sound you learn to store moments like these so that you can pull them out months later during the fifty-sixth straight day of stubborn rain and shrinking daylight. I saw a seal's tail swirl and a school of tiny silver fish break the surface and then some brown and white duck with frayed wings vanish like an arrow into the sparkling cove.

I saw everything.

CHAPTER 15

W HEN SOMETHING TURNS out well everyone dwells on
what went right. It's like reading about a ball game you
saw. If a team wins, it's all about what they did well, even though
defeat was just a weird bounce or a bad call away. It's the same way
with almost everything. Who highlights the bums and thieves in
their family tree? Everyone dwells on the doctors and mayors and
the others who fit into some show-dog lineage that makes us feel
more significant. It's the way we are.

So, of course, the sheriff's rescue team focused on my brainstorm
to get Phelps that PVC pipe. Only later did they ask why we were
out on the mudflats before dawn in the first place, and only after
that did they wonder if we were aware of the dangers of the mud,
and only then did they call our folks to ask if they knew where the
hell their boys were. Luckily, none of it made the newspaper, which
I was learning was primarily reserved for scary crimes, boring
politics and cute animals.

It took two days to find the guts to call Professor Kramer to ask
him about the fish I thought I'd seen that night, but I couldn't get a

call back. Meanwhile, I read up on turtles, eels and barracudas, and every other long silvery fish I could find, including a rare skinny deepwater creature the Chinese mimicked at festivals. When the professor finally did call back, I told him I thought I'd seen an oarfish in Chatham Cove.

He snorted, then lectured me on how easy it is to be fooled at night.

I let his words hang out there to see if he realized how silly they sounded considering all that I'd already seen after dark. "I saw it lift its head," I said.

"Did you see an eye?"

"I don't know."

"Was probably a fin or a tail or even a branch," he said vaguely. "You were under a lot of pressure."

Something had snapped between us, and I had no idea how to glue it back together.

Phelps suffered a tiny bit of hypothermia, which worked out perfectly. It landed him loads of attention from his brother, who taught him how to play the opening riff to "Smoke on the Water." And he watched tons of TV while grounded, which is why he was the first to warn me that Channel 7 was airing a special feature on a *remarkable* Olympia boy.

The mannequin sashayed onto a beach near the tavern explaining how she first met little Miles O'Malley at dawn on the first day of July on these exact same mudflats along Puget Sound's southern-most bay.

"This is where the smallest boy heading into eighth grade at Griffin Middle School discovered the largest squid ever found on the West Coast." The camera closed in on her wide-set eyes. "What has transpired since then has left marine professors and state fisheries biologists shaking their heads. Amazingly, the giant squid is just one of Miles O'Malley's recent discoveries. Others include a mysterious deepwater fish *never* seen before in our waters, as well as the unsettling invasion of some Asian crabs, which may already threaten dozens of seaside houses near here.

"How has this little Olympia boy stumbled onto some of the most dramatic marine discoveries in the history of Puget Sound? Who is Miles O'Malley? And what does this thirteen-year-old make of all this?"

The next image was the stranded squid. She fired off its length, weight and other stats and let Professor Kramer put it into historical perspective. Then she showed me calling it a cephalopod—to set up the book-smart kid—and aired that comment I regretted about the earth trying to tell us something.

"Less than three weeks later, Miles O'Malley came up with yet another discovery near dawn while kayaking alongside the beaches of Evergreen State College."

At first I didn't recognize that bizarre ragfish—indoors on a long metal table with some state biologist I'd never seen before explaining how it'd been considered possibly extinct. He then used a pointer to note how the circular welts on its side were indeed similar in size and shape to some of the suckers on the giant squid.

Chatham Cove was the next twinkling backdrop with distant silhouettes of me and Phelps on the flats. I couldn't believe it, but there I was, slapping him on television. From a distance, it looked like horseplay. *Kids.* Her voice-over explained that after hearing about the ragfish discovery, she decided to get to know Miles O'Malley. "I truly had no idea," she teased, "where this story would lead."

She explained in far more detail than I thought she knew how I'd created my own summer business by selling clams to a local restaurant and collecting tidal life for Tacoma, Seattle and Port Townsend aquariums.

"Not only has this precocious scientist-slash-entrepreneur found a market for his beach finds, but he has even convinced his buyers to drive to his home to do business—seeing how he's much too young, and probably too short, to drive."

She had an uncomfortable-looking Professor Kramer explain my "gifts," and showed Phelps furiously digging up a geoduck as if that stationary clam were a runaway mole. "What's different about your friend Miles?" she asked him.

The camera crowded Phelps's face. He took a breath. "The better question is, what's normal about him?"

She asked if I amazed him with my knowledge of marine life.

"Ask him anything." Phelps swept his bangs aside and smiled. I hated to admit it, but even with brown kelp caught in his eyetooth he looked like a dang movie star.

"I think Miles even knows more about all this stuff than the people who write all those books he reads," Phelps said. "What cracks me up is that he's clueless about just about everything else."

What a friend, huh?

Then came the sunflower star. It didn't look as stunning on television, but it still startled me. She pointed out how unusual it was to find such a big sea star that high on the beach. Then it was all me, talking fast and excited, face pinkening, nose peeling, answering her big questions and telling her about the new crabs at Whiskey Point and the new seaweed in Flapjack Bay and exactly where to find everything.

"We received a very interesting response," she said, "when we asked state fish and wildlife officials about the strange crabs and seaweed that Miles told us about: *They hadn't heard about them.*

"So we asked if they'd be willing to take a look with us, and this is what we discovered: The crabs are called 'Chinese mitten crabs,' and they are *not* native to this area. They're what biologists call an 'invasive species.'"

Then came the close-up of the tiny crabs. "They look harmless enough, right?" She awkwardly held one in her hand. "They only grow to about three inches across, and their hairy pinchers aren't big or intimidating. So how could a little crab like this be of much concern? Well, for starters, it bullies native crabs, and more importantly to locals perched above this beach, it *tunnels*."

The next footage showed hundreds of four-inch-wide holes I'd never noticed bored into the base of the sandy bluff. "If enough tunnels are dug they create instability, erosion and landslides," she said. "As unlikely as it sounds, these little crabs may have been responsible for the mysterious bluff collapse earlier this month just around the point here, which destroyed Joe and Edna Stevenson's four-hundred-thousand-dollar retirement home."

She then cornered two shy biologists to explain why the state had been unaware of the invasion of the Chinese crabs if it was already common knowledge among thirteen-year-old beachcombers. "We can't be everywhere at once," one of them explained. "This is actually an example of the system working. We rely on the public to keep us informed. And we appreciate the help." That's what he said, but it looked like the subject gave him a sunburn.

Then Wide-eyes was out on Flapjack with a handful of that strange seaweed. "The proliferation of this *Caulerpa*, which Miles had pointed out to us, also was not known by the state. And it appears the weed is already spreading across the channel toward tribal shellfish grounds. The same seaweed reportedly took over portions of the northern Mediterranean where it grew so fast it threatened *all* marine life."

Then she showed me giddy again with that sunflower star, head backlit, hair glowing, eyes sparkling. It's not being melodramatic to say that I looked possessed, maybe even holy.

"Why is it that you always seem to find amazing things in these bays?" she asked.

"Because I'm always looking," I said, "and there are so many things to see."

"But you keep seeing things that people shouldn't normally be able to see, right?"

I rambled.

"So, maybe," she continued, "like you said the other day when you found that squid, 'maybe the earth is trying to tell us something.' And if so, what do you think it's saying?"

"It's probably saying, 'Pay attention.'"

"Professor Kramer *agrees*," she said dramatically, noting that he'd told her that it was obviously *high* time for a fresh inventory of sea life in South Sound. "In fact, the professor says he intends to push for something he called a '*BioBlitz*,' in which a variety of scientists would team up to perform an animal census of sorts in the Sound's southern bays."

The feature ended with me talking about Rachel Carson, followed by that phony chitchat in which one of the anchors congratulated the mannequin for her *amazing* story and mentioned that he found it fascinating that a thirteen-year-old was a huge fan of Rachel Carson.

She nodded so vigorously it looked like whiplash. "His sidekick Kenny Phelps told me that Miles can quote long passages from Rachel Carson's oceanography books—*from memory*. And when he was given the honor of naming that giant squid still being examined at the University of Washington, I'm told Miles didn't hesitate to call her Rachel."

Even the weatherman loved that crap.

I waited for my parents' response, hoping I wouldn't puke up my share of the tuna loaf in the meantime.

Amazingly, they didn't lecture me again about sneaking out at night or badger me about how much I was pocketing from my collections or ask any of the other questions for which I'd rehearsed answers.

My father pointed out that while I might be the smallest kid around, I apparently had a bigger brain than anyone working for the state, which sent a quiver across my mother's forehead. Then he asked nobody in particular how it was that the only thing he knew beans about was baseball and beer when his son somehow knew stuff big-shot professors and fancy-pants scientists didn't? He sipped a flat beer, his face stuck in a lopsided grin that made me wonder if he'd had a stroke. "You realize how many people might have seen that broadcast?" he asked. "The Seattle area has what, Helen, a million people?"

"But it was just on in Olympia," I said.

They laughed and told me that Channel 7 was a Seattle station.

It creeped me out to think of all those strange eyeballs looking at me and our bay up close like that. I felt that odd sense of loss and betrayal you feel when you see a bad movie of a book you loved.

Mom told me that I amazed her, but it looked like I troubled her. She reached for my shoulder, but didn't quite touch it. "What do you want from us, Miles?"

When I hesitated, she said, "I mean what can we do to help?" Her nose twitched, and I knew she smelled the rising bay through the floorboards.

The phone rang. She ordered Dad to ignore it.

"I'm fine," I said.

"Are you challenged in school?"

"Sometimes."

"Should we look into getting you into a private school?"

"I'm *fine*."

The machine picked up, and some work friend of hers babbled about how her "boy wonder" looked like a miniature Michael J. Fox.

"You want to try to get an internship with Talcott Seafoods?" Mom asked, then sneezed.

The phone sounded again.

"Billy Eckert lives next door to one of the Talcott brothers," Dad blurted. "I could talk to him about it."

"I'm all right. Really."

"You need us to take you to the library more often?" Mom pressed. "You need money for books?"

The answering machine kicked on again, and Aunt Janet asked in her party voice who the heck would have thought that her little nephew would be the family's first television star.

"Come on, Miles," Dad urged. "We had no idea you were getting so damn smart about all this. We really had no . . . If you've already found your gift, son, let us help."

I probably should've felt flattered, but instead it stung that it took some mannequin on some crappy television program to make my own parents realize I might be somewhat special.

"For God's sake," Mom persisted, "there must be something— even if it just makes *us* feel better. A bigger aquarium?"

"No," I said. "Just . . ."

Dad froze mid-sip. I heard the tide settling beneath us.

"Yes?" Mom whispered. "What is it? Anything."

What did I truly want? A twelve-foot Lund with a red stripe and a six-horse Evinrude so that I could take Angie Stegner out for a boat ride. I also wanted a dog.

"Just stick together," I said, louder than I'd intended, "and don't move out of this house."

That left them speechless as the phone begged for more attention and I slipped outside to the bay where the tide brimmed so high and smooth it looked like pale green Jell-O.

CHAPTER 16

THE JUDGE AND I were cleaning and sorting his oysters,
discarding the dead, crating the mature ones, reorganizing
the young and playing our roles, him talking authoritatively with
his French-horn voice, me sunburning and listening along with the
gulls, the herons, the nudists and the rest of creation.

"Well, we now know that Angie is as bipolar as they come," he
suddenly volunteered. "See, it's all about chemicals, Miles. That's all
we really are upstairs, as much as we'd like to think there's all this
magic going on up here."

Bipolar? Was he telling me that she was crazy?

"The only way to manage something like that is with more
chemicals," the judge continued. "It's not hard to figure out what
somebody needs, but the catch is *they* have to take it. And you can't
make Angela Rosemary Stegner do anything. Least I've never been
able to. My three boys combined were easier than her. I don't know
if that says something about boys and girls or something about me."

He looked up, face reddening, as if lifting something much
heavier than oysters. "I was having lunch last Thursday with Judge

Crosby, and we were arguing again over whether judges should be elected or appointed when Angie waltzed in. Crosby gave her a look like she was some street kid panhandling for bus money even though she gave him a smile that should've floored him. 'Saw you through the window, Daddy,' she said. 'Just thought I'd say hello.' I was so flustered by how gorgeous and poised she looked at that moment that all I could come up with was, 'Thanks.' She laughed the way she does and everyone stared, but she couldn't have cared less what anyone thought. She bent down to kiss my forehead the way she used to before bed, then waltzed back out as Crosby leaned across the table and asked, 'So when're you gonna spring for an eyebrow ring, Norman?' as if she'd embarrassed me, as if I felt anything but gratitude."

The judge picked up another oyster, turned it over in his rubber gloves, then looked at me so intensely I glanced away, straight into the pulsing late-morning sun, and burned my eyelids trying to piece together what he was saying and why. I was used to adults spilling oddly intimate stories around me, as if I were too small to gossip, but this was unusual, even for the chatty judge.

"All she has to do is take her medicine and we can all move forward, but I know full well that she mixes Clozaril and the other one with whatever she's into that week. Part of me wants to know everything, of course. Another part doesn't. The problem with Angie is that making smart choices bores the hell out of her. I imagine you heard she passed out during one of her performances?"

"No," I lied.

The judge removed his sunglasses and methodically cleaned each lens with the bottom hem of his paint-speckled T-shirt. He looked so ordinary when he wasn't talking, his small cloudy eyes recessed in a fleshy chinless face. His jawline started out fine, I noticed, then lost its way. He wasn't fat, just unfinished.

He half-smiled, then crouched in his rolled-down rubber boots with four oysters that he surgically pried open. He displayed the raw, glistening globs on their shells in the mud, set perfectly equidistant, before nodding at me to begin.

I hated raw oysters, but ate them countless times with the judge. Always two oysters staged momentously in the mud like some grand sacrifice to Poseidon. It was a thrill he assumed I shared— eating his oysters, by God, straight from the bay. I threw those slippery blobs down, chewing as little as possible, trying not to squirm or wince as they slid into place so easily it felt as if they might slide right out of me. I studied the insides of the shells for pearls, but found only miniature purple murals.

"Good?" the judge asked.

"Tasty," I said.

Before I could figure out how to ask him if he was warning me that Angie was psycho, he was on to something else.

"Friendships can ruin you," he announced.

I smirked unconvincingly, assuming it was some witty aside about our oyster ritual.

"You have to be careful who you help," he said, "even when acting on principle."

He must have seen my bafflement, because he then loudly confided that he'd aggressively persuaded his fellow judges on a property-rights case that involved a college buddy by the name of Luther Stevens.

"Good for you," I said.

He liked that. I could play the judge even when I had no idea what he was talking about.

"No." He grinned bitterly. "Good for Luther, not for me. Loyalty and principle can come back around on you all gussied up as scandal—especially if you're running for reelection."

I was so lost I avoided eye contact. Again, I wanted to ask about Angie, but by the time I picked the words and readied my throat he thanked me for visiting Florence so often.

That struck me as beyond peculiar. Why was he *thanking* me? I'd rarely heard the judge mention her, and I never saw him at her cabin—although Florence often brought him up. Then it hit me: If he knew how often I visited, then he knew all about her condition, right? I felt the way I imagined people feel after confession. I couldn't wait for the judge to tell me that she had the wrong doctor or was taking the wrong medicine, and that he'd straighten it all out by the weekend.

"She really should be in a nursing home already," the judge half-hollered.

It took me a moment to find my voice. "Really?"

"Oh yes. I spoke with her neurologist last month. There's nothing more he can give her. It's dangerous for her to be alone, and it only gets worse."

"She doesn't want to go to a home," I whispered.

"Who does?" he bellowed.

I think that was the moment I stopped admiring Judge Stegner.

"Want to know something about that woman?" he asked, as we shuttled six buckets of oysters to his boat.

"Okay."

"Fifty years ago I considered her the most beautiful woman I'd seen in person. A young Sophia Loren had nothing on her." He raised his right hand. "I swear."

I tried to picture the face that went with a name like Sophia Loren while wondering where she or Florence fit into the judge's confusing lecture. Was he commiserating with my crush on his daughter? Was he warning me about her insanity and temporary beauty? Had he seen me peeping at her window?

Someone like Rachel Carson came straight at you and told you exactly what she wanted you to know in the clearest language imaginable. The judge surprised you with statements, then waited for you to connect the dots. I gave up trying to see his point and offered mine: "I'll help you with Angie."

The judge tilted his head, as if draining water from an ear, started a laugh, then smothered it. It was clear I'd misread him. There was no master plan, no collective message behind his midday ramblings. He'd just been babbling like anyone else who'd lost his footing.

"You are something else, young man," he told me. "Something else, indeed."

"Well, the offer stands," I said, and turned toward the boat so he wouldn't see the emotion twirling inside me.

The judge let me steer the Boston Whaler back toward Skookum-chuck Bay. He stood upright the whole way, balancing himself with three fingers on the steering column as yet another show of his faith in me. The tide was still low. If I accidentally hit one of the ever-changing sandbars or a half-submerged log he'd vault into the suds at thirty miles an hour.

Mallards, gulls and Canada geese flapped clumsily from our path as the judge and I strained to see Evergreen's five nude bathers—four bony men and one lumpy woman—sizzling like sausage links within twenty-five yards of where I'd found that ragfish.

It suddenly occurred to me that the judge would know exactly how fast divorces happen and who decides where the kids live and under what conditions judges insist that couples stay together, but I would've had to shout the questions over the howling outboard and I couldn't imagine doing that.

The bay's only hint of business, as usual, was the old, wind-peeled Mud Bay Tavern. Any renovation required bringing it up to code, the judge had explained, which was impossible seeing how there were no sewer lines that far west of downtown. So, year after year the tavern remained the same, without even a change in its two fading signs—one that said CHICKEN AND STEAKS, the other that just said EAT—or its fifty-five-year-old septic field buried in soil too soggy to absorb the sewage of more than a couple small families. Yet the tavern still somehow hosted overflow *Monday Night Football* crowds and the entire membership of the Bad Dogs, a motorcycle gang that showed up the first Thursday afternoon of every month for shuffleboard and clam chowder, which explained the fourteen Harleys lined up in front.

What distracted me, though, were the two pickups parked in the back gravel lot. They appeared to be moving, not backward or forward, but bucking on their shocks. By the time I glanced at the motorcycles again, they were toppling into each other in an avalanche of glinting chrome.

I started attempting to point all this out to the judge when I saw the telephone lines undulating like whips and steel light posts swaying like rubber tubes. "Judge!" I slowed the boat and pointed wildly at the tavern as it began its own left-right shimmy and spat leathered longhairs out its front door. The trucks continued bouncing so wildly we heard their shocks groan. The judge saw my stricken confusion, grabbed the wheel and explained in one word what was happening.

You can't feel an earthquake when you're on water unless it's big enough to trigger a freak wave, but even then you might not think *earthquake* unless you could see what I was seeing.

I pointed at the wobbling Heron bridge, the shaking tree limbs, the dinghies rubbing against the tavern's tiny floating dock. Dogs barked, the sky fluttered with agitated birds and someone shouted instructions across the bay. The next thing I saw made me think the earth was coming apart for real: Mud fountains sprang out of the tavern parking lot and out of the sidewalk leading to the bridge. This all carried on for what felt like five minutes. The experts later said the whole thing lasted thirty-four seconds.

"Florence!" I shouted once the trembling stopped.

The judge sped toward her cabin, picking a reckless route through the shallows. I braced for impact, but said nothing, even after the prop struck the mud twice. As we passed my house, I noticed that our front stilts appeared to still be doing their job. Amazingly, nothing looked out of place. The judge's house loomed as impressively as ever on the knoll. Even Florence's rickety cabin was still in its spot when we beached the Whaler and jogged toward it across thousands of broken shells.

Opening Florence's door required the judge's shoulder because so many books had spilled behind it. He gasped at the mess, but I could see it wasn't so bad. Three bookcases had collapsed. The rest of the clutter was just slightly worse than usual with the dust from old hardbacks whirled into slow-motion tornadoes.

She was in her chair, head tilted back, a washcloth and a bag of ice in her lap. She looked alarmed to see us, as if we'd come to kidnap her. She also didn't look like herself as a result of her nose being twice as large as normal.

"Florence!" the judge cried. "You hurt yourself!"

She shook her head, her eyes reflecting so many lights they looked like kaleidoscopes. "No, Norman, I didn't 'hurt myself,' but I'm considering filing charges against Mother Earth."

"We'll get you to the ER and get that looked at right away," he promised.

"No, you certainly won't." Her voice was a tight whistle. "Dr. Pendergast is making a house call. Thank you for your concern, Norman, but I'll be fine, just a little less glamorous than usual."

The judge's cheeks collapsed, as if she'd sucked his authority right out of him. "That was a doozer, wasn't it?" he said finally.

She sighed. "Shook this little house like it wanted to break it."

"Your stilts look okay." He wiped his forehead with the back of his hand. "But they should definitely be checked by an inspector."

I started picking up books: *Psychonavigation, Creative Visualization, Dream Mail.*

"Well, I'll be sure to do that, Norman."

The judge then, for whatever reason, gave her the play-by-play of our day—our four-oyster ritual, the dancing telephone lines, the motorcycle dominoes and the mud fountains. Take away his voice and he sounded like any boy in need of attention.

"Thank you for sharing, Norman. Now go check on your house and the others—and quit looking at my goddamn nose. I'll be fine here if Miles is kind enough to help me get my books back to a more familiar disorder."

The judge didn't know where to rest his eyes. "I'd be happy to drive—"

"Shoo!" she said. "The doctor *is on his way.*"

"There might be aftershocks," the judge warned, then sneezed.

"No there won't," she said.

The judge sniffled, then mumbled a few uncharacteristic *well-well-wells.* "It's not too hot in here for you?" When she didn't respond, he told her to call if she needed anything, then left us in the wake of his shrinking voice.

That's why he'd thanked me for visiting her, I thought. Florence is way too much for him.

"The earthquake had nothing to do with your nose," I said, without looking up from the books I was stacking: *Spirit of the Witch, Destiny of Souls, Miracles Do Happen.*

"How do you know?" she asked. A test, not a denial.

"Your ice is already half-melted," I said. "Your scratch is scabbing. And your black eyes are yellowing. Do you want these in any particular order?"

She waved a dismissive hand. "Don't dote on me, Miles. Go check on your own house."

I ignored her and sorted titles into whatever piles made sense, creating an aisle for her to shuffle through. *Psychic Wars, Numerology Secrets, Tantra: The Art of Conscious Loving.* I stared up at her lopsided face and tried to imagine what Sophia Loren looked like. "That doctor isn't coming, is he?"

"That was the biggest quake in forty years," she said. "That's what they'll say."

I reflexively glanced around for a television or a radio before remembering she had neither. She didn't want big business hypnotizing her: *Everything's better with Coke* was her favorite example. *Grab life by the horns: Get yourself into a Dodge* was another.

"So," I repeated, "the doc's not coming, right?"

"You might find me much worse than this someday, Miles. Are you prepared for that?"

"Is he coming?"

Her voice climbed. "There's nothing anyone can do for a broken nose other than tell you to ice it and try not to bang the stupid thing again. Answer my question, Miles."

I kept stacking.

"Miles?"

"I'm prepared to find you walking around your house without fear of falling."

She snorted. "If I'm supposed to sugarcoat things for you more than I already do, forgive me for overestimating your maturity. Didn't you read what I gave you? Look up the word *degenerative!*"

I was speechless. She'd never scolded me before. What she had wasn't actually Parkinson's, but some other neurological freak-out with a long crazy name meant to describe her brain's diminishing ability to tell her body what to do. Her right side would continue to stiffen, the articles predicted, and then her left side would soon do the same. Eventually, she wouldn't be able to move or swallow. It was like watching the Tin Man rust.

Nobody knew how anyone got it, but Florence had her theories. Car exhaust and hamburgers were her favorites.

"It's okay," she added after a deep breath. "Nobody's counting on this spinster—not even a goddamn cat."

"*Right,*" I snapped. "Rachel Carson never married either, but the whole planet missed her, including the nephew she'd adopted."

I finished stacking the books and didn't respond to any more questions. I left one of the fallen bookcases on its side, partly because it was too heavy to maneuver, partly out of protest. Then I banged out some ice, stuffed the cubes in a bag, slammed it on the counter three times and brought it to her.

I asked, in a demanding voice, if she'd been taking the pills her neurologist, a guy named Dr. Pack—which struck me as way too close to Dr. Quack—prescribed.

"They make me groggy," she mumbled.

I found the Sinamet and Mirapex in the bathroom and set them and a glass of water on her cluttered chairside table. "You should take them," I said, tapping out two tiny pills from each vial.

"How'd you know?" I asked, finally getting around to it, although I was still furious. "You told me 'something big' was gonna happen on the bay. Was it a voice? A feeling? Did you know it was gonna be an earthquake? Was it a guess?"

She didn't hide her disappointment in me. "I don't guess."

"Then what?"

"Don't push."

"I share everything with you."

Smiling looked like it hurt. "It's not that it's a secret, Miles. It's that it's fragile. It's like holding any image in your head. If you try too hard you lose it. The last time I talked about it too much I lost it for a long time. I can't risk that again."

Within an hour, I learned that the Capitale Apartments, the construction of which Florence had warned against, were so damaged by the quake that the county was likely to condemn them.

CHAPTER 17

T HE O'MALLEY HOUSE looked as if it had hopped up and down and landed on the same high wire. Three beer steins had rattled off the shelf and two candles lay on the carpet, but beyond that it just looked like it did right before my mother started yelling at us to pick up after ourselves. After calling my parents and reassuring them that the house and I were fine, I bicycled into the city to see as much as I could see.

Most of downtown was built as if it didn't expect to be there long. While Seattle built into the sky, Olympia stayed limbo low, perhaps because nobody wanted to throw too much money into buildings that sat just three feet above the highest waters, or perhaps because nobody was allowed to put up anything that pulled people's eyes off the sandstone capitol, built on sturdy higher ground to give it prominence as well as protection against a freak wave or record tide. And that's where we all rushed to gauge the worst of what the earthquake could do to us.

What I found was a stiff-necked mob gawking at a startlingly visible crack in one of the four-foot-wide pillars holding up the dome. People stared big-eyed at the flaw, as if they'd witnessed the cracking of the Liberty Bell. I rode around the building looking for other damage that maybe only I could see, then gave up and coasted down Columbia Street to the Capitale Apartments where some of its walls had shifted more than a foot and the penthouse had collapsed into an elevator shaft. I watched police stretch yellow tape across its entrance and firemen shuttle in and out. I wanted to shout *I told you so!* for Florence. I looked at everything twice so that I could describe it perfectly for her, then I rode on, surrounded by breathless, chatty strangers filling the parks, streets and alleys with their astonishment. I overheard the same numbers over and over: Six-point-eight! Six-point-eight! And the warning: *There may be aftershocks.*

News arrived in bursts and spread by mouth. The exact same earthquake had crumbled Seattle's oldest brick neighborhood and shoved seven Tacoma houses into the Sound. Airports closed, Highway 101 caved into Hood Canal and 230,000 households were suddenly unplugged. A total of eighty-three buildings were ultimately taped off in Seattle, another thirty-two in Olympia where the Deschutes Parkway looked as if it'd been riddled by meteorites. Even cities as far away as Portland and Spokane vibrated enough to crack windows. Yet despite all the wreckage and more than four hundred reported injuries, not a single person died at the will of that quake.

The sunset that night was a long blackberry stain beyond the hills behind our bay. People lingered outside, exclaiming, sharing, testifying, as if we'd survived a bombing raid together.

For once, everyone had a story.

My mother's was that she'd apologized for being so fat after her friend's Fiat started bouncing when she climbed inside it. My father said a friend of a friend was getting a vasectomy—which had to be explained to me twice—when the quake hit. That story was enough to double over my mother and make my father groan and grab his crotch. Then Phelps called to tell me that he'd been stealing some Kents when the entire fucking carton started shaking and spilling packs onto his parents' bedroom floor. He asked me how many people I thought were having sex when the quake hit. "Hundreds? Thousands?" Angie Stegner's story was that she'd slept through the whole dang thing.

By the time we finished sharing tales and inspecting our houses, a bearded University of Washington seismologist was on every channel asserting that the epicenter was in the Olympia area.

"More specifically," he said, pointing at a South Sound map, "it appears this earthquake originated about twenty-three miles beneath Skookumchuck Bay." That put a shiver through me. No wonder Florence *knew*.

The seismologist called it the biggest quake in the Northwest since Alaska's 1964 whopper that killed 125 people and triggered a two-hundred-foot tidal wave. He called our earthquake a gentle giant by comparison, considering, he said, that it, amazingly, killed *nobody*.

It shook us just long enough and hard enough to make us feel helpless, I thought, and just short enough and mercifully enough not to kill us. But it wasn't until I heard what happened to my school that I started thinking about the choices the earth made.

Overhead lights had crashed onto dozens of desks, but Mrs. Guthrie's portable classroom actually fell off its blocks and split in two, as if struck by a huge axe. The Ice Queen didn't smile once during the 181 days of my fourth grade. So why was her classroom singled out? Or what about the stretch of crumbled chimneys the quake left behind on just one side of Jefferson Avenue? And why did the brand-new fake fountain at the entrance to Sunset Estates crack all the way through?

Reporters, photographers and television vans wheeled up to the bay soon after it was hailed as the epicenter, just in case there were aftershocks or the bay itself released a formal statement.

We continued to flip between newscasts until a red-faced man told us what I'd been waiting to hear. "KING Five has learned that more than a decade ago an elderly woman, who used to give psychic readings in Olympia, predicted that the then-*proposed* Capitale Apartments would be particularly vulnerable to an earthquake *if* it was constructed. Well, it was indeed built and today it was as seriously damaged as any major structure in Olympia. KING Five's efforts to reach Florence Dalessandro for comment have been unsuccessful so far."

Soon one van, then two more, and finally eight people on foot sped down Florence's gravel.

There were no lights on, and the urgent knocks went unanswered. What they got instead of old Florence was Judge Stegner swaggering into the clearing in charcoal slacks and black suspenders to cheerfully announce: "Fortunately for Flo's sake, she isn't home right now. She's at a friend's house. And *no*, I'm not going to tell you which friend or exactly where she is. Florence has asked me, however, to tell you that she won't have any comment for public consumption on this or any other matter, but sincerely thanks you for your interest."

The judge then rattled on in front of the cameras in Florence's driveway, commenting that he'd never expected little Skookumchuck Bay to become the center of any universe. He kept mentioning the squid discovery, as if it'd just occurred, and observed that seismologists hadn't been aware of any fault line in the immediate area. "So either the fault is different than previously mapped, or *perhaps* we've discovered a new fault altogether," he said, as if he were heading up the investigation.

I watched from a safe distance as the judge milked attention. It was easy to forget that he wasn't the psychic who'd warned about the construction of that apartment building in the first place.

More than a dozen people took frantic notes. Behind them, others rehearsed in front of a bank of cameras, stressing that they were *live* at Skookumchuck Bay. "I'm standing in front of the home of Florence Dalessandro, the Olympia psychic who predicted in 1989 that the Capitale Apartments would be destroyed in an earthquake . . . We ready?"

I pictured Florence waiting it out in her chair without any temptation to answer the door or hear the details about her news-making cameo. I put a sign on her door the next morning that said she wasn't home and had no comment, but a Tacoma reporter eventually got inside with a knock that sounded like mine. He described her menagerie of books and her swollen nose. He got all that right, but he couldn't coax more than two sentences out of her: "I'm glad nobody died in those apartments. And that's all I have to say." It seemed like a crumb of news, but it landed in the paper and might have had something to do with the visit Florence later received from a state case worker.

At least that's the way I remember it. Time was jumping around on me again. The day of the quake itself felt like a week, and it still doesn't sound possible that I ate raw oysters with the judge during the same twelve hours that included that first visit from the cult.

When we heard the knock at nine-thirty we assumed it was another chatty neighbor, but my mother opened the door to strangers—a tall older lady and a stumpy, lipless man in a tie. The lady apologized for calling on us so late, then explained that they were members of a community school that hoped to speak to Miles O'Malley.

"Which school?" Mom demanded.

"We're with the Eleusinian School," the lady said gently. "We'd just like to talk to your son, if that's okay with you."

"You're with *the cult*?" Mom half-shouted, then laughed so abruptly the lady flinched. "I'm sorry, but my son won't be talking to any cults today. Thank you very much."

"We're not a cult," the lady patiently explained. "We're not a religion either. We're students at a school." The open door sucked wind and her soapy perfume into our house. "And our teacher is interested, with your permission, in conversing with your son."

"And why is that?"

"Well, she saw the television special on him, ma'am, and she simply wants to be open to the possibility that he is tuning in to the natural world in ways most of us aren't. And then with today's earthquake right *here* and all, she just wanted us to say hello, and to let you and Miles know that we'd like to open a dialogue, if that's okay."

My mother's laugh was cold. "We're not interested in our son being part of your freak show. *No thank you very much.*" She shut the door and vibrated her lips, then congratulated herself for telling the cult to shove it. Finally, she looked at me. "You didn't want to talk to them, did you?"

"I don't know anything about them," I said. The day had been so crazy, having some cult come looking for me didn't seem all that peculiar.

What I learned from my mother's subsequent rant was that the Eleusinian School was a cult of *loons,* including Australian loons for some unknown reason, who followed a local crazy lady conveniently named Mrs. *Powers* who claimed to have visions about the secretive rites associated with the so-called Eleusinian mysteries of ancient Greece. My mother called the cult's fenced compound a nuthouse for suckers and psychic wannabes. "At least Florence only charged ten bucks for her mumbo jumbo. This woman takes your life savings." Mom then mimicked the tall lady who'd just left: *We're students at a school.*

My mother's impersonations were often entertaining, but never flattering. She was so good at the rhythm of the judge's words you forgot her voice was so much higher. She could flutter her eyelids exactly like Florence and talk without vowels like one of the three Dons after his second Crown Royal. She did Phelps once right back at him, flopping bangs in her eyes and asking, *What's up,*

Mrs. O? and followed that with a long smile that, amazingly, matched his.

"It's getting to the point, though," Dad said cautiously, "where you've got to be careful what you say about that place. I just discovered, for example, that Nellie Winters is a student. And Nellie says it's basically good self-help information that a lot of people need to hear."

"They're a *joke,* Sean, and don't let loony Nellie tell you otherwise. It's new age bullshit at its worst. She mixes ancient rituals with the latest hokum. She blindfolds 'students' and sends them through mazes to teach them how to read minds! She makes them sit in bathtubs of seawater and scream while they listen to Yanni! She's been married twenty-eight times! She's a high-school-dropout-Rolls-Royce-driving con woman! Either that or she's got an amazing multiple-personality disorder—probably both—all of which suggests to me, at least, that we shouldn't let her anywhere near our son."

"Shirley MacLaine swore by her," Dad said sheepishly, lighting a candle.

"Shirley MacLaine," Mom hissed, as if the words were more than a name. "Why is it, Sean," she asked softly, "that you always believe the last person you talked to?"

"All I'm saying is that I don't know that they're any more ridiculous than a lot of other things going around these days." He lit another candle. "And old Florence sure isn't looking like such a crackpot tonight."

Mom groaned. "You make enough predictions and something's bound to come true! Everybody eventually wins at roulette if they play long enough, Sean. You think I was rude to them, don't you?"

"You were fine." He wouldn't look at her. "It's late."

I eased toward the door to check on Florence and to step into a night where beauty loitered and the sun took its time setting, as if it, too, didn't want to miss anything.

"Do you think I was rude, Miles?"

I looked past her to the trembling candle flames. "You didn't seem to bother them."

In other words, I knew they'd be back.

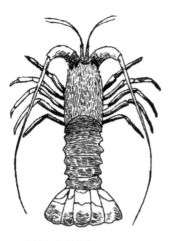

CHAPTER 18

THE NEXT DAY the bay swarmed with boaters, rubberneckers and three television crews, as if a Loch Ness monster or a Sasquatch might appear, or a prophet might speak, if they just hung around and didn't blink.

Several minutes after my parents sputtered off to work the same odd duo that visited the night before moseyed to the door. I noticed another eleven cult members beyond them, including one with a drooling baby in her backpack, shuffling in our driveway. The tall lady introduced herself as Carolyn and asked if she could talk to me for a minute.

We did that while the others sheepishly loitered, their hands folded in front of their privates, as if waiting on a principal or a priest. They all looked normal enough, other than that they seemed too friendly. Whenever I glanced in their direction they smiled the way Aunt Janet did if she hadn't seen me for months.

After hearing Carolyn's boring talk about their school and her exhausting apologies about their "intrusion" the night before, I asked whether their leader had a personality disorder. That answer got so long and boring, with all sorts of filler about religious mysteries and some "goddess of life," that I interrupted to ask if she wanted me to show them the flats, seeing how it was an hour before low tide and I couldn't bear listening to her any longer.

Her face bloomed as if I'd flattered her.

Once we shuffled to the beach, I treated them like third-graders. I told them to stick their heads between boulders to listen to the barnacles slamming their doors shut. Like most people, they couldn't believe the crusty little bumps actually housed live animals, much less critters who sealed seawater inside their shells whenever the tide rolled out. I also explained how tube worms recoil and trap water with filaments that work like corks, and how snails contract and slide doors shut too, and how crabs and sand fleas burrow beneath rocks to stay as moist as possible until the tide returns.

Then I strolled onto the flats, showing them exactly where to walk and how to avoid sinking in the mud. I pointed out how tidal life descends into everything, every crack, every shell and even between grains of sand, how if they slowed down and relaxed their eyes, they could see that much of what looked stationary was moving, like the thirteen tiny hermit crabs I pointed out in identical brown and white checkered periwinkle shells. I showed them life on top of life, barnacles and limpets stuck to oyster shells, clinging to each other, piggybacking on larger shells and barnacles on top of everything, as if there'd been a Superglue party the night before.

Most kids just want to know about the biggest and grossest stuff. This group was interested in *everything*. They jockeyed for position to actually *see* me explain things to the point I wondered if some of them were lip-readers. Carolyn was the only one who asked questions. The others smiled whenever I poured on the details. One of the ladies kept glancing around and chewing the side of her mouth. My guess is she was imagining aftershocks. I suspect we all were. It didn't help that Fort Lewis kept firing mortar rounds thirty miles away, with each blast sounding like a heavy table skidding across a wooden floor above our heads. But it was more than that. It takes time to trust the earth again once you've seen it move. It even looks different, the way your father looks different after he spanks you.

I pointed out how the eel grass lay flat on the beach, and asked them to imagine what it must be like to live in a forest that worked like a folding stage prop, going from three-dimensional to two-dimensional twice a day. And I asked them to consider that the hundreds of stranded moon jellies, scattered like palm-sized transparent blobs on the mud, would all be dead by the first fall storm if they even survived the wait for the next tide. I picked one up and showed them its torn underside. "They don't live long, but they got it pretty easy once they get to a size where nothing wants to eat them." I gently tossed that jelly into deeper water. Carolyn followed my lead, then all of them were hunching over, scooping moon jellies into their bare hands and ferrying them to deeper water like some jellyfish rescue squad. If Phelps had been there he would have laughed himself breathless.

I told them how the *Cyanea* jelly grows from the size of a gum ball to that of an umbrella in a few months. "And when they're full grown," I said, "they trail these long poisonous tentacles behind them that some smart baby fish use to shelter themselves from predators."

After I warned them to try not to crush the sand dollars—though there was no avoiding them completely—they tiptoed across the flats, as if sand dollars were an endangered species. One of the ladies limped slightly, and I noticed that her left ankle was twice the size of her right. I watched her pick up a sand dollar, turn it over and gasp at its tiny shimmering legs quivering in the sun like a stadium audience seen from above.

"You all probably know this," I said, knowing none of them would, "but the moon's influence on the tides is twice as strong as the sun's. Distance is more important than size when it comes to gravity. So it's obviously no coincidence that the tide and the moon usually rise about fifty minutes later than they did the day before."

They looked at me like I was Copernicus. Why did my mother mock these people? If they were crazy they seemed crazy in the right direction. I dodged their eyes and looked around my feet for clam signs. Even a middle-aged horse clam would get an ovation from this bunch. They mimicked my clam-hunting stoop and followed my path so precisely I made sure to traverse only solid mud, which was what I was concentrating on when I spotted the mermaid's purse.

I'd seen them on the flats before, but never this late in the season. Yet there it was, looking like a leather satchel some child had left behind. They crowded me as I kneeled to study it. I glanced up. "What is it?" I asked.

A stubby man cleared his throat and said, "Petrified bark?" Another one said it looked plastic. "It's not manmade?" Carolyn asked.

I opened the purse to what I expected to see, two baby skates set like human eyeballs against a black backdrop.

Carolyn gasped and tripped into the man behind her who stumbled into the lady behind him which set off a series of apologies that took a while to settle. When everyone crowded forward for a better view they were beyond startled and gawked at me as if I'd unwrapped the beginning of time.

"They usually show up in the spring in rockier areas," I explained, "but every now and then they wash up down here. They're egg cases for baby skates, better known as rays." I mimicked their kitelike glide through the water. "They come out soft, then harden into purselike pouches to protect the eggs. But these ones are very dead. I'm surprised nothing's eaten them yet."

I closed the purse and set it back in the mud, then splashed the stink off my hands.

"Where'd you find that giant squid?" Carolyn asked. "Around here, right?"

I pointed in the general direction.

"Could we see that too?" someone else asked.

"See *what?*"

"Where you found it." More heads nodded.

"Why?" I stalled. "There's nothing to see, and most of you don't have the right shoes."

"We don't care if we get wet." More nodding.

"You wanna risk getting stuck?" My eyes settled on the lady with the snoozing baby on her back, then on the limper with the huge ankle.

The nodders won, and I led them out. We had to help the fattest one out of two sinkholes, but eventually we all stood on the mud bar where the relentless tides had erased almost every sign of the squid, the TV crews, Professor Kramer's news conference, the judge's coffee stand and the rest of that morning.

I showed them exactly where the squid beached. I described its size, how my flashlight bounced off its purple skin, how its siphon quivered, and the loud sigh I thought I heard come out of it.

Then Carolyn talked quietly to all of us, although mainly to me, about the way their school viewed nature and particularly seawater. She said they were having a special gathering in two weeks, and that their leader herself had hoped I could attend and discuss sea life with her.

"Take me to your leader," I said in my best alien voice, which dazzled them all over again. Two weeks was a long ways off. It was so easy to say yes.

The backpack baby yawned into the next lull and peeked over her mother's round shoulder at me. I didn't make any faces or anything, but she broke into this gummy, fat-cheeked smile to the point people started giggling and I blushed so hard I must have looked like a cartoon character.

Florence had told me that babies often look slightly above your head because they're checking your aura to see if you're friendly. She claimed it's a skill we all lose and have to relearn. I admit it: I gave Florence's psychic lessons a second chance after she predicted that earthquake. In fact, I'd tried to meditate earlier that morning, although I couldn't even settle on a mantra. And the truth is, babies had always made a huge deal out of me. But until then, I'd assumed it was just because I was usually the closest one to their size.

I took a break from their relentless friendliness by resting my eyes on the next mud bar and a shimmering rectangle swaying along the tide line. It didn't look like an oarfish at first, but the more it shimmered and the more I studied its length, the more it looked like the same long silver creature I still couldn't shake from my mind.

I walked toward it, without excusing myself, and was almost upon it before I gave up. The light on the ripples, and the way it lurked an inch beneath the surface had been enough to trick me. It was nothing more than a five-foot-long four-by-four, which wasn't unusual at all, especially with all the waterfront construction past the college and along Sunset Estates. Yet it definitely wasn't new lumber. It was actually remarkably weathered with strange faded designs on one end. As I got closer, I saw they looked like those angular characters above Chinese restaurants. A souvenir, I suspected, that someone had carted home from the coast then lost off their dock. When I picked it up, though, it was obvious that wasn't the case.

Two men splashed out to help carry it back while the others continued rescuing jellies. A murmur spread, then they all eyed this weird, waterlogged post.

I tried to hide my excitement, but heard myself talking fast and loud about the odds against it showing up in Skookumchuck Bay. I explained how the coasts of Washington and Canada are separated by the fifteen-mile-wide mouth of the Stait of Juan de Fuca, and how Asian debris occasionally shoots that gap, but rarely, if ever, corkscrews all the way down the entire eighty-mile fjord to our southern bays.

"How do you know someone didn't bring it home from the coast?" Carolyn asked.

I pointed at the gooseneck barnacles stuck to its backside. "These guys cling to stuff that floats in the ocean. That's what they do. I've never seen them in the bay before, or anywhere around here. And they're still healthy, which means they probably haven't been out of the water until now."

"It's a street sign!" one of them cried. "It's an old Japanese street sign!"

After a long pause in which we all stared at that post and its odd, angular markings, Carolyn said: "You found it for a reason, Miles, didn't you? Just as you found the squid and those other discoveries. You've been *selected*, haven't you?"

What *was* guiding me to everything? My subconscious? Something from above? And, if so, what if there'd been a mistake? What if the wrong person had been *selected*?

A heron squawked past right then, as if to say it couldn't wait to flap out of earshot of such nonsense.

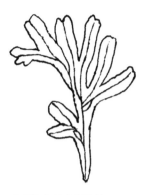

CHAPTER 19

I T WAS PHELPS'S "brilliant idea." That's all he'd say about it other than to instruct me to meet him at the Heron bridge with my bike. I hadn't seen him since he'd nearly drowned, so I didn't care what he had planned and didn't ask questions.

We glided through flickering daylight, the wind bending pines as we coasted across the Fourth Street Bridge, everything lodging in my mind; the girls smirking out passenger windows at us, Phelps humorously oversized for his bike, his brown hair flying behind him like a torn flag, Mount Rainier an enormous boulder in the sky on one side, the wounded capitol looming on the other, and beneath them both, the largest ship I'd ever seen docked in Olympia, a red and black freighter two blocks long and taller than half of downtown.

I'd read how Puget Sound was created by glaciers thousands of feet thick that advanced and retreated from Canada to Olympia again and again, dredging bays and carving passages over ten thousand years. I could almost picture it if I squinted, but it was much easier to visualize a tidal wave—maybe half the size of that two-hundred-footer that whacked Alaska—roaring down the Sound's main trunk, squeezing through the Narrows, then rolling up Budd Inlet, a cliff of angry water shattering downtown windows and splashing up against the capitol with kelp and jellyfish flying everywhere.

We pedaled through Sylvester Park, then toward the Sound, the sidewalks uncommonly busy, the horny wind lifting skirts high enough to turn Phelps's head. I looked away when I saw one of the three Dons pop out red-faced from the Eastside Tavern, and ducked when I saw my mother's friend Alice on the same sidewalk with her brat kid I used to have to entertain. People were just out strolling, but it seemed like more was happening, or about to happen. Phelps kept flashing his maniac smile as if we were getting away with something.

Earthquake wreckage still cluttered taped-off sidewalks, but most of the damage involved old brick facings of buildings nobody wept over. I was enjoying the motion, not even thinking about where we were headed. If Phelps had turned around and pedaled home, I still would have considered his idea brilliant, but it was clear he had something else in mind.

We turned down a surprisingly noisy alley where music was bursting out of somewhere. I followed Phelps behind First American to a green Dumpster where we chained our bikes together. Then we strode, wobbly legged, thighs sizzling, toward the sound of crashing drums. As we got closer, he finally revealed that his brother had told him that The Sisterhood was the easiest club to sneak into. "The back-door bouncer is a head case," he said, "and the place gets so loud and packed it's a free-for-all."

I said the obvious before we went any farther. "I can't fake twenty-one. I don't even look thirteen."

"Nobody will even see you, Squid Boy. That's your advantage." He handed me a black hat with a Rolling Stones tongue on it, then instructed me to follow at his left heel like an obedient dog. I adjusted the hat to its smallest setting, then pulled it as low as it would go without blinding me.

Phelps waited for a cluster of loud older kids to make their move, then squeezed behind them once one of them got stopped by some thick-chested guy. I followed, and we somehow jackknifed past everyone through the far side of the door while the bouncer checked invisible hand stamps with a tiny flashlight. And suddenly there were too many people and too much noise in a place way too small to handle it.

Thick bluish smoke swirled beneath ceiling fans that looked as if they were about to wobble free. The noise made more sense inside, but it was more violent and personal too, the bass guitar rattling my ribs. People wiggled and swayed in place, all staring in the same direction. Nobody was sitting, and nobody was covering their ears but me. Phelps pulled me closer to the noise, slithering toward the front where the stink of spilled beer and cigarettes thickened. Some woman wailed above the bass and the drums. I couldn't make out a word.

I tried to keep up, but people fell back onto me twice, knocking me over once, all without ever seeing me. Still, I kept following, peeking through the tangle of shoulders, breasts and elbows for a glimpse, trying to see everything I could before I either got crushed or plucked out of there. It helped that everyone's eyes were above me. The crappy part was I was at armpit level, and there was a whole lot of BO that didn't seem to bother anyone else. Everyone was touching or almost touching. It reminded me of the awkward moment when I had opened the wrong door and saw thirty greasy middle school wrestlers panting and grunting on a thick maroon mat in a windowless room where the only air must have been recycled fourteen thousand times through the same noses and mouths. This was worse. Not as sweaty, but hotter and darker and so smoky my nose stung. Plus, the music *hurt*. Still, everyone pressed forward, as if they couldn't quite hear it, as if they wanted to *feel* it.

Phelps grabbed my arm and snaked closer to the stage until there were just these three girls short enough for him to see over. Everyone half-danced, facing forward, moving disjointedly, as if to different songs. When the girls in front separated enough to give me a brief view of the stage my lips went numb.

Angie was wearing that same striped dress she wore when I saw her perform outside in the spring. Her hair was spiked and tossed, eyes closed, neck glistening. Her new eyebrow ring was neon green.

Phelps lunged into my view and yelled, "Gotcha!"

Maybe I should've guessed what was up, but Phelps was easy to underestimate. The posters outside hadn't said anything about L.O.C.O. or Angie Stegner, and I still didn't recognize most of her songs. But there she was, head cocked, her heavy boots set wider than her shoulders, her dress bunching high on tanned thighs. She suddenly screeched the way people screech when they jump off a high dive. Then her hairy drummer ended his frantic banging at the same time her bass quit throbbing through speakers that were as tall as me.

The applause was pretty loud, I guess, but it was nothing compared to the music. I waited for Angie to shout something like, "What's up, Olympia!" But she didn't say anything. She waited for the applause to fade, then casually asked if we'd noticed her new screech. "A baby barn owl taught me that one the other night," she told us. "It was the cutest damn thing." She ripped another impression of it, then coughed and laughed into the microphone, which made everyone laugh. It felt like an invasion of my privacy to hear my favorite laugh shared with all these clammy people, as if someone had split open my head and passed my fantasies around like breath mints.

Angie turned around to drink something, leaving us staring at the back of her dress that had such narrow stripes it seemed to move on its own. Some guy screamed, "Angie, I love you!" More people laughed, then yipped and hooted rodeo-style. I was hoping the music would start again before anyone noticed us, or someone else confessed their love. I looked around for phony Frankie, but I couldn't make out a face. Every second the music didn't play felt like our last. How long could it take to spot two thirteen-year-olds? At least they hadn't turned on the lights. A stink rose up. I held my breath, but it intensified and lingered. There was no escaping the deadliest fart in the history of farts. Rotting sea lions smelled better. The worst muddy, low-tide stink was refreshing compared to this. But nobody cussed, muttered, screamed or even covered their noses, as if getting dunked in the old fart tank was just part of the whole rock 'n' roll ritual.

My stage view vanished with the return of the beer-spilling boyfriends of the girls in front of us. And that's when I overheard some guy behind me asking who brought their "fucking kid brother." When one of them tapped my shoulder I ignored it. Then I heard somebody whisper that maybe I was a "tiny chick" or a "dwarf," which sent them into nose-snorting giggles.

Luckily, the next song came almost right on top of the last. It just felt like a month. The problem was I no longer had a view of anything but the wide denim backs of the annoying boyfriends. This time, I could tell, the drummer was singing. He and Angie took turns banging out rhythms and he kept saying *pass out* every ten seconds or so. There were no other words. Just *pass out*. People howled. It was the song they'd been waiting for. The couples in front of us squatted and the stage opened up better than ever. Angie struggled to keep her eyes open. Her swaying seemed excessive. *Pass out*. I noticed Phelps chatting with a woman crouched to his right, and by the time I looked back to Angie I'd lost sight of her in the tangle as the couples rose again, smelling like what I assumed was pot. I overheard Phelps asking that crouching woman if he could have some of her secondhand smoke. The song throbbed on. *Pass out*. I had no idea where it was going or if it would ever end, and I couldn't find an angle to see more than flashes of Angie. I focused on the thud of her bass, hoping to learn something about her from it, but there was too much going on. I watched that woman rise next to Phelps, grab his chin and cover his lips with hers, as if performing CPR. It lasted a long, long time. I had time to think seventeen thoughts and feel everything from fear to jealousy before smoke leaked out of Phelps's mouth and he started coughing wildly. I wasn't sure if he'd been assaulted or initiated, but once his smile surfaced I felt nothing but envy. He stuck out his hand for five. I gave it to him hard enough for it to sting, then refocused on the stage until I found an angle to see *my girl*, who I told myself was far smarter, cuter and ten times cooler than Phelps's *dundula* even if she wasn't filling me with smoky kisses.

Angie studied her strings, her left hand sliding up and down the long neck. *Passout.* The new lighting somehow made her look soaked, like some musical mermaid fresh from the bay. The boyfriends rose in front of me again, and the music seemed louder when I couldn't see her, because then it was just noise and sweat and another fart that belonged in the Guinness book. Phelps flipped me a thumbs-up because he, of course, was tall enough to still watch Angie jam. He air-guitared her for me in between glances at that girl who'd lit him up. I watched her hug some other guy and blow smoke inside him. Then she hugged a woman. I turned away, overwhelmed, as they kissed too. The gang in front of us crouched to smoke again, but I didn't like what I saw. Angie was swaying, and not to the beat. She and the drummer were slowing down. *Passss ouuuuut,* he said. Then again, even slower. As the song ended, Angie teetered and the drummer rose, leaning toward her with his hands out. The applause swelled, and I started scrambling through the dipshit denim boyfriends toward Angie, not excusing myself, moving through limbs, stench and smoke. Then I heard laughter and I caught a glimpse of her smiling. Soon everyone was busting up, and she said, "Thank youuuuuuuuuuu." The drummer leaned back, smirking all over himself.

When I turned around and exhaled, some older guy was lecturing

Phelps and waving me toward them. Then the thick bouncer barreled toward us, the crowd fanning from him as if he were on fire, as the band kicked in again and Angie's bass shook my bones and her voice rose above the bedlam. "Life sometimes feels like too much worry," she yelled. The thick-chested man steered us out with fat hands that had huge rings on every finger. I missed half of Angie's next line, then heard, "So what's the hurry?" Once we were completely out the back door I heard her croon, "Just give me twenty good reasons to keep onnn livin'."

"Names?" the bouncer demanded.

"Seymour Butts," Phelps said, then giggled as Mr. Thick started jotting down *Seymour*. The bouncer suggested we fuck ourselves and beat it before he rang the cops.

We strutted down the middle of Capitol Way, feeling the way Butch and Sundance no doubt felt after a little run-in with the authorities, with Phelps crowing about simultaneously making out and getting stoned, although he later admitted he didn't really feel anything from the smoke and was so startled by her lips he hadn't kissed her back.

"So what'd it feel like?" I reluctantly asked.

"You know how that first sip of Pepsi fizzes in your mouth?"

"Yeah."

"Kinda like that."

I doubted it, but what did I know.

"Could feel her knockers rubbing against me when she laid that smoochy-smooch on me," he added.

"No you couldn't."

"How do you know?"

"The story's good enough without exaggerating."

"Yeah?"

"Yeah."

"She definitely liked me," he said, running his hand through his hair the way he did when he thought hard about something.

I didn't tell him I saw her filling all kinds of people with smoke, but I did boast that I helped Angie come up with the song she was singing when we got booted. Phelps surprised me by how thrilled he was for me.

"Maybe you and me are gonna be a band, Miles. I'll be the lady-killing guitarist and you'll write lyrics, although there are probably only so many songs people are gonna wanna hear about barnacles and starfish."

"I read a book last night," I said, "called *Tantra: The Art of Conscious Loving*."

Phelps digested that. "What's that all about?"

"Sex, basically, but it's also about yin and yang and goddess energy and chakras."

"Slow down," he said. "Where'd you get it?"

"Borrowed it from that old lady friend of mine."

Phelps laughed. "'Hey, Granny, can I borrow your sex book?' How many pages?"

"Hundred and twenty-nine. It was weird. They called the G-spot the 'sacred spot.'"

"Like it's got some religion to it?"

"They had crazy names for everything."

"Like what?"

"They call a dick a 'wand of light.'"

A Starburst flew out of his mouth. "You gotta be making this shit up. What'd they call a pussy?"

"The 'precious gateway,'" I said, "or the 'golden doorway.'"

Phelps roared. "My lady, may I brighten your golden doorway with my wand of light?"

"There's all kinds of tips in there too," I said. "Like you're supposed to always keep your eyes open when you're making love."

"Doesn't that depend on who you're with?"

"You're supposed to breathe together too."

"Come on!"

144

"Why would I make this up?"

"What else?"

"You know how I was telling you that G-spot book talked about women ejaculating?"

"You said it was gross."

"Well, it's not so gross the way the Tantra people talk about it. They call it 'divine nectar.'"

Phelps giggled himself off balance.

"They say it can come out of their precious gateways like a mist. Sometimes it's even like a fountain that shoots divine nectar six feet into the air."

"Stop!" Phelps choked. "Enough!" He found his breath. "What else?"

"They say men should ejaculate less often."

"What?"

"Yeah, they say we should orgasm within ourselves sometimes."

"I don't even know what that means."

"I don't either, and I read the thing."

"How are we supposed to stop ejaculating?"

"By focusing on the higher chakras in our chest and neck."

"That is some outrageous bullshit."

"They say the best way for men to attain higher spirituality is through long periods of no sex."

"So we must be fucking saints already!" Phelps bellowed.

"Yes," I agreed, "we must be."

We took the longest route imaginable to the bikes, talking in circles about the sneak-in, the smoky kiss, the songs, the Seymour Butts line, the golden doorways and the divine nectar, recycling it, refining it and reliving it, each of us, in our own way, flattered beyond recognition.

CHAPTER 20

I'D ALREADY BIKED to the library and read everything I could find on oarfish by the time my mother informed me that Angie Stegner had her stomach pumped earlier that morning at St. Pete's hospital.

"She almost OD'd," Mom said, as if Angie deserved it.

I tried to picture a stomach pump, but all I could see was the little bilge pump I carried in the kayak.

"That girl's crazy," Mom said, while updating her to-do list. She was sitting cross-legged, her bare left foot bouncing noticeably from the thump of her oversized heart.

"You think everybody's crazy," I mumbled.

"*What?*"

I didn't say anything.

"She has no regard for her father's reputation. She has no personal accountability. She has no cares for anyone but herself, and her only concern there is apparently to see how many illegal drugs she can consume. I'd call that crazy, Miles."

"Why are you so mad," I asked, "at someone who's sick?"

"I'm not *mad*. Who said I'm mad? Did I say I was mad?"

"She's bipolar," I said. "Lots of people are."

"*Bipolar?* Who told you that?"

"I don't need to be told everything."

"Of course. I forgot you're a psychiatrist *and* a marine biologist already."

"She cares about *me*."

That surprised her. "Angie Stegner cares about you?"

"We talk lots."

My mother rolled her eyes and something flickered inside me. "What?" she demanded.

"You shouldn't talk about people you don't know," I said.

There must have been something in my tone because her lips paled. "I've known Angie since she . . ." Her voice rose, then halted. "Dammit."

Whenever she sputtered my instinct was to apologize and get past it. I'd seen her ignore friends for months because of one imagined insult. But anger was blowing through me too. "You call Angie crazy. You call Florence crazy. You call all the cult people crazy. You think you're the only one around here who's not crazy?"

"Just because you got on television," she barked, then said, "Dammit, Miles!" and stopped again.

"I hated being on television," I yelled, "and if you don't know that then you don't even know your only kid."

With that, I marched out of the house, my feet making a whole lot more noise than usual, my thoughts shouting in my head to the point that I couldn't make out her words behind me.

My stomach burned all the way to the Stegners' door, which was open such that I could see Frankie Marx slouching on the brown leather couch.

"Hey," I said.

Frankie glanced up, then popped upright as if I outranked him. "Miles! What's up?"

I couldn't come close to matching his enthusiasm. "Angie around?"

After some shuffling overhead, the judge leaned over the balcony, his face a heavy mask. He didn't have his glasses on, and he was squinting, a vein swelling diagonally across his forehead. "Mr. O'Malley," he purred, starting for the stairs.

I looked back at Frankie and almost felt sorry for him. He didn't look anything close to cool. He wasn't sure how to sit or stand, much less what to say.

"She out of the hospital?" I asked.

He hesitated, then glanced upstairs, and we listened to the judge's leather soles tap down the steps.

"She okay?" I asked.

Frankie's circular head movement, neither a nod nor a shake, alarmed me.

The judge extended his hand as if it were still a gift. Then I heard more stepping behind him and Angie's oldest brother descended. I shook Brent's hand too, as if we were all agreeing to something important, before the judge quietly explained that it probably wasn't the best time to visit.

I'd never heard Stegner men whisper before. Back when all the boys lived at home, I could overhear their daily conversations from our yard. It wasn't that they yelled at each other in a combative way. The house was just so big, and they were so sure of what they wanted to say, that there was a whole lot of shouting.

"You've grown up a good bit," Brent said.

"Not really," I said, "not as much as you have." That shook a grin out of all of them. "Just want to tell her about this fish I saw." I wished my voice didn't sound so insignificant.

The Stegner men swapped eyebrow shrugs, then the judge cupped my shoulder with his warm hand. "Give it a try, young man, if you're up to it, but don't be offended if she's not a gamer today, understand?"

149

Stepping into her bedroom disoriented me. I'd obsessed over it so much that to actually be inside it was like standing on the deck of a ship in a bottle.

It smelled like beer and smoke mixed with old stuffed animals, although I didn't see any. Her head was propped awkwardly on two pillows and her body lay flat beneath girlish flowery sheets. A poster of Chrissie Hynde hung behind her. I recognized her because Phelps spent an afternoon educating me with a stack of his brother's *Rolling Stone* magazines. All I knew about her was that she played guitar and growled like a bobcat when she sang about doing *it* in the middle of the road. Everything else on the walls looked dated, including faded gymnastics ribbons and a dusty painting of a wedding procession in which frogs held up the sweeping train of some rabbit's dress.

Angie didn't look anything like herself. Even something as seemingly permanent as her eye color was off. They were *black,* not green, and her skin had lost its tan overnight. I'd heard about babies getting switched at the hospital, but never teenagers or adults. She sighed when she focused on me and said, "Ahhh, shit."

"Sorry," I said vaguely. "I can go."

"It's not you," she rasped. "It's that it's all so repetitive. How *is* she? How *could* she? Over and over and over."

"I understand." My voice shook, but I kept going. "Just wanted to tell you about this oarfish I saw." It sounded ridiculous, but it was part of what I'd set out to tell her—the easy part—and I didn't know how to change course once I was that nervous.

She stared at me through crow eyes in a bloated face, her lips chapped and parted. "I'm sorry," I said.

"Quit saying that! What the fuck did *you* do? I'm the one who fucked up! And I, for one, am sicker than hell of saying *sorry*. The world is overflowing with sorry people, Miles. Everyone's so fuckin' sorry." A huge housefly buzzed my forehead, bounced off a window, landed on a curtain rod, then flew off again, buzzing louder than ever. "So tell me about your fucking fish."

Her eyes, I realized, had changed from green to black because there was nothing left but pupils.

By then I definitely wished I hadn't come, and I could tell by the way my stomach was still a hot fist that I wasn't even over my mother's words yet.

Still, I told her every last thing I knew about oarfish, how the one I saw looked like a shimmer of light drifting behind Phelps, how it lifted its head in a way driftwood can't, how I didn't want to scare him worse than he already was, but how I saw what I saw, even if I thought I saw it again and it turned out to be a Japanese street sign.

I took a breath then told her how seeing an oarfish was almost as crazy as finding a giant squid, how oarfish grow to fifty feet and swim almost vertically and dive like dropped swords. Then I told her that what I'd read earlier that morning had planted a seed in my head that was blooming out of control. I took another breath, then shared the revelation that some Japanese believe that if you see an oarfish it means an earthquake is about to hit.

There was no sign she heard any of that. I might as well have told her about my imaginary friend or my revelation that ice melts in the sun. I continued anyway, like an actor who wants to finish a scene he's already bombed. "Angie, I saw that oarfish—at least what I'm pretty sure might have been an oarfish—just five days before that earthquake hit *right here!*"

Still nothing. Her eyes were open, but unfocused. "I didn't really know what I was taking," she said in a raspy monotone. "I mean I knew, but I didn't know it could do what it did. If something feels good I want more. I don't understand people who don't want too much of something that feels good. I'm told I have an addictive personality."

I started talking because I was afraid of what she'd say next. "A lot of coastal sea life is like that," I said. "Razor clams and certain kinds of fish get addicted to the high oxygen levels generated by the crashing waves." Now I really hoped she wasn't listening.

"I mean I knew I was mixing things I shouldn't," she whispered, "but I didn't know it could kill me."

I couldn't have scripted a better cue for me to deliver the hard part of what I'd come to say, but nothing was anything like I expected. Even the air wasn't right. I desperately wanted to open a window.

"For guys, an abortion is like getting a tooth yanked," she suddenly said in that same sore-throated drone. "And it's not even their tooth. Even if they do stick around, it's still not *their* problem."

She looked at me, waiting. My mind scrambled and came up with this: "Not all males are like that." I sounded defensive. "Male sea horses carry the eggs around in kangaroolike pouches that work like placentas until they're ready to hatch. And by then, the females are long gone."

She let my blush burn holes through me.

"Do you hate yourself much of the time?" she asked.

I didn't say anything, because *no* didn't sound like what she wanted to hear and *yes* wouldn't sound honest. I peeled dead skin off my nose.

"I hate myself pretty often." She tilted her face back on the pillow, damming tears and attempting to smile at the same time. "Pretty fuckin' often."

I searched desperately for something helpful. "Meditating might push those bad thoughts aside," I said. "At least that's what Florence tells me—not that I'm any good at it."

"*Florence,*" she said, as if it rhymed with *ridiculous.*

"Have you tried crossword puzzles?" I mumbled.

"Crossword puzzles?" She'd never looked at me with less affection.

"My mother says they make her feel good about herself." I wished a trapdoor would open beneath my feet. "She tries to finish one before she goes to bed every night. Says it makes her feel good . . . about herself."

It looked for an instant like she might laugh. Instead she silently cried, her face aging and collapsing. "The best thing you can do for me right now," she said in an odd small voice, "is leave me alone."

I was grateful that she didn't look at me when she said that. That crazy fly beat its head against the window while I muttered something useless about hoping she felt better.

I floated down the curved staircase into that high-ceilinged living room where the judge and Angie's brother gave me some false assurances about how she'd be better in a couple days, as if solving her problems were just a matter of picking the right sentences, the perfect tone.

I shuffled outside on stiff legs, my ridiculous words spinning through my feverish head. Oarfish? Sea horses? Razor clams? Crossword puzzles! No matter how I rehashed it, there was no getting around the fact that it was the most pathetic cheer-up effort of all time.

Frankie was smoking alongside the house looking like a sad Marlboro man in need of a hug. There wasn't anything phony about him that day, and I was truly curious how his dog was doing. If I'd asked about Lizzy it would have made things easier for both of us, but I didn't even give him a nod, a grin or a grunt, which made me feel even crappier. I couldn't fake anything for anyone, especially not for Frankie Marx. I shuffled home wondering what I'd do with myself if Angie was never herself again. I guzzled milk straight from the carton until my stomach cooled.

"I'm sorry to hear you got a little smart-mouthed with your mother today," Dad said. I was in such a blind funk I hadn't noticed anyone else was home. I stuck the milk back in the fridge, then started for the door.

"Hold on, Miles."

"What?"

"You have anything you'd like to say to your mother?"

I looked at him, then at her. "Angie asked me to say hi to you, Mom."

My father cleared his throat and asked how she was.

"Fine," I said.

"Glad to hear it," Mom added.

It was as close as we'd get to apologies. I tucked my lips against my teeth, then headed toward the door again.

"Miles," my father said. "It's already the fifth."

I had one hand on the doorknob. "I haven't grown, Dad."

"I beg to differ. Look at him, Helen. Isn't our boy sprouting?"

My mother hummed a neutral response and started fussing in the kitchen.

"Later, okay?" I said, afraid of what I'd do if he didn't agree.

"Won't take a second."

I kicked off my shoes and stood like a prisoner against the broom closet. I didn't bother to fluff my hair or sneak air beneath my heels. I just stood and glared, my insides wheeling, while they discussed whether the hardback was level.

"That's it, Sean. Right there."

"Well, he hasn't shrunk, has he? I'm pretty sure of that. Come on, sailor. Stand tall."

So I did, to get it done, then listened to him exhale as he darkened the same four-foot-eight-and-seven-sixteenths-inch line he'd darkened the prior month and the months before that.

"Don't be discouraged," he said, masking his disappointment. "Your spurt is coming."

I unloaded. "Deng Xiaoping was five feet tall! Buckminster Fuller was five two! So was Napoleon! Beethoven was five four! So was Houdini! You don't have to be a giant to be a wild success on this planet! And there's no such thing as being smart for your *size!*"

His eyebrows twitched, as if tuning in to a radio station. "We're not going to love you any more or less," he said, "if you end up six one or five seven."

154

Five seven. That was the shortest he'd allow himself to imagine me ending up—two heavenly inches taller than himself.

I knew I had to check on Florence, but my mind was overheating, so I slipped between the barbed wire behind the Stegner property and into the pasture.

I figured out how to approach cows after I read about their vision. They can see just about everything that isn't directly behind them, but their depth perception stinks. They can't tell if you're five feet away or twenty feet away. That's why they startle so easily, and if one startles they all jump, and then you're in trouble. And that's why cowboys move so slowly. They're not just trying to look cool.

I moseyed toward the three largest cows in the low grassy depression closest to the bay. Whenever they glanced up, I stopped, letting them adjust to the sight of me before easing forward. One snorted finally, and dared me to keep coming. She snorted again, fiercely this time. Her head alone probably outweighed me. I plucked a tall blade of grass, stuck it between my teeth and waited. After a long pause, the others resumed eating, and she eventually joined them.

I stood among those cows for almost twenty minutes, wishing I could get a do-over on the entire day to see if I could walk through it without making everything worse. House lights flickered on around the bay. Sunrise to sunset now took just fourteen hours and forty-two minutes, and my summer was down to thirty-four days.

I slowed my breathing, then my thoughts, until I cooled enough to leave the cows and traverse the pasture toward Florence's cabin where high tide hovered a half foot higher on her stilts than the tables had predicted.

CHAPTER 21

I FELT FOOLISH standing outside the tavern waiting for a lady I barely knew, but I'd slept so little the night before all I could think about was napping on the way to wherever she took me.

By the time I woke we were already there, but it was hard to see any of it from behind the long stucco wall that flanked the compound. When Carolyn had to speak into an intercom to get an iron gate opened, I wished I'd told someone, at least Florence, the truth about where I was headed that morning.

I was so flattered by the attention Carolyn and the others had given me on the flats that I hadn't worried about the cult visit I'd agreed to. Plus, I didn't know anything about this *conversation* we were going to have other than that it was something my mother wouldn't have allowed, which appealed to me until we wheeled through that gate.

The main building looked more like a castle than a house, and the large barns beyond it were surrounded by dozens of tents and tarps. A pack of ladies older than my mother watched us roll up. The sky was scrubbed so clean I could see more detail in the moon than I could on most nights.

When we entered through a heavy door the music reminded me of the background sounds on those stargazing shows. Glass beads dangled from chandeliers, and the ceilings were twice as high as they needed to be. I saw huge dark paintings with little museum plaques beneath them. All the furniture was covered with the same maroon velvet. Carolyn whispered with three women who all had the same gray haircut and gray pantsuits and see-through necklaces. A stooped lady asked me if she could get me a Pepsi. I said sure, to be polite. I was still waking up.

Carolyn led me into another room and then through a passage with a fake waterfall and some smelly hyacinths into a curved auditorium with a half-bowl of sloped theater seating. People were straightening a stage and double-checking microphones, *testing, testing, testing*. Meanwhile, that same endless stargazing song played on. I saw a whole lot of whispering, eye-swiveling and those pleasant zombie smiles that the jellyfish rescuers had bombarded me with on the flats. The stooped lady handed me a Pepsi and a plastic cup. I set the cup aside and drank from the can. Phelps had to be bluffing. Nobody's kisses felt like that first sip unless maybe they'd been rubbing their feet on new carpet.

Carolyn left me with the Pepsi lady while the auditorium filled with peculiar-looking grown-ups, most of them fancy-dressed women, some with funny accents that made it sound like they were performing while introducing themselves. One man with a hamster-sized mustache told me to keep up the "terrific work." It took five of those miniconversations for me to realize a line had formed to greet me. It reminded me of the time I went to church with the Stegners when visitors were singled out by the preacher. Afterward, people shook my little hand as if I'd won some medal. This welcoming, though, was more like those boring wedding lines when the couple begins their marriage by smiling and shaking and making crappy small talk with a line of ridiculously happy friends of their parents. I didn't like shaking hands, but once it started the hands kept coming—some big and callused, others soft and even smaller than mine, or worst of all, damp. One lady, with a mole so close to her mouth I wanted to get her a napkin, stared down at me over small round glasses and informed me that she'd been looking forward to hearing what I had to say ever since she saw me on television.

"What do you want to talk about?" I asked.

She laughed quietly, as if not to wake anyone. "I'll wait, young man. I'll wait."

Suddenly Carolyn peeled me away to meet the lady with the biggest hair in the room. She had shapely eyebrows and skin so evenly tanned it was hard to tell it was makeup until I got up close. She looked like an older, fuller Fairy Godmother, and introduced herself as Delia Powers.

Her hand was so warm and soft it relaxed me. She asked if she could get me a Pepsi. I said sure, and someone next to Carolyn departed without saying a word.

"It's an honor," she said to me.

"Yes," I said. I had no clue what honor we were discussing, but I was pretty sure that she was the leader who wanted to chat with me. "I need to go to the bathroom."

She smiled, as if I were delightfully clever, and Carolyn showed me where it was.

The urinal was too high so I went inside the stall, sat down and couldn't believe it. That sickening stargazing tune was even louder in there. I looked around for speakers, then saw a damp flier on the floor next to my feet that I strained to read in the weak light. It mentioned upcoming classes on enlightenment, and below a wet blurred splotch was a schedule of "special events." I read down the list: A discussion of quantum physics with Dr. Sinclair Freeman on August 5, a lecture on numerology by Brenda Pryor on August 9 and a conversation with thirteen-year-old ecologist Miles O'Malley on August 16.

I read the same words three times.

It was way scarier than seeing myself in the newspaper or on television. This was something that was *about* to happen. And nobody even knew where I was! I pictured myself on the back of a milk carton and my stomach cramped.

When I came out, Carolyn asked if I was all right.

"You tricked me," I said.

She pretended to be surprised. "How?"

"You know."

She gave me a whole bunch of words next, including all sorts of crap about how informal and relaxing it would be, but I didn't hear most of them. Once someone lies it's hard to care what else they have to say.

"Take me home," I demanded.

"If that's what you want, Miles." Her eyes shone. "I just wanted to share you with others who I know would love to listen to you as well." She said a whole lot more, but I didn't make her feel okay about any of it.

"I want to go home."

When we returned to the big room it was almost as noisy as a school assembly, but there wasn't another kid in there and nobody else wore shorts or a T-shirt.

Mrs. Powers smiled down at me from the stage. "Ready?"

Someone handed me a new Pepsi, and Carolyn explained that there'd been a misunderstanding. She looked so pale and embarrassed I thought she might collapse. "Miles wants to go home. He didn't think there'd be an audience."

Surprisingly, Mrs. Powers was fine with everything. "You're the boss," she told me, "but before you go, just do me the favor of talking to me long enough to finish your Pepsi. That's all I was hoping for anyway, just to hear your thoughts on things most of us rarely think about. So, please come on up here and enjoy that nice cold Pepsi."

She walked toward center stage, assuming I'd follow. Everyone started clapping until she turned on a microphone next to her chair, thanked everyone for coming, then asked them to continue conversing while she got acquainted with her guest.

I hesitantly slouched into the chair across from her as she confided that she knew what it was like to be thrust into the spotlight, seeing how she'd experienced her first visions while washing dishes in her tiny Seattle apartment.

Something about her sparkling eyes reminded me of the *Jesus freak* who'd visited our school during recess when I was a fifth-grader, but something about her words reminded me of Florence, which relaxed me. She asked where I lived and how I got so interested in sea life, and suddenly I was explaining Professor Kramer and Rachel Carson and even telling her about Phelps. She listened a whole lot like Florence too. When I paused, she covered my Pepsi-chilled hand with her hot one and said, "This is all I want to do, and it's so much easier to turn on the microphones than it is for me to try to recount what you've said. But if you want to leave, that's obviously up to you, Miles O'Malley. You're the boss."

I shrugged. She nodded at someone, the lighting shifted, her voice amplified and people quieted the way they do on television when a golfer is about to putt.

She asked me why I was so interested in marine life.

"Well, I live on Skookumchuck Bay," I said, then paused. "I've never heard my voice so loud before."

The audience snickered. "You won't even notice it in a minute," she promised. "Don't pay it any mind."

"Well, I live on Skookumchuck, like I said, and I read a ton. I've read every book in the library on marine biology and quite a few they don't have, but I guess what got me going is when I learned that about eighty percent of life on earth is in the ocean, and that about half of the ocean is so deep that sunlight never even reaches it, and that it's been dark down there from the very beginning. Plus, we still don't know that much about it, really, which makes it a whole lot more exciting than land." I was full of Pepsi and talking so fast I didn't know where to stop or even pause. "And since I live on the tidal flats it's hard to resist, because that's where it all comes together. It sounds phony, but if you're out there enough you eventually think about the beginning of life on land too, because it probably started with stuff like mussels and barnacles so there was something for the first land scavengers to eat. You know what I mean?"

I sipped Pepsi to give her a chance to tell me to be quiet or to admit that this was a dumb idea.

"So when you found that squid," she said, "that tied some of this together for you, didn't it?"

"Well, the squid lives in the deep, so yeah, it showing up the way it did was amazing. And so was that ragfish. Everyone asks about the squid, but the ragfish was awesome too. Lots of scientists figured that fish was already extinct, see, yet there it was lying on Evergreen's nude beach. Maybe the squid and the ragfish simply got lost. A coincidence, you know? Most people think the squid is so ugly with its huge eyes and all that, but you should have seen it that morning. It was the coolest purple and such a brilliant design when you think about it. Makes sense—doesn't it?—that you should have the biggest eyes on the planet if you have to survive in its darkest waters."

The crowd giggled, but I couldn't see any of the faces, which relaxed me even more.

She asked what I meant when I said the earth was trying to tell us something.

"I really, really hate that question," I said.

Laughter bounced through the auditorium. "Okay," she said. "Try this one: You really love Rachel Carson's work, don't you?"

"She was the greatest." I felt words piling up inside me. "She's still the greatest."

"Can you quote from her?"

I smiled. I'd quoted her to people before, but nobody had ever asked for it, and nobody but Angie or Florence had ever seemed to enjoy it. "She has this one quote I really like in *Edge of the Sea* about how our search for the meaning of life draws us to the tidal flats: 'It sends us back to the edge of the sea, where the drama of life played its first scene on earth and perhaps even its prelude; where the forces of evolution are at work today . . . where the spectacle of living creatures faced by the cosmic realities of the world is crystal clear.' And then she later says, 'So the present is linked with past and future, and each living thing with all that surrounds it.'"

Mrs. Powers looked to the crowd and smiled. She could talk with her eyebrows alone. The loud clapping surprised me. I felt like a circus seal.

"What else have you seen or learned that amazes you?" she asked. "Please give us examples."

"It's endless," I said. "Abalones make shells harder than ceramics. An octopus squeezes through a hole one-tenth its body width. Arctic fish can freeze solid then spring back to life when they thaw because their organs are somehow protected. But it's the little stuff that gets me, the way that life scatters like dust in Puget Sound in the spring, that a cupful of water might contain thousands of living plants and animals, including baby barnacles and oysters the size of salt grains that already know enough to drop down during ebb tides so that they don't drift too far from their parents."

"You speak so eloquently about sea life," she said once I finally stopped talking.

"I'm just describing what's there and what I've read. When Rachel Carson accepted the National Book Award, she said, 'If there is poetry in my book about the sea it is not because I deliberately put it there but because no one could write truthfully about the sea and leave out poetry.'"

I admit it. I was indulging myself. It was my first big audience.

"What about that Japanese street sign you found near your house? What did you find out about that?"

I smiled. "My aunt Janet has a friend who was an exchange student in Japan, and her friend told me the post says 'Odyssey Drive.' At least, that's her translation. She also says Japan hasn't used that kind of street sign since the sixties."

She held up her hands, as if stopping traffic. "How about that earthquake? Why did it strike right below your bay, and what should we make of that? Or should we make anything of it?"

"I think when the ocean spits interesting stuff up on the beach it might be sending us postcards we don't know how to read yet," I said. "And when the earth shakes that violently, but doesn't kill anyone, when its tantrum is so selective that it picks which classroom, chimney and fountain to destroy, I think it's probably telling us something, but I don't know what."

She smiled at the audience. "Is he a wise child, or what?" Over murmurs that sounded like *amens*, she said, "Okay, Dr. O'Malley, now we're getting to the hard questions: Do you believe God is in all of us?"

"Wow," I said. "If there is a God I'd guess He's in nothing that lives or everything that lives. Why would He just be in us?"

She bobbed her head thoughtfully at me, then at the audience. "Should I tell him God is a *She*?" She cut short the laughter. "You quoted from Rachel Carson earlier about looking for the meaning of life in the sea. Is that what you're doing?"

"I try not to ask myself impossible questions." I was winging it. I'd never held that thought or the one that came after it. "We don't even understand everything that can go on in a drop of salt water, so it makes sense to me that we can't understand everything."

I heard sighs, then applause. "You are amazing," she told me, then to the crowd: "Isn't Miles O'Malley amazing?" She interrupted the applause to ask, "How do we know when we're moving forward? How should we measure progress?"

I frowned, my mind empty. I'd never understood the way people used that word, but by this point my goal was to not disappoint. "Crabs move sideways. They don't worry about going forward or backward." I stood up, raised my forearms at right angles and shuffled sideways with bent knees. I was good at crab impressions. The laughter was instantaneous.

"Do you fear that we're killing the ocean?" she asked once I sat again, feeling ridiculous.

"We could maybe ruin Puget Sound, and that would be horrible. And we could kill off lots of ocean species—we already have—but the oceans are way bigger than us and they'll be here long after we're gone. That's for sure."

She amused the audience with her eyebrows again. "So what should we do, Miles O'Malley? You play the teacher. We'll be your students." The crowd loved that. "What would you have us do?"

"See as much as you can see, I guess. Rachel Carson said most of us go through life 'unseeing.' I do that some days, then other days I see a whole lot. I think it's easier to see when you're a kid. We're not in a hurry to get anywhere and we don't have those long to-do lists you guys have."

She smiled that Fairy Godmother smile, patted a hand in the air to quiet the crowd, then asked if I saw things "coming." "Is there anything we should be watching for?"

By this point I was hooked on the attention and couldn't resist stretching it. I considered telling them about the oarfish, but it didn't seem dramatic enough. "You might want to watch the high tide on September eighth," I said. "It's not supposed to be a big deal, but it's gonna be way higher than predicted, the highest it's been in fifty years."

She opened her arms. "I think we have to be open to the possibility that our teachers come in all shapes, sizes and ages." Then back to me: "Thank you so much for coming to speak to us.

And believe me when I tell you that God is in you, Miles O'Malley. God is definitely in you."

It wasn't until I'd shook the last warm hand and the Pepsi jitters started wearing off that I spotted that lanky reporter who'd told everyone that the beach talks to me.

She was hunched over on the fringe of the crowd, writing secretly on something that fit in her palm. She studied Mrs. Powers, then wrote some more. When she flipped her eyes at me, she saw that I recognized her and she froze, then slowly raised a finger to her puckered lips.

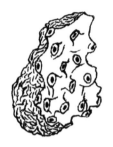

CHAPTER 22

FLORENCE SWORE her nose felt terrific, but that was just her toying with perceptions again because it looked worse than ever. Two weeks since her last fall, and it was still turning darker shades of yellow and purple and muffling her voice and blocking her vision whenever she tilted her head back to make a point.

I'd rehearsed the best way to tell her what I'd told the cult, but chickened out and said this instead: "The judge says fifty years ago you were as pretty as Sophia Loren."

Smiling looked like it hurt. "Norman always saw what he wanted to see. Still does."

"Does he visit you?"

"Used to be a regular," she said, "before he got elected. Norman has always been keenly attuned to public opinion. His affection knows many boundaries."

"You used to give him readings?"

"Of course."

I felt like an anthropologist digging up some ancient civilization.

"So when'd he stop coming?"

"After I told him he was gonna lose."

That blindsided me. The judge was gonna lose? "Why doesn't he help you?"

She snorted and her eyes bulged. "I've had people coming to me for *help* for as long as I can remember, but I've always considered it conversation. Life is something you do alone, Miles. You can only help and be helped but so much."

I avoided her scolding eyes and drifted toward the kitchen. She'd said she wasn't hungry but I didn't see any signs she'd eaten. There was nothing in the fridge beyond moldy cottage cheese, a hardened wedge of cheddar and some slimy romaine stinking up the produce drawer. I stuffed it all into the overflowing trash bucket and set it outside. "Want me to call Yvonne to pick up some groceries?"

"She's coming later in the week."

"What'll you eat in the meanwhile?"

"All kinds of stuff—almonds." She picked up a sack next to her chair to prove it. Her left hand shook more than usual.

"You're not a squirrel," I said, absently finger-drumming my chest. "You can't live on nuts."

"What do you think the cavemen did when they couldn't hunt?"

"Ate almonds?" I played the countertop as if it were a tall piano.

"That's right," she said. "Say whatever you want to say, Miles."

I hesitated, then confessed: "I stole your prediction about that superhigh tide in September, and acted like it was mine so that the Eleusinians would think I could see the future."

Her laugh released me and I told her the rest; how I'd relished an audience, how I'd performed for it, and how exhilarated and guilty and dishonest I felt afterward.

"You were as honest as you could be," she said. "It's not your words that matter anyway. It's your outlook they're after. It's you."

"They said God was in me."

"Of course they did."

"You're not mad?"

"I didn't realize you had so much faith in me, Miles." She smiled wide enough for me to see she'd chipped a tooth.

"I pushed it though," I whispered. "I said it was gonna be the highest in *fifty* years."

She lowered her head and wiggled her skinny eyebrows. "Perhaps it will."

"I think my parents are getting divorced," I blurted.

She nodded, as if I hadn't switched subjects.

I waited. "Did you hear me?"

"There's nothing wrong with my ears," she said. "True love is a tiny pearl, easily imagined and easily lost. But that's for your parents to sort out, not you. I'm sorry for you, Miles, but I'm not worried about you because you don't get in your own way. You never have, and believe it or not, that makes you extraordinary. The Eleusinians are going to school to try to become what you are when you wake up."

I blushed because it sounded like flattery even though she'd lost me halfway through. But there wasn't any time to dwell on any of it before we heard gravel crunching.

The lady who knocked was just a couple inches taller than me with perfectly spoked eye wrinkles that made her look tired of seeing whatever she saw.

She introduced herself as Julie Winslow, then explained with dramatic hand gestures that she was a case manager with Adult Protective Services, and that her supervisor had asked her to see if they could be of any help.

I watched Florence tighten, then speak in a strangely formal tone. "Thank you very much for your concern, but I am actually doing quite well. However, if I do find myself in need of some assistance I would certainly appreciate having your card handy."

The lady's smile was no bigger than a coin slot on a pay phone. She said she'd definitely leave a card, but she'd sure like to ask a few questions, if that was all right, of course. She looked for a seat that wasn't covered with books, then asked who I was.

"That's Mr. Miles O'Malley," Florence said. "He's my best friend."

I would have done anything for her at that moment. If she'd asked me to chase this lady off with scissors, I would've.

Julie Winslow stepped forward and extended a small white card. Florence's hand fluttered toward it. She now preferred her trembling left over her stiffening right? When had that happened? I saw her concentrate, but she couldn't control the spasm. Her hand was a wounded bird coming in for a bad landing.

The lady could have made it easier. Instead she watched the card fall from Florence's twitching fingers, then hunched forward to peel it off the floor, her nostrils flaring. Florence didn't smell terrific that day.

"Do you have the heat on in here?" the lady asked. "Sure is hot."

We shouldn't have let her in the house, but we did, and that was that, and there we were, and her questions kept coming.

"How's your nose?"

"Looks like hell," Florence said, "but works just fine. That earthquake knocked me around a bit."

"Where were you?"

Florence hesitated. "Near the kitchen there."

The lady squinted in that direction, as if looking for evidence—a dented countertop, a cracked window.

"Have you had someone look at it?"

"Oh, yes."

The lady waited for more, then said, "What does Miles here do for you?"

"Keeps me company mostly. Saves me a few trips to the refrigerator. Don't be fooled by him. He's older and wiser than he looks." She winked. Florence never winked. "I also have a friend who picks up my groceries and prescriptions, seeing how I try not to drive anymore—not that I can't."

That led to a flurry of questions about Florence's neurologist, medications and diagnosis, which Florence waved off as a mild variation of Parkinson's.

"So you're ambulatory?" the lady asked.

"Oh, yes." Florence smiled. In all the hours I'd spent with her I'd never seen half as many forced smiles. "Want to see for yourself?"

She took a breath, pushed down on both chair arms, then fell back into the cushions. She got up on her second try and gingerly steadied herself, feeling for that sweet spot on the balls of her feet that kept her upright.

I started to rise to steady her, then caught myself and recalled the judge telling me how helpless he felt watching little Angie teeter on a balance beam.

Florence forced another smile and took a huge breath at the same time, which made her look bug-eyed crazy. Then she rocked side to side until her right foot lifted enough to slide forward a few inches. She did the same to budge her left, then shuffled forward. There was tons of head and torso action, but her feet never left the floor.

The state lady glanced at me, her expression convincing me that Florence should have stayed in her chair.

The worst part was Florence thought she'd done pretty dang well. When she got to the counter, she clutched it, turned and beamed for real, as if she'd proven something. "I'm a little slow, but I get around." She leaned against the counter and breathed, reading our faces, disliking what she saw.

This Julie Winslow said all sorts of encouraging crap, but it was easy to see beneath the words that she had a job to do, and that she was very confident in her ability to make decisions about other people's lives.

"So, what about your perspective, Miles? Has Florence been getting worse, better, or staying the same?"

The question sounded harmless, but tightened everything inside me.

During the prior week, I'd started tapping her pills out almost every morning. Otherwise I found them on the floor. I loosened food lids and tried to leave her at least buttered toast or an apple if I didn't make her a sandwich. I helped her to the bathroom twice and even pulled her off the toilet once. She'd claimed she was unusually stiff that day and promised she'd never ask me to do that again, but I wondered how long it would be before she couldn't bring a spoon to her mouth or get up without me. Plus, I didn't know how to get straight answers about how she truly felt, and didn't know who else to ask, especially seeing how she'd sworn me to secrecy, without ever saying as much, about almost everything.

"Some days she's stiffer than others," I said vaguely. "The good thing is she doesn't really have to get around that much because she reads most of the time, and even the fastest reader only has to get up so many times to pick out another book."

We all laughed, but everyone looked sick, and I realized that I hadn't seen Florence with a book in weeks. Could she even turn the pages anymore?

"Parkinson's is a cruel affliction," the lady said after a clumsy silence.

"It's not actually Parkinson's," I offered, before I could stop myself. "It's cortical basal ganglionic degeneration. And her neurologist isn't even certain it's that."

The state lady looked astonished, glanced at Florence, to see if she'd challenge me, then pulled a pen from nowhere and wrote on a small pink pad.

Florence blinked slowly at me and swung her heavy nose a quarter inch from side to side.

After Julie Winslow finally left, I told Florence it was good that the state lady saw that she wasn't completely alone. I don't know if she heard me. She was as distracted as I'd seen her, half-lidded and alone with her thoughts or wherever she'd gone although her body remained a couple feet from mine.

I ran home, made her a tuna sandwich and ran back with it. Then

I shook out her pills and left the vials open beside her next to a coffee mug half full of water. (I didn't give her water glasses anymore. She needed handles.) I told her again that she did pretty well with the state lady, but she wasn't listening.

Her dentures stuck in the sandwich on her first bite, forcing her to pull the bite out of her mouth and clumsily tap her teeth back into place as my stomach rolled. She looked up, big-eyed, as if something just occurred to her. "I feel so grateful."

"It's just tuna," I said.

She laughed and everything felt normal again, so I told her more about how my conversation with the cult made me feel terrific and phony at the same time.

She listened intensely, and when I was done, said, "I just realized something."

I waited.

"You were the love of my life," she said.

It wasn't just the words that startled me, it was the tense. She talked for a while in that same tense, summing up her life. I let her go on, not out of respect, but because, like I said earlier, I was never any good at pretending. Finally, her eyes focused and she asked me to please finish stacking her books.

She chatted on in an untroubled voice about a dream she'd recently had in which her grandmother was a young woman again riding a red bicycle and waving at her. It was obviously a phony dream she invented to make herself appear distracted, to make me feel comfortable finding and setting aside her tiny Kama Sutra guide while I restacked the others.

After I finished, she sighed and asked me to please help her to the bathroom. Once I got her lined up, I left her to lower her pants and do her thing, but waited around just in case. After a long silence during which I worried she'd fallen asleep, she called for help. I came in, held my breath, braced my feet against the toes of her shoes, pulled her up by her bony wrists, then reached behind her and flushed. She apologized cheerfully and kidded herself for being way too old to let someone like Julie Winslow rattle her, as if getting on and off the toilet were a matter of confidence.

Before I left, she asked me to bring her one of the blue pills from the closet. "Sleep will give me strength," she said, but didn't sound convincing.

Glancing back through her cabin window, I saw her trying to shield her eyes from the late sun, or possibly from me, her hand bouncing lightly, trying to land, as if it were loose at the wrist and about to wobble off.

CHAPTER 23

THREE OF US huddled eagerly above a speakerphone in the tidy den belonging to the parents of Phelps's obnoxious neighbor Blake "Blister" Cunningham. As soon as this girl named Ruby got on the line, Phelps took over. He introduced himself, told her two of his friends were listening in, then said, "Would you please fake an orgasm?"

Ruby giggled through the speaker, then started panting lightly, as if climbing steps. That was enough to make us blush, although she still sounded pretty phony to me until she started whispering, "Oh yeahhhhhhhh," before yipping like a puppy and mewing like a hungry kitten. Then came a series of jolting breaths as if she'd touched something hot, followed by long, supersatisfied noises that came from somewhere below her throat, as if she were lowering herself into a hot bath or had just tasted the world's best soup.

Suddenly there was nothing funny about it at all, and we dodged each other's eyes until Phelps leaned toward the speakerphone and said, "We give up. Thanks. That was pretty convincing."

Her laugh sounded almost manly for some reason. Then she told us she hadn't finished yet.

"We get the idea," Phelps said. "Great work. Really. Best I've heard in a while."

The phone call, of course, was Phelps's brainstorm after he heard Blister's folks had flown to Reno for the weekend. He talked Blister into it by convincing him there was no way the 900 number on the ad—which featured some remarkably limber Asian girl—would stand out on a phone bill. And if in the long shot it did, Blister could say he'd ordered vintage baseball cards like the ones Phelps swore he'd ordered on a similar 900 number earlier in the summer. Once Phelps pointed out again that the call would cost just $2.99, Blister agreed his parents wouldn't notice.

Blister was a wrestler, not a genius. He loved to ask if you wanted to learn the fireman's carry. Then he'd grab your right bicep, drop to a knee, swing a forearm under your balls, roll backward and fling you onto your back. It was Phelps who first observed that Blake Cunningham was as annoying as a blister.

After that phony orgasm, Phelps pointed to me, and said, "Ma'am, my good friend Squid Boy here would like to ask you some technique questions."

"Hello there," I said timidly.

She giggled. "Why do they call you Squid Boy?"

"Because I have ten arms and two hearts." That killed Phelps to the point he knocked his hip into the heavy wooden desk and started cussing.

"*Okay*," Ruby said. "Let's hear the questions."

"When we're kissing," I asked, "when exactly should we get the tongue involved?"

"For real?" she asked.

Phelps nodded approval of the question.

"Yeah," I said.

She giggled. "Well, that all depends."

Phelps looked at me, agitated. "Depends on what?" he asked.

"On how aroused I am and how aggressive your tongue is."

Phelps looked disappointed.

"What about breasts?" I asked. "When should they be squeezed and how hard?"

Phelps nodded again.

"Depends on the time of the month," she said. "Sometimes even a light touch is too much." Her voice turned breathy. "Sometimes you can almost *bite* them."

"What time of the month can you bite tits?" Blister asked. "The last week of the month or what?"

She laughed herself into a cough.

"Just so you know," Phelps said, "the Einstein who asked you that question has just one eyebrow."

Until then I hadn't noticed Blister's left eyebrow was nothing more than a gray smear, the result, I learned, of him getting so excited lighting a joint he'd stolen from his sister that he hadn't noticed his eyebrow burning until it started to stink.

Phelps waved his hand to silence Blister's noisy counterattack, then urged me to ask more questions.

"How much moaning should the guy do?" I asked.

She laughed her manly laugh. "As much as he wants."

"What about talking while you're doing it?" Phelps asked. "Is that expected?"

"You mean like dirty talk or chitchat?"

"Yeah."

"Which one?"

"Both."

"Not expected."

That was a relief to all of us.

I asked more questions, including how best to remove a bra, until Phelps got bored and asked: "Do you ever call the penis a 'wand of light'? And what can you tell us about your fountain of nectar?"

"What are you even talking about?" She sounded annoyed.

Phelps stopped laughing long enough to say, "Just tell us how important it is that your boyfriend knows his way around your G-spot."

Ruby sighed, then said, "You guys aren't eighteen, are ya?"

I was afraid she was about to hang up on us, so I asked, "What's your favorite Kama Sutra position?"

"Come again?"

I pulled Florence's little picture book out and flipped through pages. "Do you like the 'crab's position'?"

The boys crowded me, demanding to know where I'd come up with the guide, struggling to glimpse the drawing that showed some bored woman with her feet on her belly and her bored boyfriend inserting himself.

I'd committed almost every position to memory, but it was hard to pick which ones to ask about. To be honest, most of them didn't look that fun. I mean these people were all dressed up in these silly hats and still looked as bored as seventh-graders during the second hour of social studies, the only difference being they were mostly naked and stuck together like dogs.

When she didn't answer, I asked, "What about 'the embrace of thighs'? You like that one?"

Her lips smacked twice and she exhaled, as if she'd lit a cigarette. "You boys know this phone call is two ninety-nine a minute, right?"

Blister flashed as red as a stoplight. "It's two ninety-nine for the *whole* call," he said unconvincingly.

"A minute," she said. "It's two ninety-nine a *minute*."

That was the last we heard of Ruby before Blister hung up and glanced wildly at the loud antique wall clock and slowly figured out we'd been talking for at least fourteen minutes.

Then he shouted at Phelps who shouted right back that he'd read the ad the exact same way. Blister found a tiny solar-powered calculator and twice screwed up punching in numbers with his thick fingers before letting thirteen fucks and shits fly after announcing that the call was gonna cost his parents $41.86!

Phelps shrugged and said, "Ruby didn't really sound all that Asian, did she?"

"I am in such deep shit!" Blister shouted.

"Personally," Phelps soothed, "I'd be more worried about explaining how you lost an eyebrow."

Blister chased him around the couch and outside before tackling him near the gazebo and twisting him into a painful double-arm bar that had Phelps laughing and screaming for help all the way onto his back.

I took the long way home so I could get a look at whatever the highest tide of the week had stranded.

Every week left behind more shells, bones, seaweed and litter. If the weight of the bay's tidal debris had been charted weekly that summer the line would have sloped relentlessly upward from June through August.

It wasn't my imagination.

I was accustomed to beach buildups after winter storms dragged bushes and trees into the bay. This was different. There hadn't been any big blows since April, so most of the tidal slop was broken-down sea life.

I found a four-foot-long tangle of driftwood, barnacles, crab backs and oyster shells lassoed together with mussel threads. And I saw an amazingly intact large sculpin skeleton, as if whatever ate it had vowed to preserve its architecture. I poked a stick into the bulge of seaweed next to it, expecting to find a dead salmon or gull. But it didn't smell and it was too firm for flesh. I parted the seaweed and picked up yet another barnacled hockey glove.

I studied it quickly to make sure it wasn't the same one I'd stuck in the garage, then glanced around to see if anyone was messing with me. One strange hockey glove was interesting. Two was a bona fide mystery.

But now that I didn't feel comfortable calling Professor Kramer about big stuff like oarfish sightings, I definitely couldn't call him about an invasion of hockey gloves.

I crossed the Heron bridge and hopped log to log past the sticker bushes, seeing how far I could go without touching sand or water, until I smelled that the blackberries had finally sweetened. After gorging on them, I dropped the hockey glove next to its dried twin in the garage and climbed my stairs to get out of my wet sneakers. I'd almost pulled off the second soggy tube sock before I saw the fancy *M* on the front of the envelope on my pillow.

The card was a close-up of red sea stars and green anemones. Inside were these words in green ink: "Sorry for being so rude the other day. Sometimes not even you can make me feel better or act right." Below that was a stylish heart next to the letter *A*.

I studied the handwriting. It was as if she'd invented her own slightly offbeat alphabet for me. Part of it, I knew, was that she was left-handed, but it also just made sense that Angie Stegner's letters wouldn't look like everybody else's. I read and reread those twenty words (not counting the *A* or the heart), searching for meaning or emphasis I'd missed. The heart was code for *love*, right? I mean, she wasn't encouraging me to eat healthy and it wasn't Valentine's Day.

When I skipped inside, my parents were sitting formally across from each other, eating silver salmon covered in that gross gray fat that oozes out of them sometimes. Their wooden postures told me they hadn't spoken in a while, and my father didn't even look up to greet me. He was so absorbed in the teamwork between his knife and fork it was like watching someone stitch a wound.

"Grab yourself a plate," Mom said. "We couldn't wait any longer."

"Sorry," I mumbled. "Lost track of time."

Nothing else was said while I scraped fat off my fillet and choked down a few bites.

"Miles, we need to discuss something," Mom said.

Her firm tone and my father's bloodless expression suddenly made sense. Blister's parents had already found out about the sex call somehow and had already called to complain!

"Yeah?" I said warily.

"I'm going to stay with your aunt Janet in Seattle."

"For the night?"

"For a while."

I felt dizzy and slid my chair back from the table. "Is this a—"

"No," they said simultaneously, cutting me off. Dad piled on a few extra *no, no, nos* and a *not at all*. Then Mom said, "We're just taking a break, Miles."

"From what?" I asked.

"Don't make this difficult," she scolded. "It's best for everyone, including you."

They watched me swallow. "Is there anything I can do?" I asked.

They hesitated. "It's not about you," Dad said. "Not at all."

"But Mom just said . . ." Then I stopped and stared at a place between them until I could speak without stuttering or yelling. "I ate too many blackberries. I'll eat something later."

"Are you excusing yourself, Miles?" Mom asked.

"For God's sake," Dad hissed, "let him go."

They stared at me as if I were staggering too close to a flame, but the truth was I'd already been dealing with what they thought I was facing for the first time. And once I stepped outside, it surprised me how quickly my anger turned to unexpected relief: I wouldn't have to leave the bay, at least not yet.

Later that night, I heated a can of split-pea-with-ham for Florence and, after watching her spill twice, fed it to her one spoonful at a time without looking away until she sneezed out her dentures.

CHAPTER 24

THE STORY THAT changed everything came out the next Sunday, with the first heart-stopper being the photo of me with a golden halo around my head. Another one showed me sitting in the back of Carolyn's car, leaving the cult compound, looking thoughtful, the way Kennedy looked in those motorcade photos before someone shot him in the head.

I knew another story was coming because that lanky, always-rushed *Olympian* reporter had come out to chat again. You'd think I would have been suspicious, but I was in love with words that day. I took her out to Chatham on a decent low and explained everything until her notebook was full and she had to go. See, I figured I was a harmless piece of her big story about Mrs. Powers. Of course, that's not the way it unfolded.

The article included plenty of what I told the cult and listed off my marine "discoveries"—including the invasive crabs and sea-weed—which she called the sole reason for an upcoming examina-tion of sea life in South Sound bays. She even recounted the details about me reviving a drowning Lab and saving Phelps with a makeshift snorkel. Then she had some cult member calling me a "child prophet" and Mrs. Powers herself saying, "God is in him." (The article didn't mention that the Eleusinians said that sort of thing all the time, that they believed God is in *everyone*.) Then there was Judge Stegner, of course, calling me the next Cousteau. Even Florence picked up the phone: "Miles has one of the brightest yellow auras I've seen," she'd said, adding that she wouldn't trust any spiritual leader who lacked a yellow aura.

And I thought "the beach talks to Miles O'Malley" was embarrassing.

Near the end of the article, for no reason at all, she described me strolling "pensively" on the beach, pointing things out and wishing aloud that "everyone" would spend a half hour on the flats at low tide—ten minutes listening, ten minutes looking, ten minutes touching. I said it, sure, but I came off like one of those schmaltzy naturalists I couldn't read more than three pages of without barfing. Yet sure enough, there I was, insisting that such an exercise should be a "minimum requirement" for anyone living near salt water. Maybe that's just how ridiculous you sound if you keep talking and someone is taking notes and you want to say something that makes them write faster. She also had me saying this: "If you don't feel any connection to the ocean, then ask yourself why your tears, blood and saliva contain about the same percentage of salt." The article ended on the craziest note possible, with one Eleusinian describing me finding that Japanese street sign, and another one swearing that the gout in her left ankle subsided after wading with me.

The calls came so steadily that morning my father finally ordered me to stop answering "the damn thing" because he was having one "helluva" time getting through the story with so many "goddamn" interruptions. His breath smelled like charcoal-lighting fluid, and he kept guzzling pints of water and farting as he read and reread the same paragraphs.

He'd talked to the reporter too, but he also hadn't sensed where she was headed, even though he apparently told her that ever since I was about seven he'd thought of me as an adult trapped in a child's body. By the age of ten, he said, my vocabulary surpassed his.

After he finished the article, he swallowed three Motrin before saying anything. When he spoke, it was to gently scold me for visiting the cult without telling him. Then he twitched his head, blew his nose and asked, "Do you feel like maybe something supernatural is going on with you, Miles?"

I gave that some thought. "I feel like I always feel."

"So then where is all this headed?"

"What?"

"Well, where do you come up with comments like the one about God being in nothing or everything?"

"I was answering a question."

"Why are you telling a bunch of strangers some crazy prediction about the tide coming up too high in September?"

"It just came out that way."

"But, I mean, what is your goal? Are you trying to scare people or change people—or *change* society?"

He hadn't raised his voice, but I was getting yelled at.

"I don't want to change anything," I mumbled. "I like things the way they are—the way they were."

He stopped, pressed a finger against his temple, then said, "Your mother loves you, Miles."

I looked past him to the sparkling bay. "Can I go outside?"

He held up the newspaper. "I'm uneasy about all this. Okay? And I don't know if it's because I don't like it for you, or if I don't like it for me, but I don't like it. I've never wanted attention. Okay? The worst part of getting married was having everyone looking at me. And I can't even eat before staff meetings because I've got to pretend I've got the answers. Okay? And I'm such a lousy reader I have a hard time reading a goddamn newspaper article. So I guess I'm uncomfortable being the Joe Blow father of some speed-reading genius or child prophet or whatever it is people are trying to turn you into."

It was more than I'd ever heard my father tell me about himself, so it took me a few breaths to respond. "You don't have to talk to anyone," I said. "And I don't want to talk to anyone. And this should blow over pretty quick anyway, right?"

He smiled for the first time that morning, rubbed my head too hard, gave me a clumsy half-hug and returned an urgent message from my mother.

She kept asking if I needed help. Her voice was always louder on the phone, as if she barely trusted the technology. She said while it was flattering that so many people had said such nice and bizarre things about me, it had clearly gotten out of hand.

Then she warned me to stay away from the cult. She tried to pick her words, but I knew her lips were bloodless before she sputtered to a stop, then asked to speak to Dad again.

"Well, we are *separated*," he whined. "Yes, I know I was quoted in the damn story, but I didn't *know*." Then he shouted: "How could I know?" He shoved the phone back at me.

She asked again whether I *needed* her.

The night she left she'd argued with my father for so long in the driveway that I'd had time to look for things she forgot. It wasn't easy. She'd obviously packed for a long stay. Even her sweaters were gone. When I stepped outside and handed over her favorite pillow, she looked away and dabbed at the corners of her eyes. Then she just pushed meaningless words around until she kissed the top of my head and stranded us in gravel.

I weighed her question. Did I need her? Whatever she wanted to hear I wanted to tell her the opposite. "No," I said firmly. "I really don't."

It sounded like a salmon bone caught in her throat, then she told me to remember to eat, and to tell any reporter who wanted to interview me that they needed to talk to my mother first. She gave me Aunt Janet's number—even though I'd memorized it years ago—and made me repeat it. She said she'd try to make it down during the next couple days and hung up midway through her good-bye.

Dad studied me. "What'd she want?"

"Nothing."

Our house felt unbearably hot. He stared at me, waiting. "She wanted to know if I needed help."

He groaned. "Your mother has fallen out of love with me, *not you*. And I personally think she's fallen out of love with herself. So telling her you don't need her doesn't help anything."

"I'm going outside."

Florence and Yvonne treated my breathless question like a punch line.

After she stopped laughing, Florence assured me that auras can't be photographed and that nobody's was as prominent as my golden halo in the newspaper. Plus, the color was way off, a bright sunshiny gold, instead of my soft yellow.

Yvonne visited so rarely and usually so late at night that I hadn't seen her since spring, but a decade might as well have slipped past. She held a cane across her thighs and looked winded just sitting in the rocker.

She asked me if I'd noticed the color of Mrs. Powers's aura. "I haven't seen anybody's yet," I said, "not even mine. And I don't know how anyone could tell where that lady's aura begins and her cotton-candy hair ends."

Yvonne's laugh sounded so much like a duck it seemed strange to hear it indoors.

"Attention changes people," Florence said suddenly, "even strong, humble young people."

She offered more vague warnings that I ignored while I surveyed the fridge. I was relieved to see milk, bread, eggs, apples, cottage cheese and lots of almonds, but something about Yvonne's ability to deliver groceries made me feel lazy and useless until I heard Florence telling her how great she'd been feeling, how well she'd been getting around, and how a pleasant state case worker by the name of Julie Winslow was outfitting her with all sorts of helpful items.

Maybe I didn't show up with magical bags of food, but I was the only person Florence Dalessandro trusted.

Phelps swung by later with Blister, Bugeyes, and the Collins brothers, who were a year apart but still looked like twins or at least splices from the same plant.

Phelps had them all bowing and addressing me as "your lordship." It was ridiculous. I told them to knock it off, but I didn't see the downside yet. I didn't hear the avalanche coming.

By Monday, variations of the same story were reprinted throughout the country, including a brief article on the front of *USA Today* with a headline that just said: KID MESSIAH? So many people called—none of them paid attention to time zones—that my father had our number changed before he'd finished his second cup of coffee.

See, it was late August, and there were no hurricanes or elections or wars or Olympics or little girls caught in wells to report. Amazingly enough, I was the story of the day. And it wasn't just reporters wanting a slice of me. The Washington Environmental Council, Greenpeace and the Sierra Club all wanted me to praise their causes, which I usually didn't understand even after they explained them. People for Puget Sound showed up to crown me as the state's Environmentalist of the Year, which seemed odd seeing how the year still had four months to go. I held up that award and smiled, but didn't know where to put it afterward and noticed their smirks when I folded it into a square small enough to cram into a pocket.

Strangers clustered around the bridge and the tavern like fish around pilings by late afternoon. Some even ventured down our driveway, then returned to the tavern, the bridge or vacant beach lots when their knocks went unanswered. As the tide fell, people waded out toward where six of us were goofing on the mud bars. Most of them either cut their feet or retreated once the mud softened, but several eventually made it. They weren't actually interrupting anything special, but it felt like an intrusion, and Phelps intercepted them with his fuck-you bangs to inform them I wasn't doing any more interviews.

They, of course, insisted they weren't reporters—three called themselves Eleusinians—but they repeated the same boring questions. And I said as little as possible until all of them lost interest except for the intense, long-necked, black-haired man who resembled a cormorant at feeding time.

"Do you believe some higher force is guiding you?" he asked.

"No."

"What about visions? Do you have visions?"

I shrugged.

"Do you talk to God?" he pressed.

"I talk to myself at times, and maybe He overhears some of that."

Phelps snorted behind me.

"Then how did you hear about that extraordinary tide on September eighth?" He sounded urgent. "Who or what made you predict that?"

"Someone I trust."

"A voice?"

"Yes."

"What did it sound like?"

"Like an old lady."

"Yes?"

"Yes."

"Has that voice steered you right before?" he asked.

"Yes."

He bent toward me, unblinking, his nose packed with so many black hairs I was surprised he could breathe. "Do you believe this bay has healing powers?"

"I'm not a doctor."

"Are you a child of faith?"

"I don't know."

"But—"

"That's enough." Phelps stepped forward. "Sorry, but Mr. O'Malley is answering so many questions that he isn't getting a chance to make new discoveries. You understand. Thank you for your interest."

Phelps ushered me away, carrying himself in a way that you didn't notice he added up to just 118 pounds. "That fucker was freaking me out," he said. "We're charging for interviews from now on. Ten bucks a pop. No discounts."

"*We?*" I said.

"Everything's fifty-fifty with us," Phelps replied. "Deal's a deal." He lit a Kent and popped two smoke rings through a larger one over water so calm they hung in the air like thought bubbles.

We waded farther out as the tide continued falling on its way to a minus-two-point-seven. There were far more people watching us than I'd realized. Spencer Spit twitched with spectators, and I counted three kayaks and two canoes gliding our way.

"Keep the riffraff off our lordship here," Phelps instructed Blister and the rest of our posse, then urged me to do something freaky. So I squatted, spread my arms out as if performing some martial arts warm-up and started slapping the smooth water top. I drummed hard. It made a more interesting sound than you might imagine. Once Phelps and the boys stopped laughing they mimicked my stance, and soon all six of us were splashing the same rhythm. "Skoo-kum-chuck!" I chanted. They joined me in their deepest cannibal voices. "Skoo-kum-chuck! Skoo-kum-chuck!" Binoculars and cameras popped out along the shore. Two canoes closed on us, and someone jogged out on the flats with a television camera. "Skoo-kum-chuck!"

After our arms tired, I watched the water recover around us, waiting for it to clear and the sun's reflection to settle until I realized it wasn't the sun's image at all. It was orange and shimmered on the surface, but its light came from below.

The closer I got the brighter it looked. I assumed it was a sunken fluorescent buoy or a bottle of orange soda until I saw how it waved in the current like a giant foot-high feather.

Bugeyes was the first to notice what I was marveling at. "What the fuck is that?"

Two canoes unloaded and the jogging cameraman puffed to within fifteen yards of us. Others scampered—three limped—more easily across the mud now that it was less than an hour before low tide.

"Here we go again, ladies and gentlemen," Phelps said in his best circus voice. I looked up at an audience thick enough to block the sun. TV cameras rolled. I recognized some of the heart-attack faces as cult members.

"What is it?" someone asked.

"A *Ptilosarcus gurneyi*," I said, and smiled.

"Would you repeat that?"

I did, and spelled it too.

"So what exactly is that?"

"It's also called a sea pen, because, I guess, it looks like one of those old-fashioned pens."

"Tell us more," someone with a microphone pleaded.

"Well, for starters it's an animal, not a plant." People hummed and tittered. "And it's actually dozens of animals in one. Each one of its little branches is an independent mouth. So it's kinda like a bunch of sea anemones who got together and decided to dress up like a colorful plant so they could trick small fish and other sea life

191

into swimming close enough to grab them. And all the mouths share one digestive system." I smiled and heard camera shutters. "Weird, huh?"

It was probably my speeding heart, or the way people blocked the glare, but the closer everyone huddled the brighter the sea pen looked. "And this is the biggest and orangest one I've seen," I said, "although all the others have been at aquariums."

"What led you to it?" someone asked.

"I thought it was the reflection of the sun."

"Is there a voice in your head telling you where to look?"

I didn't answer that.

"How old are you?" someone else asked.

I didn't answer that either. I didn't want to hear murmurs about how I looked younger than someone's ten-year-old when I was a month and a half away from fourteen.

I waded to the far side of the sea pen so everyone could see it, then squatted behind it. I reached down slowly, stroked it gently and it gave off a green light, a sudden, unmistakable green flash.

People swore, the cormorant crossed himself and my scalp tingled the way your foot does after you sit on it too long.

"Why'd it turn green?" someone demanded.

The sun sparkled through the crowd and blinded me, so I rested my eyes in the other direction long enough to make out the red sea star, poking three legs out from beneath sea lettuce fifteen feet from the sea pen. It wasn't a big star, but big enough. I waded toward it, waved the lettuce aside and pointed it out to more gasps.

"What kind of starfish is that?" someone demanded.

"A *Master aequalis*," I said. "It's one of the few stars that eats sea pens." I smiled again for the cameras. "They smell like firecrackers if you hold them up to your nose."

I handed it to some lady who looked like she had the chicken pox.

"Why'd that plant turn green?" someone asked again. Others echoed the question.

Through a gap in the mob, I saw Angie and the judge shuffling along their waterfront, their somber gaits making them look like impostors. When Angie turned, I waved theatrically, but got nothing back and instantly felt ridiculous. And selfish. And motherless.

It surprised me to already miss her, though not in the way I expected. It was more like the hollowness you feel when you've misplaced something important.

I was so distracted I didn't hear the questions other than what to do with the sea pen. "Leave it alone," I said, "and keep that star away from it."

I strode, head down, toward Florence's house, hating myself for not having checked on her all day, ignoring the pleas to coax me back, questions and demands flitting around me like bats.

My eyes blurred counting shoeprints on the flats. People were everywhere. I didn't recognize the bay or anyone on it, including myself.

CHAPTER 25

T HE BAY CONTINUED to attract strange crowds for days, so I either collected clams in Chatham Cove with Phelps or hid behind curtains with Florence to avoid the questions. My father got so fed up he chased a herd of reporters off our doorstep and shouted: "It's over!" He also posted No Trespassing signs in the driveway, and one of the Dons staked a poster with a red slash through the word *media*. And the story finally eased away from me to the sudden pilgrimage of Russians to Skookumchuck Bay.

There were still curious cult members and locals wandering about, but we increasingly saw old cars full of people who crawled out speaking some loud language with voices that could motivate sled dogs. The old ladies wore huge scarves on their heads, and the men were wide-boned with large faces. TV told us most of them were Russians and Ukrainians who'd settled south of Seattle and who routinely drove across the state to Soap Lake, where even some doctors claimed the lake's silky mud and mineral-rich water healed certain skin conditions. All sorts of other people showed up on the bay too, including Canadians who'd heard things were *happening* here, that the mud or water had cured gout, and that people were *seeing things*. One of the most-repeated stories, unfortunately, was about a little boy who not only discovered a giant squid but turned a large underwater sea plant from orange to green just by touching it.

The murmurs kept people coming, and no announcements or denials or TV reporters explaining the color-changing capabilities of sea pens discouraged them. Skookumchuck Bay turned into the last stop on the summer road trip for people hoping to see miracles or to find relief from psoriasis, arthritis and everything from cancer to diaper rash. Caravans of dusty cars filled the meadows and sandy lots around the tavern and packed the overgrown driveway leading to the cabin rented by Hal Clinton, better known as Hallelujah Hal because of the way he routinely prayed beneath a massive cross he'd built out of four-by-fours and hung from a cedar limb near the beach.

It was obvious Hal had welcomed the visitors because whenever the wind and traffic died, we could hear Russian voices praying beneath his cross. We also saw the strangers in front of his cabin, splashing into our cold, muddy bay as if it were a community pool, swimming aimlessly or wading to their hips and dunking their heads and especially their babies until their cries blended with the whining gulls and the scolding herons.

But that wasn't the weirdest part.

The Russians started it, but soon there were others wading to their knees, scooping up the slickest, stinkiest, blackest mud they could find, and rubbing it over themselves and each other as if it were sunscreen. Some covered their entire bodies, then baked in the sun along the scrubby lip of the shore. Once they were stiff and flaky dry, they waded back out, rinsed off, lathered up with a new batch and did it all over again—no matter how ridiculous it looked or how many television cameras watched.

My reports on all that revived Florence, or perhaps her growing fear of nursing homes scared her body into improving. Regardless, she was a different lady for a few days: joking, shuffling with confidence and even eating more. But when I swung by that Thursday to make lunch, Julie Winslow opened the door as if she owned it.

"We were just talking about you," she chirped. "I'm delighted you're here."

Florence was in her chair, forcing a smile, smelling like pee.

Julie Winslow showed off the new equipment she'd brought: an elevated toilet seat, a walker, an aluminum shower seat and even new silverware with oversized handles.

She also told me Florence's "team" now included a nutritionist, an occupational therapist and an equipment specialist. The hardest part of it for me was watching Florence fake gratitude.

"She seems nice," I said, after Julie Winslow left.

"Exactly," Florence said. *"Seems."*

"You still don't trust her."

"I don't want to talk about it."

So I talked about how I was dreading the dang "BioBlitz" that was supposedly coming to town in less than ten days. I couldn't even stand the name of it.

We kept hearing about what a huge deal it was going to be. Never before had more than seventy scientists agreed to assemble to survey the biology and botany of a public waterway on such short notice! And never before had the findings of one child galvanized such a grand response from the scientific community! That one killed me. What if they went to all this trouble and didn't find anything the slightest bit unusual? What if I'd already found the few peculiarities in our bays? What if these superimportant scientists interrupted their mankind-saving work just because some stupid reporters wrote some ridiculous half-true stories about me?

"Stop it!" Florence snarled. "Quit being so childish."

I would have rather been slapped.

"You are not responsible for what happens on this bay, or for what people do based on what you find or what you say about what you saw. Do you understand?"

I didn't risk a response. I just waited for whatever else she had for me.

"Julie Winslow is determined to put me in a home," she announced.

"She said that?" I whispered.

"Of course not."

"Then why'd she bring out all this stuff to make it easier for you here?"

"To create a file. She can't just send me to a home, thank God, but if I ever take a ride in an ambulance the hospital discharge officer will review her file on me and recommend assisted living. And you know what that is, don't you? That's a nice way of saying *nursing home*, which is a place where people sit in wheelchairs shitting themselves. You do realize I eventually won't be able to talk, right?" Her voice strained. "How am I going to tell them what I need if I can't talk? You're smart, Miles. You know me. Don't look away! You think I haven't seen the way this ends? Eventually I won't be able to swallow! You think I would allow that?" Her big eyes twitched. "Have you told anyone about my falls?"

I was blown back by her question and frightened by her tone. "You told me—"

"Yes, I know what I told you, but perhaps you asked your parents or Norman what to do, and one of them called the state."

I wanted to tell her what the judge had said about calling her neurologist, and remind her of the reporter who'd written about her living conditions. Most of all, I wanted to ask her how she could doubt me.

Her glassy eyeballs reflected light from everywhere. "I'm sorry, Miles." She reached for me, and I flinched. "The books will be yours," she said calmly. "So will the cabin and the land."

I wasn't about to argue with her or thank her.

"There might be something to clean up," she said after a sigh so long it made her slouch. "I'm sorry about that. I truly am. It's unfair for me to burden you, but I already have and I'm not through yet." She slowed her breathing and drifted into her half-lidded state.

"Please don't say anything," she said. "Just get me some water, and let's enjoy some silence together. Doesn't that sound good?"

It sounded like the terms of our friendship had changed yet again.

CHAPTER 26

P HELPS TURNED UP his radio and shouted insights about the
double meaning of the lyrics, all of which, of course, had to do
with sex.

"Turn that crap off," I said after the second song.

"Crap?"

"It scares clams. They're sensitive to vibrations."

Phelps snorted. "So what?"

"So they'll dive down," I lied, "and we won't make any money."

"You don't even give me regular smoke breaks, and now you want
to turn off my lunch tunes? You know what the National Labor
Relations Board would say about that? Music is my future."

"Yeah, I hear tons of guys make a good living playing air
guitar."

"You're a jealous fuck. And you know why? You have no musical
talent."

That was true. I'd played the trumpet for three years, and all I was
known for was getting a silver mute stuck on my left pinky. Try
hiding that in your armpit during algebra while your finger swells. I

eventually had to go to the fire department to get the dang thing sawed off.

"Would you play Zeppelin in church?" I asked.

"Of course not."

"Well, this is my church."

Phelps glanced around at Chatham's half-exposed flats. "I don't see any crucifixes."

I started to tell him about that blue sea star I'd found, then fortunately caught myself. "You are one sorry . . . *fuck*," I said.

He told me that he should stomp my puny ass, but I could tell he was flattered that I'd used his lingo, and he turned down Zeppelin, then shut it off once the song ended.

As we grabbed our shovels, I loosened him up with more stories about the mud healers, then got around to asking him how often he saw his real dad.

Phelps gave me the only laugh I ever heard him fake. "Let's see," he said, pretending to count with his fingers, "the answer to that would be . . . never." He dug harder than usual for the next couple hours, as if he were pissed at the clams, stabbing and scooping sand and mud with the intensity of a swordsman.

There was an excited pop to Pansing's voice later that afternoon when he saw the two geoducks Phelps had unearthed. His restaurant was hosting something called a "trade delegation," and the Chinese, he told me, couldn't resist geoduck caught the same day.

He packed the huge clams in a cooler along with a half-bucket of manilas and eighteen butters, then handed me two creased twenties and waved off my ten.

I told him I'd take him fishing on Skookumchuck once I saved enough to buy a Lund. "The twelve-footers are perfect for fishing," I explained. "They're so sturdy you can stand up in them. And I bet I can get one for about five hundred, maybe four-fifty, if I wait until somebody gets tired of watching one rust in their yard."

"Okay." He nodded. "I bring the rods."

He didn't look at me when he said that, and no matter how much I stalled, he still only stayed long enough to roll and smoke one cigarette, which screwed me up because I'd hoped he'd still be there, puffing casually, when B.J. showed up.

My problem was the aquariums wouldn't send anyone down anymore. So unless I got a ride to Tacoma I couldn't sell the white sea cucumber, the two sea lemons or the enormous Bering hermit I'd found. So I'd reluctantly called B.J.'s answering machine, laid out the prices and gave him a time to swing by if he was interested.

I noticed the fresh dent in the driver's door when he pulled up, then watched him crawl across his shifter so that he could shoulder his way out the passenger side. He wore oil-stained cowboy boots and a dirty tank top that showed off explosions of red armpit hair. "Let's see 'em," he said, then burped.

"You owe me five dollars." I dragged my sneaker in the gravel like a bull preparing to charge.

"Yeah, yeah, yeah. We'll work it into the total."

"No, I want it now." I was surprised by how firm I sounded.

B.J. mock-laughed, as if I'd shared a bad joke. "Let's see what you got."

"You owe me five."

He narrowed his eyes, then started toward the garage door.

I redesigned the gravel at my feet. "It's locked," I said.

That turned him around and sent him back to me with long purposeful strides, squiggly veins bulging at his temples. "You playing hardball *with me?*"

"I'm not getting ripped off anymore." I hadn't even practiced that line. My heart felt like a fan with something stuck in it.

"You ungrateful little shit." He smelled like old milk. "You're lucky I even waste my time coming out here."

I didn't risk trying to speak, but I didn't look away either.

Finally, he pulled out a fold of bills, found a five among the ones, wadded it up and flung it at my chest. I caught it on the bounce and stepped back.

"Now open the goddamn door," he hissed.

Something in his tone stopped scaring me. "It's twenty-five for what I got in there."

"You already told me that! Open the fucking door—now."

Nobody had ever ordered me to open a door before. "Not unless you give me the twenty-five up front."

B.J. spoke through his teeth. "I'm not buying a damn thing I haven't seen."

"I'll give you your money back if you decide you don't want 'em," I said. "But I'm getting paid up front from now on."

"Open the door." There was a crazy light in his eyes, and his nickel-sized nostrils quivered like he was getting ready to do something that required a lot of air.

I strolled head down toward the garage, surprised I could walk, surprised my hand was steady enough to insert the key and surprised how quickly I slipped inside, slammed the door and flipped the dead bolt.

B.J. told me to open the motherfucking door. Then I heard his boot heel ram it. The whole garage shook. He did it again, the door rattling. Then he tried to reason with me in that teeth-clenched way before halfheartedly kicking the door one last time. After some muttering, he shouted that I now owed him twenty for wasting his fucking time. He laughed until he spat, then I heard him climbing into his car. Finally, he revved his engine so loud that I scampered to the far wall of the garage just in case he rammed that baby-blue El Camino right through it.

I watched a whole Mariners game that night with my father. It was the first time I'd seen nine entire innings—all 238 pitches—of baseball. The game took three hours and eighteen minutes, or more than half the time it takes for the moon, the sun and the earth to perform an entire tidal shift.

We watched from our couch with the sound loud, which was comforting because the house had turned into a library without my mother's rants, impressions and one-sided debates with newscasters. Not even the phone was ringing. Nobody but Phelps, the three Dons and Mom knew our new number, and she hadn't called or visited during the five days since I'd told her that I didn't need her. My father added to the strangeness by pacing in his slippers and talking in a wet mumble that didn't sound like anyone I knew. He'd picked up a cold that kept getting worse, which I considered further proof that my mother was already the doctor she'd wanted to be.

Colds, flus, sprains, cuts and other illness or ailments were helpless against her. She killed viruses with garlic, grapefruits and her "fix-me-up" soup—some tasty mush of carrots, potatoes and onions. She second-guessed doctors, built her own splints and plucked our stitches herself. Our miseries brought out a side of her she rarely wasted on the healthy. More than once, I hoped my fever wouldn't break because my mother only sang to me when I was burning up.

I washed our clothes between innings, all my father's first, then all mine. My mother would have flipped, but I never understood why whites had to be washed separately. How white do underpants really need to be? I waited until the seventh-inning stretch to ask if we could get a dog yet.

Dad teared up at the question. Like I said, it didn't take much. United Airlines commercials could break him. "You know your mother doesn't want a dog, Sport."

I stared at him until he said, "What about when she comes back?"

I stalled and waited and rehearsed, but I didn't find a single moment in that marathon evening to ask him what to do about Florence.

"Wake up, Angie."

She was facedown in her thick pink pillow, trying to suffocate herself.

I tapped the arch of her right foot dangling off the mattress and asked her again to get up.

Then I tried once more, and she finally rolled onto a shoulder and slitted an eye.

"Got something to show you," I said.

"Later, Miles," she mumbled. "I'm crashed."

"It's eleven forty-five."

"Why do people always tell me what time it is?" She rolled back into the pillow.

"You've gotta come see this."

"Later."

"It won't be there later. It's a right-now thing. Might already be too late."

"What is it?"

"That'll ruin it."

She rolled her head to my side. "You've already ruined my sleep."

"Please."

"I'm not getting up to see some *interesting* starfish," she whispered. "I don't care if you found a sunken pirate ship. Got it?"

"You're awake now anyway."

Her entire right leg slipped out and my breath popped out of me. She then rolled onto her back beneath the sheets until her left leg swung over the side and hinged at the knee. Her hair was matted, curly and everywhere, like a drawing I'd seen of Medusa. She opened her eyes enough to squint all the way down to my dripping feet. "You dragged mud through the judge's house?"

"He's not here," I said. "Won't you get up?"

She stretched double-jointed arms toward the ceiling. "This is the only time of day I feel like me." I could see all the way into the hollows of her armpits, and it occurred to me that she slept naked. "Those pills take the *me* out of me. And if I'm not me, I don't even want to be around me. You know what I mean?"

"I'll wait outside until you get dressed, but hurry, okay?"

206

"You've got your mother's impatient eyebrow," she said.

She didn't leave the house until she'd reheated coffee that the judge had left her before he'd gone to church. She poured it into a Styrofoam cup, but it was still too hot for her fingers, so she slid the first cup into a second one that took forever to find. By the time we finally got way out on the flats in front of Florence's, the egg sacks were partially submerged, yet still clung together like the head of a huge daisy with see-through petals encasing what looked like lentils.

"They're butterfly squid eggs," I said. "And they're not eggs from just one little squid. That's the crazy part. It probably took eight females to lay this out."

"No way." She studied me. "How could they time their spawning together, and why would they bother to make it look pretty?"

I shrugged. "Maybe their eggs have a better chance of surviving when they're laid alongside others. Maybe it's group art, like when the whole fifth grade painted that mural on the side of the Morningstar restaurant. Who knows? I just read about this tiny salt marsh snail that has to climb a tall blade of grass or drown every time the tide comes in. So what sort of alarm warns it to start climbing to safety every twelve hours?"

I wasn't sure if Angie was smiling with me, at me or at something completely unrelated. "Is this it? Is this what you woke me up to see?" She tried to sound pissed, but it was easy to see she was savoring her moment on the mud the way a deer savors daybreak in a field when it doesn't know you're watching. "Isn't it late in the summer to be spawning?"

"Yeah." I nodded. "It's a weird summer though."

I'd barely talked to her in the weeks since she'd almost OD'd, and the few times I had she'd seemed dazed or disinterested, as if she'd forgotten about the card she gave me, as if I'd lost whatever pull I'd had on her.

She'd been spending time with some "boring therapist" and

sleeping most nights at her brother's house in Tacoma because the judge was so busy campaigning and everybody insisted, for some reason, that she shouldn't be alone at night. It was obvious she knew very little about the crazy articles on me, or anything about the Russians, Florence or my mother.

"Get closer," I said. "Down here."

She squatted until her eyebrow ring was near enough to kiss. "You can see them moving in there!"

I felt her breath on my face. "Which means?"

"They're about to hatch?"

I rinsed her two cups, stuck brown kelp on the bottom of one, filled them both partway with bay water, then scooped the busiest pod into one cup and the second busiest into the other. Then I placed the cups back in her hands, and we watched the tiny gray squid twirl in their membranes. Within seconds, eggs in the white-bottomed cup started whitening while eggs in the other cup darkened.

"Oh, my God!" Angie held the cups away from her as if they might explode.

The dark ones started popping out first and miniature squid squirted around the cup. Angie stood speechless and calf deep in the incoming tide, her face brightening as the white eggs hatched in her other hand.

"If even two of these survive to be adults that's a success story," I said. "Mostly, they're protein for everyone else." I reached into the kelp-bottomed cup, plucked an unhatched egg loose and dropped it onto my tongue.

Angie laughed. "You're crazy."

I swallowed. "Bipolar," I said, then told her to let the squid go whenever she was ready.

She didn't do anything for a while, other than give me a glassy look. Everything had gone so well that I froze at the moment I'd intended to tell her that it was worth living just to be able to watch butterfly squid hatch. The words sounded so corny in my head that I waited a few beats and said: "I know it sounds ridiculous, but I can take care of you."

She squinted, as if attempting long division in her head, then looked away, bent over and freed every last one of those tiny squid.

When I got home, my father sheepishly asked if I knew what day it was, then blew his nose so hard it sounded like someone shoveling snow.

I knew it was six days from the BioBlitz, seven days from the stupid flood that Florence and I had predicted and eleven days before school started. And I knew that we were down to thirteen hours and nineteen minutes of daylight and that, of course, it was the first of September.

I didn't give my father any grief about all the successful runts in the world this time. I took off my shoes and straightened until my spine ached. He balanced some musty hardback that he'd never read on my skull, studied the broom closet door, then accused me of sneaking air beneath my feet.

"Take a look yourself," I said.

He examined my heels, glanced at the top of my head then at my feet, then back up again before asking me to slouch and step away to verify the book was level, which I did.

"Stand under there again." His voice rumbled with excitement.

I stood as straight as anyone ever stood. "It's dead-on level right now," he whispered, then instructed me to step away again and scratched a thin line beneath the book edge that was a whopping *nine sixteenths of an inch* above the prior one.

We stared at the new line as if it were a comet.

Dad later called one of the three Dons over to make double-sure the measurement was precise. There was no question about it. I was a sliver over four feet nine inches and growing like a goddamn blackberry vine, as Don Isaacson put it.

Dad didn't try to reach my mother. He didn't want to hear that the book was probably sloped. No, he and big Don poured Crown Royal into water glasses, then laughed wildly at nothing in particular and called me their "main man" until I climbed the steps to my room, ducking slightly as I entered, to make double-sure that I didn't whack my forehead on the top of the doorframe.

CHAPTER 27

THE CLOSER WE inched to the BioBlitz the more it looked like some confusing festival assembling on Spencer Spit. On the south side, more than fifty people squatted near Hal's cabin in dirty tents, cars and RVs with bug-splattered windshields. Meanwhile, Blue Moon Outfitters strung huge bright tents and canopies on the north side in meadows soon overrun by new strangers wearing sensible shoes, clean jeans and handy vests crammed with gauges, vials and pocket guides.

As scientists congregated, local families loitered and snapped photos, as if something worth remembering was in the making. And curiosity usually pulled them toward the odd drone of prayers and singing around Hal's cabin, where the sight of mud-covered bodies made children giggle or cry, depending on their age. I stayed away from Hal's camp to avoid the creepy sound of people pointing at me or murmuring "there's the boy," even if they didn't badger me with questions and often just smiled.

It was hard to wander among the scientists without getting pointed out too, but that was fine because most of them were pals of

Professor Kramer's who simply wanted to say hello or ask about the flats. The professor, I was slow to realize, was in charge of the whole dang thing. And whatever problems he'd had with me had vanished, which came as such an unexpected gift I confused him by thanking him.

The goal of the exercise, as the professor kept repeating, was a "snapshot census" of the animal and plant life of the Sound's southernmost bays. Yet despite all the serious grown-up talk, it still sounded like a silly game designed by children because this so-called census had to be completed within twenty-four hours.

Similar "snapshots" had been performed on Long Island Sound and Lake Superior, but as the professor reminded everyone, those exercises took much longer to set up. Ours was scheduled to begin nine-thirty Saturday morning because the next twenty-four hours included the lowest tide of the month. And the best part, from my vantage, was that everyone was so distracted by the scientists and the healers that nobody seemed to recall my ridiculous prediction that the highest tide in fifty years would blindside Olympia late that Sunday.

As Chatham Cove filled with people in boots and waders carrying buckets, vials and nets, the flats greeted the mob of scientists and volunteers with a faster striptease than usual, the tide rushing out, stranding veils of glittering sea lettuce and purple Turkish towels beneath the cool, restless Saturday-morning sky.

It had been a long time since I'd stepped on the Chatham flats when I wasn't *the* expert. Now there were biologists of every flavor, including people who could name all forty Puget Sound jellyfish or explain the sex lives of nemertid worms or the odd-couple, home-sharing relationship between horse clams and tiny soft-shelled pea crabs. Still, nobody was as familiar with those flats as I was, so in the minutes before the exercise officially began, Professor Kramer asked me to give an overview of what was likely to be seen where.

When I started to speak, I recognized all sorts of volunteers I never thought I'd see on the mud, including my second- and fifth-grade teachers and friends of my mother's who'd asked with wrinkled noses about that "rotten-egg smell" outside our house. Blister, Bugeyes and the Collins brothers were out there too, looking thrilled to help count sea plants. If you'd asked them to do that a month earlier they would have spat and cussed, but now, for some reason, it was an honor. Even my father and two of the Dons volunteered to barbecue burgers and brew coffee around base camp. And my father had assured me twice that morning that he expected my mother to be there by lunch.

As many times as I'd been out on the cove, I'd forgotten parts of it. I knew which clams lived where, but I didn't know where *everything* was the way I thought I did, especially seeing how rapidly the tidal life was changing. And I got so excited trying to explain what I knew for sure that I wasn't clear about anything other than that I was excited. Plus my voice wasn't strong enough to reach more than half the crowd, but nobody seemed to mind.

Twenty minutes after we spread out across the flats, everyone gathered to listen to a mollusk biologist rave about a piddocks colony.

Piddocks are clams, but what you usually see looks more like rubbery plants waving in shallows, or like half-buried human hearts with their aortas sticking straight up. I'd seen a few in deep pools near the clay banks before, but this patch covered an area half the size of a tennis court.

It's not that piddocks were all that rare or valuable, but this freckled, pigtailed scientist picked her words as if she were lecturing in some grand hall where only piddocks were discussed. Just as she was about to call it the largest documented piddock colony in Puget Sound, the leader of the porifera team couldn't resist interjecting that the nearby purple sponge—an animal that resembles fake rubber puke—was as *shockingly* bright as any he'd seen.

Scientists rubbed beards and hyperchewed gum, and everyone talked and worked faster as if the stakes had risen, as if the piddock discovery needed to be topped.

The annelid team drew the next crowd when its leader gushed over a nereid brandti she'd found. She had flatworms and ribbon worms in her bucket too, but she couldn't get over this green and blue worm that was the size of a skinny ruler and writhing like an eel.

"I didn't know they grew this large in the Sound," she said, backhanding frayed bangs from her narrow face. We edged closer. "It's really quite spectacular."

I waited for an opening to say, "I've seen bigger ones than that out here."

Voices rattled to a stop, and the annelid lady squinted suspiciously at me. "Are you sure they were nereid brandtis?"

"I saw a bunch of them swarming at night." I felt their stares and saw Phelps trying to distract me by sucking on bull kelp. "It was mid-July," I said, "and there were so many convulsing on the surface that they actually created phosphorescent waves, which made me notice them in the first place. I couldn't tell what was going on until I got close enough to shine my headlamp on them, and then I kinda wished I hadn't."

People chattered in hushed tones about headlamps and giant squid and "he's only thirteen" until the team leader said something about it being easy to confuse worms with eels, to which I responded that all I knew was that I saw larger versions of the exact same blue and green creature wiggling in her bucket. After answering a few more questions, I returned to my assignment—to count and catalogue as much life as I could find in one square yard of tidal flats.

I framed a particularly lively patch with four PVC pipes, then counted seven pink and white anemones, twenty-six hermit crabs (most of them in periwinkle shells), 109 barnacles, thirty-six mussels, twelve clam chimneys (three squirting), four snails (two dire whelks) and a blue-gray troscheli sea star slowly separating a mossy chiton from its shell.

Everything seemed quicker and brighter than usual, as if the flats were *performing* for us. Even the snails were quick, the whelks lunging their gleaming white bodies ahead of their spiraled shells, moving almost as fast as the hermits. The gravel shook and sprayed with the restless jostling and squirts of manilas, and the ochre sea stars glided along the browse line at speeds they usually only managed underwater. Gulls and herons swooped lower than usual too, their wing thrusts making us all look up and wonder what they saw that we didn't. Even the weather added to the drama, delivering the coldest morning we'd felt since June as the retreating bay darkened with northerly gusts and hunkered toward low tide.

I was close enough to watch Phelps show off the variety of mollusks he could uncover in one modest hole and noticed afterward how he coaxed half of the bivalve team into a smoke break and had three of them leaning on shovels, puffing his mother's Kents, laughing at his story about being stuck in the mud and breathing through a PVC pipe "like some motherfucking clam."

By eleven-thirty the crustacean team boasted it'd already found every brand of Puget Sound shore crab and even a few baby Dungeness they assumed never roamed this far south. But what they corralled us to announce was that they'd found a *green crab*. Not the ho-hum green shore crab I often saw—although it was easy to confuse the two—but the dreaded European green itself. At least that's what this owl-eyed biologist said at least six times when people badgered him to be certain he was sure.

The crab looked harmless, just three inches across the back, but to listen to this scientist describe its powers you would've thought that we should've taken three steps back and drawn pistols. Its pinchers were as sharp as can openers. It ate three oysters and thirty mussels a day. It dug down six inches to murder clams. It even ate other crabs! It sounded like some over-the-top cartoon villain—a Mighty Mouse who'd gone so bad he'd even turned on other mice.

Suddenly this fun snapshot census had turned into a grave mission to save the Sound from evil crabs. The crustaceans team leader reassigned half of us counters to hunt exclusively for the greens. But after twenty minutes of searching, I admit that I lost focus and watched hermits fight over shells.

There must have been a shell shortage going on that morning because everywhere I looked some hermit was hauling around an extra shell or bullying another hermit out of its home. And two of the biggest bullies, a hairy hermit and a blue-handed hermit, faced off in a tug-of-war over a lurid rocksnail shell, which at the time was the shiny castle of a smaller hermit who'd been minding its own business. I played God and lifted it away from the bullies, but they found it again and resumed their duel. Finally, blue-hand grabbed the victim and slammed it facedown into the poisonous flower of a large sea anemone, then held it there, smothering the poor hermit in the anemone's poison. I snuck back fifteen minutes later, and blue-hand was still applying the pressure, waiting for the trapped hermit to surrender its shell. I didn't get to witness the ending, with the anemone, no doubt, swallowing the poisoned hermit and the bully moving into its new shell. Unfortunately, there was way too much going on, and it was killing me to not be everywhere at once.

The cnidaria team finally pulled us way out on the flats after one of its biologists waded to his knees to examine what he proclaimed was an Australian jellyfish. Either he couldn't remember or didn't know its species, but he kept repeating in a voice twice as loud as it needed to be that it was indeed an *Australian* jelly. He was so worked up spit whistled in and out of the corners of his mouth, and his belly looked like microwave popcorn about to burst. The jelly was definitely unusual, with a spotted white bell the size of a basketball and long frilly tentacles. I'd seen at least fifteen different jellies that summer, but never one so large, so ball-like or so fast.

It struck me that perhaps we were the victims of some crappy prank, that some jerk like B.J. the Drywaller had stocked the cove with exotics the night before.

Professor Kramer must have heard about our findings, because he returned from base camp to long-step it out onto the flats, first studying the piddocks, then the green crab, then wading out to us, volunteers and scientists dragging behind him.

"A boat team in Budd Inlet just identified three black dolphins," he announced before he even saw the Aussie jellyfish.

"Black dolphins?" someone asked. "Aren't they southern hemisphere?"

"Indeed," the professor said. "They're usually only seen off Chile, and they're not seen much period, especially not around here."

"Neither is this," said the fat biologist, gesturing toward the large pulsing jelly. "What the hell's going on here?"

We waited, but the professor didn't come up with an answer before a member of the cephalopod team suddenly showed us an old Rainier bottle with a baby octopus crammed inside it. Then he reached down and held up another Rainier, home to a second tiny octopus.

We all quit talking and quietly looked for beer bottles around our feet.

CHAPTER 28

BASE CAMP OVERFLOWED that afternoon with scientists, volunteers, reporters and waves of spectators including the governor, the sheriff, the middle school principal and people dressed in nothing but shorts and mud. Specimens of every worm, jellyfish, anemone, clam, crab, isopod and other invertebrates cluttered five conference tables in tubs, pans and jars alongside three tables buried with rockweed, eelgrass, feather boa algae and other plants. Scientists sorted specimens and hunched over microscopes studying tiny and invisible creatures while two speedy typists catalogued everything we'd collected below the high tide lines.

So many people packed onto the spit that afternoon that five Olympia bicycle cops showed up to monitor the swarm, and lines to the Sanicans grew so long that men stood shoulder to shoulder behind the tavern as if the blackberry bushes were urinals. Almost everyone was there except my mother and Angie, who I feared had already left for North Carolina.

I saw plenty of Eleusinians, including Carolyn, who obviously wanted to hug me, but wanted it to be my idea. I saw Pansing shuffle past the specimen tables, hands respectfully behind his back, until I called his name and he smiled longer than I thought he could. I watched Judge Stegner greet everyone with firm, gracious handshakes, as if they'd come solely to show their support for him. And I watched astonished locals stare at sea life for the first time. Most of them had no idea what this was all building toward, but they saw the scientists' excitement and they sensed the crescendo.

Word had already leaked about some of the discoveries, but after Professor Kramer stood on a picnic table to give the four-thirty P.M. status report, our findings became national news. Two hours later there was more to report. Divers found *Caleurpa* seaweed—"killer algae," as the newspapers called it—along the bottom of Squaxin Cove across from Flapjack Bay where I'd first seen it. And the Chinese crabs that I'd noticed near Whiskey Point were caught tunneling in cliffs near Altman and Japhet creeks too. Then a boating team spotted what it assumed was a sick shark off Cooper Point. It had the signature dorsal fin, but divers swiftly confirmed it was something altogether different.

Mola molas look like ugly whales cut in half. And their behavior is just as bizarre: They like to munch on jellyfish while drifting on their sides out in the ocean. I boated out with Professor Kramer and two other biologists to see it ourselves. This time the freak was netted, weighed—672 pounds—and photographed, before being freed. Even then it clung to the side of the boat like some confused alien and smelled like it had already died.

Our census also turned up exotic litter, including two softball-sized glass floats Japanese fishermen once used to hold up nets, a forty-three-year-old sake bottle with a smeared message inside, two mannequin heads, a violin and three barnacled hockey gloves like the two I found in Skookumchuck.

And at dusk, a kayaking botanist noticed a flotilla of what she assumed were leaves surfing past Penrose Point. A closer look revealed shiny blue bodies with clear, saillike protrusions and dangling tentacles. She collected them in jars and paddled back to surprise the cnidaria team.

The five *Velellas* were an instant hit, examined beneath lamps and gawked at by people who'd never even heard of them. Strong westerlies often beached thousands of *Velellas* along Washington's sandy coast. But these little jellies—which looked like miniature spinnaker-flying yachts—had apparently crossed the Pacific and sailed all the way to the very entrance of Skookumchuck Bay, making them navigational wonders.

Classmates who considered science the most boring subject of all lined up to see them. And kids I'd never spoken to, including the owner of Phelps's favorite chest, surprised me with smiles, hand-slaps and big howdys. I'd never even seen Christy Decker's lips move other than to chew gum in a lazy, sexy way before she swiveled up to me and spoke in clear English, like anyone else might, about how cool the little jellies were. She got close enough for me to smell her spearmint gum, then asked if we'd ever know the whole story behind that blurred message in the sake bottle.

I mumbled a few vague sentences that may have given the impression I was heading up the team looking into that mystery. It would have been hard enough to talk to her without Phelps waving his arms and air-sucking enormous imaginary breasts a few strides behind her, but I still managed to offer a few more nonsensical answers without once looking directly at her mouth-level cantaloupes concealed beneath a COUGARS sweatshirt and no doubt locked up behind some multiclipped bra that would have taken a safecracking genius to unhook.

As the evening cooled and the disheartening smell of autumn wafted past, Professor Kramer gave the last media briefing of the day just outside the main canopy.

He admitted right off how surprised and excited everyone was, but he didn't need to speak. His tall, kinky hair, which he kept tugging higher, said as much. "One thing's for sure," he said, "you don't have to go to the Galápagos Islands to see exotic sea life." People chuckled. "Just walk out on Chatham Cove," he said, "and you might see something nobody else has. For example, despite all the biologists we have here, we still haven't identified this tiny eel we accidentally netted near Whiskey Point."

By the time the professor got around to describing the European green crab, people started twitching and murmuring then suddenly abandoned him. I assumed it was out of disbelief or boredom, but then I saw cameramen and others hustling toward the *Sanicans* to huddle around a stout bald man with restless eyes who sounded the way people sound on the news after a tornado spins through their trailer park.

"Like I said, I haven't heard out of my left ear for seventeen years." His scalp gleamed in the camera lights. "Ask my doctor if you want. I'll give you his number here in a minute so you can call him yourselves. And you gotta understand that I've never tried anything like this before. Being a man of modest faith, I didn't have high expectations about any so-called healing waters. But I heard some things were happening out here, so I drove up from Grants Pass to see for myself."

He had a singsong way of talking that pulled you close then punched you back with a mild roar. "I used to fly-fish, so I had these waders in the back of my truck, and I was just up to my knees, out past Hal's cabin, about twenty minutes ago, maybe twenty-five, when this big wind stopped, and I suddenly *heard* out of both ears." He covered one ear, then the next. "And I still can!" His teeth were the color of rust.

He deflected questions with hairy hands, bobbing his head until everyone quieted, then said he'd already talked to people who swore the mud had cleared up their psoriasis. He also said a woman from Utah claimed the arthritis in her knee had vanished after wading for a half hour. He then confided, in his come-closer voice, that word was spreading—not that he necessarily believed it—that the bay's healing powers were likely to peak at high tide the following day.

He kept talking beneath the lights long after the scientists lost interest and returned, snickering, to their monotonous tally.

Once darkness settled, the news crews left and rain fell hard and fast in marble-sized drops that made us stop counting to stare up at our thin plastic ceiling that had turned so noisy we had to shout species' names to each other.

Soon camp thinned to a couple dozen bloodshot scientists and volunteers sorting and counting while night teams continued dropping crab pots, dragging plankton nets and shining massive flashlights into black water. I helped dizzy biologists keep track of what they'd already counted. Nobody needed to point me out anymore, which was nice. Even my father, whose cold had dropped into his chest, urged me to stay as long as I wanted and just reminded me to eat, which I hadn't.

I took a break after eleven to call my mother. It'd been building in me for hours, this desire to share every last highlight of the day with her before she went to bed. I also intended to at least try to apologize for being ungrateful when she'd offered to help, knowing she'd hold on to that until I said something that helped her let it go.

My cousin complained about me calling so late, then informed me that my mother and Aunt Janet had flown to Chicago for the weekend.

Chicago.

It'd come up that spring when my mother abruptly pointed out to my father that she never traveled anymore, that she hadn't even gone to New York, Chicago or any *real* city *since Miles was born.*

My father shuffled out in boxers, a toothbrush in his mouth. If he noticed the phone shaking in my hand, he didn't say anything.

"What's their phone number in Chicago?" I asked my cousin.

"What?"

"I need their number."

"You can't call them *now*. It's two hours later back there."

"It's an emergency."

"Yeah?"

My voice rose. "My father is real sick."

Dad didn't say anything as I dialed and told some lady my mother's room number. It took a few rings until I heard Mom's hushed voice and groggy Aunt Janet in the background demanding to know who was calling.

"It's Miles," Mom whispered away from the phone, then to me, "What is it? What's wrong?"

"Dad said you were gonna be here today," I said. "Everybody else was."

There was a long pause in which I heard Aunt Janet's muffled voice and Mom responding to her again, then to me: "That isn't why you called at two in the morning, Miles." There was worry in her voice. "You didn't get hurt, did you? Is your father all right?"

"Even Alice McDonald and Annette Rankin were there," I almost shouted. "There were like seventy-three scientists and maybe a hundred volunteers on the flats, in the water and at base camp. And Professor Kramer had me tell everyone where to find everything."

After a pause, she whispered, "Tell me what happened, but *softly*. I'm right here."

I listed off as much as I could remember. It must have taken five minutes. And I didn't quiet down or apologize for anything. Every sentence rang like a pounded nail.

When I ran out of air, she said, "Sorry I missed it." She wasn't whispering anymore. "And sorry for leaving the way I did. It was something I had to do, Miles, but it wasn't fair to you."

I was so startled I wanted to ask her to repeat herself. I felt the way fish must feel when they jump from heavy water into ridiculously light air, but all that came out was: "Me too." When she didn't say anything, I added, "Dad's got a bad cold. I think he needs your magic soup."

By the time I returned to base camp, the scientists who weren't insomniacs had already peeled away for naps. So there were just six of us at the end, counting to the rhythm of rain determined to make up for its two-month absence in a single night.

Olympia rain rarely calls for hats, much less umbrellas, but this was a waterfall. And by one forty-five in the morning I saw the auras of the remaining biologists, or maybe it was just backlit mist. What I do know is that I saw a blue light around every one of their heads. And Florence had taught me that people with blue auras are relaxed and ready for anything, which suited these people perfectly.

Professor Kramer ordered me home an hour later. I took the long way, splashing past our house and Angie's dark window, through the deep puddles and all the way to Florence's cabin.

I had to duck out of the rain beneath an eave to see her, mouth open, in her chair behind the curtains. It relieved me to see her chest rise. I thought about waking her and helping her to bed, but decided against it. I didn't want to scare her, or lift her. Plus, I knew she preferred to sleep in her chair.

My boots felt so heavy climbing my stairs that I wondered what Florence's feet felt like on a bad day. I tried to imagine her as a cartwheeling young woman resembling some beauty with a musical name like Sophia Loren. It was impossible.

I left my clothes in damp clumps and collapsed, but, of course, I couldn't sleep.

Images of my mother played on my eyelids. I tried to *see* her in our house. I saw her frowning at her weedy garden. I saw her in Aunt Janet's huge recliner. I marched her apology back through my head so many times I couldn't remember the differences between what she'd said and what I'd hoped to hear. But I still couldn't put her inside our little house. And I still couldn't sleep.

So I read about the deepest canyons in the Pacific, about trenches so vast you could hide Mount Everest in them, about scalding vents on the floor of the abyss where, amazingly, life thrived.

Diagonal rain kept the crowd small for the closing ceremony the next morning when Professor Kramer rattled off the final species tallies: 314 invertebrates, 32 fish, 7 mammals and 186 plants for a total of 539 species of tidal and subtidal life. He also listed thirteen invasive species, another eleven rarely found so far north and mentioned that we still had no idea what to call a two-inch translucent eel with lime-green eyes.

About fifty scientists, volunteers and spectators applauded the findings, or maybe it was an ovation for life itself—or for the record-breaking rain, which continued falling so hard it knocked pinecones loose, ripped leaves off madrones and made it hard to hear the professor.

"As much as anything," he told us, "this exercise serves as a reminder that we are just one of hundreds, and actually thousands, of species who call South Sound home. And I also hope it teaches us that we need to keep better track of invasives or risk further jeopardizing our waters."

When his hooded eyes found me, he waved me forward until I sheepishly obeyed and climbed onto the table in my mother's huge yellow raincoat. He then wrapped his long arm across my back and shouted, "None of this would have been possible if Miles O'Malley hadn't put his love for sea life into action. If Miles hadn't spent his summer trying to see what's out here, there would have been no reason for us all to . . ."

His words didn't sound or feel real. What the exercise had proved to me was that what went on that summer had nothing to do with me. Not a little. *Nothing*. What I'd seen was just a sliver of the new life bubbling in our waters, and the only reason I'd seen more than most was because I was the only one looking.

It was a huge relief, in a way, to know that I hadn't actually been *selected* for anything, but I admit being disappointed to know, for certain, that I was as ordinary as I felt.

I was too tired to concentrate on the professor's voice and the rain at the same time, so I just listened to rain until applause hammered me from all sides. Then either the professor bumped me or I mindlessly shuffled because I lost my footing on that wet tabletop and skated slightly, then somehow miraculously righted myself in mid-swoon and managed to smile, which sparked even more ridiculous applause.

CHAPTER 29

R ACHEL CARSON WONDERED aloud about the romantic links
   between sea life and the highest tides.

She wrote about European oysters, North African sea urchins and tropical worms whose spawning patterns are so synchronized with the tides that if you were shipwrecked you might eventually figure out the day of the year and the time of the day by tracking their sex lives. She also marveled at grunions, flashy little fish that somehow sense the instant when waves surge highest along California's southern beaches.

Shortly after full moons between March and August, grunions gather to surf ashore. They wait for the highest tide of the month to splash as high as it can, then thousands of them ride the subsequent waves onto the beach where they lie momentarily shocked, unable to breathe. Then the female drops her eggs and the male fertilizes them in the time it takes for the next wave to arrive.

If you came across this ritual in the moonlight, it might look like thousands of distraught fish attempting suicide in unison before abruptly changing their minds and returning to sea. And chances are you wouldn't notice their buried eggs, which enjoy two weeks of peace in the sand until the next highest tide of the month washes high enough to haul freshly hatched grunions away.

Rachel Carson puzzled over whether it was the pressure or movement of the water during the extreme tides, or perhaps the brightness of the moon that told grunions when to slam themselves into the beaches and make instant love in the sand.

See, even Rachel Carson didn't understand everything.

I slept after the closing ceremonies, a dreamless, dead-boy's sleep that wasn't disturbed by the trespassers tromping to our door or by the little earthquake thirty-five miles southeast of Olympia. When I finally woke it was because all five feet ten inches of Kenny Phelps had banged his head into my slanted ceiling and was breaking his cussing record while his poncho dripped onto my filthy carpet.

"Get the fuck up," he said, as if everything were my fault. "That big-ass tide of yours is coming in."

I propped myself up and squinted out the window at broken madrone limbs surfing past our property. I checked the clock. High tide was more than two hours away, but the water was already high and swift, the wind rowdier than it had been in months and the rain still punishing gutters and manufacturing fog to the point that the steep forest across the bay was nothing more than a darker smudge between identical grays of water and sky.

Phelps told me about the three-point-two earthquake that he'd initially mistook for a Fort Lewis mortar round. "My butt is here to testify that the toilet seat shook," he said, then told me that a big crowd had already gathered downtown to greet the rising storm. "My brother says it's blowing three-footers straight down the inlet. Let's go."

I heard voices and glanced outside to see five chatty blobs of rain gear in the driveway. One knocked hard on our front door.

Phelps leaned over my bed, dripping onto my sheets, glaring out the window. "Your old man home?"

"He's got a Sunday shift."

Another one knocked harder. Then I saw the shape of a television camera bulging beneath a poncho.

"They don't know you live up here, right?" Phelps asked. "Of course not. Who the fuck would live up here but trolls?"

I tried to overhear the trespassers while pulling on my army shorts and hunting for a sweater for the first time since spring. Halfway down the back steps I whispered that I was hungry. Without looking back, Phelps silently slipped me a green Starburst.

We rode downtown until we heard, then saw, the cheering mob on the finger of land pointing north past the marina and the log yard where steel-colored waves slapped the stilts beneath the offices of KOLY 1220 AM and shattered along the bouldered shoreline, spraying sheets twenty feet high.

Phelps and I slalomed through the crowd until it got too thick and we had to walk to the front where eleven soaked men in orange Public Works vests stacked white sacks of sand. A hundred people swirled behind them, the sort of crowd that gathered at Sylvester Park whenever there was a free concert or a bad war. As the men furiously built their barricade, it became clear by their expressions that they knew the mob wasn't on their side, that people were rooting for the storm.

The second time the waves cleared the boulders they swooshed around the sandbags and across pavement toward the log yards and downtown. I saw a tattooed kid knocked off his skateboard, a lady with a camcorder washed off her feet and lots of people peeling seaweed off their faces and chests. Then a larger wave struck, cleared the sandbags and sloshed calf-deep through the crowd. Someone started shouting at us to stay the hell away from the high-voltage radio tower. People gaped up at the three-hundred-foot spire they hadn't noticed until then, spilling backward into each other until a few tripped onto the flooded pavement, sending dozens more backpedaling and tumbling into each other again as another wave washed over those who hadn't yet risen and swamped the base of the tower.

That's when I recognized Blister, of all people, babbling to someone in a blue King 5 rain jacket. He leveled a hand at his chin and scanned the hysterical mob, still yapping nonstop. I felt it coming, but it still chilled me to see him jab his finger at me, as if pointing out a bank robber.

As the cameraman and his color-coordinated sidekicks scurried my way, I got on my bike, and yelled, "Excuse me!" five straight times until I splashed through enough puddles and around enough panicked people to break free.

Phelps later said he never saw me ride any better on that oversized three-speed than when I wove through that mob, then pumped past the logs to Marine Drive and around a pileup of smoking cars, past the Farmer's Market, up Capitol Way to Fourth and across the bridge to the west side.

By the time we'd pedaled back to Skookumchuck, steam wafted off us like smoke and the storm eased slightly, the rain still falling with conviction but not showing off anymore. Even the wind relaxed, although it still heaved occasional rollers over the bay's lowest borders.

Spencer Spit had never looked so small. The rising tide had shrunk the meadows around the tavern and pulled the cabins to the fringe of the bay. And even without the scientists and volunteers there were more people on the spit than ever.

Phelps and I walked our bikes through the swarm, dazed by how swiftly so many people had congregated. A small group prayed beneath Hal's cross while dozens more lined up shoulder to shoulder along the water's edge the way fishermen did when the salmon ran—but without poles.

One had an eye patch. Two had crutches. I watched a lady cast aside her black cane and inch into the bay on legs so white and veiny they could have been used to teach anatomy. I saw another lady dunk her bald head, and a young mother in a denim skirt haul her crying baby into the bay. Still others waded back to shore with buckets of mud.

As we rolled toward the bridge, we saw a tall, bearded man practicing slow-motion karate, and behind him a pretty lady selling "self-opening miracle umbrellas" and telling everyone that it was less than an hour to high tide, which reminded me of the local oddity that the tide peaked eighteen minutes later in Skookumchuck Bay than it did downtown.

We pushed ahead. The atmosphere changed entirely near the Heron bridge where the tavern crowd overflowed into the street and older teenagers blasted Phelps-like rock just off the east side of the bridge, which hovered slightly more than a foot above the aggressive incoming current.

Phelps spotted his brother and stopped to worship the music with him, leaving me on my own to check on my house and Florence.

The tallest waves whacked the top of our stilts, but I didn't bother to go inside. If the water was that high, Florence's floor was already soaked.

I sprinted until I had to jog, then sprinted again once I saw that standing water had almost encircled Florence's cabin. I splashed to her door and burst through it without knocking.

It took me longer than usual to adjust to the gloom. I heard water sloshing against floorboards and smelled the sea as clearly as if we were rafting. Yet the floor, amazingly, looked dry.

When I finally made out Florence, it was comforting to see her safe in her chair, not waiting for me to pull her off the toilet, or worse.

I apologized for not checking in earlier as I crossed the room, panting, moving from one pool of dust-twirled light to another, until I saw her new forehead gash and noticed her nose was larger than ever.

"Ahhhh Florence." Guilt flooded me. "I'll get some ice." Her closed eyes didn't worry me. She often rested them. And I'd seen a crusty film on the corner of her lips many times. It was the set of her mouth that shook me. Had she fallen so hard that she broke her jaw?

"Florence? You okay?"

The instant I realized she was dead my stomach burned and my throat clogged, then everything slowed way down.

I don't know exactly what I did for the next few minutes other than that I eventually stopped looking at her and began lifting books off the floor and onto tables and counters.

I think I was waiting for my mind to catch up with my eyes and tell me what to do. Slowly, it occurred to me that I should've already called 911 to see if someone could revive her. Maybe she isn't dead! Yet I was too scared to touch her, and I'd seen enough dead fish and seals and birds to know what death looked like.

So I continued stacking books and listening to the tide splash beneath me until it hissed through the boards near the fridge, and I finally noticed the blue pills next to her chair.

I stuffed them into my raincoat. I don't know if Florence wanted me to do that, but I did it. Then I dialed 911 and told a busy lady that Florence Dalessandro had died.

When she asked for an address, I gave her mine and told her that Florence was two driveways over. Then I splashed back out into the rejuvenated storm to feed the rest of the sleeping pills to the blackberries.

I ran back inside, planted the empty pill vial in the middle of the kitchen garbage and flung the bag outside beyond the growing puddle. When I shut the door behind me again, I realized I was panting. I drank straight from the faucet. It felt like a selfish act. Where were the sirens? Should I call again?

The floor was noisier than ever, wheezing and gurgling like some slurping monster. Yet it was still mostly dry, except for the kitchen, where it had seeped all the way from the fridge to the tiny dinner table. Then I noticed the floor was actually damp all the way back to the bathroom, and beyond that to the bedroom door.

Florence had always kept it shut, as if hiding or preserving something. I'd never more than glanced in there, and when I stepped inside now what I saw didn't fit. The rest of the cabin felt like Florence, but her bedroom could have been anybody's— simple green curtains, matching bedside tables, a green and gold bedspread fitted at the corners and three identically framed photos perfectly spaced on the far wall.

I assumed the old man with the familiar lips was her father. The other two black-and-whites were of a younger Florence alongside two similar-looking women who had to be her older sisters. Florence still looked like herself back then, but her eyes fit comfortably in her face. They still looked oversized, but in a pretty and unintimidating way. It hit me looking at her sisters that shuffling old Florence was the last in a line, the baby of her family just like me.

A louder splash struck beneath me and snorted through planks in the living room. I burst out to see the oval rug darkening in front of Florence's chair, water beading and draining along its edges. I glanced guiltily at Florence, as if she might wake long enough to scold me for snooping in her bedroom while her house sank.

I felt as if I'd been given a test I couldn't possibly pass. I knew that I should wash her face and set her jaw straight, but I was afraid I'd make her look worse, and what if her dentures popped out? I considered trying to carry her outside, but didn't know if I could lift her without her help, and feared I'd end up dragging her across the wet floor. And what would I do once I got her outside?

The next wave shook the cabin just as I hoisted the last of her books off the floor and watched two countertop stacks collapse. I restacked at hyperspeed, knowing it was futile, but at least it kept me in motion. When I looked around again, I saw the entire floor was soaked and pooling, a couple inches deep near the fridge.

I slid the footrest toward Florence, without looking at her face, and lifted her wet heels off the floor, holding my breath, afraid of what I might smell. Her legs were heavy, as if they'd gained weight in death. I scooted the stool beneath them and heard more water spitting through floor cracks as I lowered her feet.

After another wave hissed beneath me and squirted a loud foot-high fountain in the kitchen, I burst outside for air and stumble-waded into the gravel where I waited like a mindless guard dog until I finally heard a siren.

The nodding ambulance man and his blank-faced sidekick listened to me breathlessly explain how often Florence fell, and how she'd apparently had another big tumble earlier that day. The last thing the man said to me was, "Are *you* okay?"

He probably saw guilt, not pain.

After the ambulance rolled away, I went into the world to tell someone that my best friend was dead.

Of course, there was nobody to tell.

The Stegner house was empty and my father was still at work. The only other people I saw were trespassing strangers loping up and down driveways to get closer looks at the still-rising tide.

I ran home and called my father's work number, but hung up once his recorder kicked on. I did the same with Aunt Janet's after I discovered my mother had checked out of Chicago. It surprised me to want her the most, but I'd never been miserable without her.

Being alone in our house spooked me, especially with water hissing beneath me again, so I ran toward the bridge and the music, trying not to think, kicking any images of Florence from my head before they had a chance to root, proving to my mother, even if she wasn't around to witness it, that I could handle even this without crying.

It was easy to pick Phelps out alongside his brother and a dozen others like him in identically faded jeans, rocking in unison, the water and the music rising together. As dueling guitars took off, Phelps stepped in front of the older boys, slung his imaginary strap behind his head and began to play air guitar with such convincing intensity a cheering section egged him on. Phelps couldn't have noticed. His head was bouncing, his bangs swinging, his whole body committed to the electric crescendo blasting from his fingertips.

I intended to wait the song out before pulling him aside, but it refused to end, and there was way too much blood racing through me to just stand there. So I dashed back across our land in time to watch the tide clear the frontage of the Stegner property. It wasn't a wave or two splashing over. The entire bay curled over the top, the way a bathtub will if you leave the water running, drowning dandelions and huckleberries and flat golden fields already drenched with rainwater just below where the cattle liked to graze. Two cows grunted and thudded toward higher ground. The others soon followed, except for the two fattest ones who kept eating as if grass were worth dying for.

I could tell the tide had cleared the bay's eastern banks by the way the firs and cedars dragged in the water, and I ran south along the changing shoreline, splashing past the Ericksons' horse fields where the tide was clearing that lip too, and on to the LeMays' vacant pastureland where I ran high enough on the knoll to get a full view of Sunset Estates. Five men were stacking sandbags, but it was obvious they were losing. Enough water had already pooled in the largest foundation to reflect the moody sky. I ran higher and looked wildly about, panting, doing my best to not let Florence flicker in my head.

Luckily there was so much to *see*. The bay looked half again as big as it ever did, with large branches and trees swirling toward its southern end along with two skiffs, three canoes and a floating dock ghosting toward the swamped estates. Why was the tide *still* coming?

I sprinted back to the Stegner house and tried their door and shouted Angie's name even though I knew she wasn't there. Then I saw their sun-bleached Coleman canoe wind-coasting in the flooded yard. I waded to it, found two paddles inside, dragged it toward deeper water and climbed carefully aboard without flipping it.

The wind slackened and the low gray sky began to rise and give way to blue. Even the rain turned to mist. I kneeled near the stern, with the bow aloft, paddling toward the bridge and the noise as the fatso moon cleared the eastern tree line, playing it cool, as if it were just another innocent cloud. I closed my eyes and tried to feel its pull. When that didn't work, I howled at it. It wasn't something I thought about. I just started howling.

I'd read that it was a myth that wolves howl *at* the moon. They howl before a hunt as a sign of togetherness and they howl out of loneliness, but the howling itself supposedly has nothing to do with the moon. I'd also read that some Indians think the howls of wolves are the lost souls of the dead trying to return to earth. Who knows? All I know is I howled at that moon, and I let it have it. It turned into more of a scream than a howl, and when I ran out of air I reloaded and did it again. Then again, and again, until my throat stopped me.

It was easy to see that the tide had risen well past the timbers bracing our floor beams, making the O'Malley home look like a sinking houseboat. But I paddled past it without caring about it or anything inside it and continued toward the bridge and the ruckus, battling the current with short quick strokes until I felt it surrender.

The tide, simply and finally, quit climbing.

CHAPTER 30

T HE BARTENDERS LET everyone stroll outside the partially
swamped tavern to gawk at the high water and loiter, cocktails
in hand, near the bridge where the head-bobbing rockers blasted
the same song yet again. Or maybe it had never ended, but Kenny
Phelps was definitely still the bandleader, air-guitaring his way
toward another neck sprain.

Up the shoreline, dozens, maybe hundreds, waded beyond the
swamped cabins. I didn't give any of it more than glances because I
was pretty sure I'd seen Angie Stegner strutting across the Heron
bridge with phony Frankie and my favorite dog.

I dragged the canoe into the high grass next to the nearly
submerged bridge, then ran in the direction I'd seen her strut. I
slammed into some lady reading a tide table and toppled a baby
stroller that luckily was empty. I didn't stop to say sorry. I felt the
way you feel when you're suddenly lost at a county fair and you
realize the lousy odds of ever finding your parents again. I don't
know how many people I would've normally recognized, but
everyone either looked strange or like Angie. I was so convinced

I saw her twice that I actually felt relief in my chest both times, before giving up, bending over and gasping, unsure what to do next other than find something to drink. I was returning to the bridge to try to grab Phelps when I heard a bark from the far side of the tavern and found Frankie hurling an orange tennis ball into swirling suds.

Angie was looking the other way, staring intently at the overwhelmed bay. She looked remarkably ordinary from that distance, in her baseball cap and cutoffs. When I came up on her and she slowly recognized me, her hands flew off her hips and encircled me.

"Miles," she said. "My sweet Miles." She hugged me so hard tears popped out of me. Once that started I couldn't stop. It was like the worst case of hiccups, or a laugh that you can't stop even if someone crams a BB gun up your nose. I cried so hard I sounded like a sea lion with a sore throat. Angie rocked me like she used to until I could tell her about Florence, which got me going again until I was empty.

The next thing I remember was hearing Frankie tell someone to beat it.

When I looked up, I saw a blurry couple about twenty feet from us. "Have some decency," Frankie yelled. "Back off!"

"Miles?" said the lady next to what I slowly realized was a cameraman pointing a lens at me. She sounded familiar, but looked out of focus. "Will you please talk to me about this amazing flood you predicted?"

Frankie ordered them to beat it again, and the cameraman started yelling back, warning Frankie to stop telling them what the fuck to do. It wasn't until Lizzy splashed ashore with the ball and shook the bay onto everyone that I placed the lady's voice and wide-set eyes. But by then Angie was pulling me, then running me around the wet side of the tavern toward the bridge where the highest tide in fifty-three years still hovered.

After I pointed out her canoe, Angie said we'd ride it out. I didn't understand what she meant until we were hauling it across the bridge, then paddling north, with me in the stern, even though balancewise it made sense for her to be back there.

Once we glided around Penrose Point everything quieted, and Angie kept my mind off Florence, pointing out the clusters of moon jellyfish pulsing through brown plankton blooms and the eight cormorants breaking formation, as if disoriented by the way the high water swallowed their roosts. "Look at that larch," she said, aiming her paddle at the lone yellow tree in the green hillside. "It's so bright it looks like it's on fire."

Angie left most of the paddling to me and yakked nonstop about how she'd been jamming that afternoon with a friend who played tenor sax, and how they were conspiring to pull together an all-girl band. She also mentioned that she'd decided to bag Carolina and go to Evergreen instead, for at least a semester. "My father needs me," she said, then raved about some new antidepressant called Pixie or Pixil, or something like that, which let her feel like herself even if it did make her sleepy. "For better or worse," she said, tapping her forehead, "it's all Angie in here again."

She saluted the bowling-ball head of the harbor seal that popped up to study us, then congratulated an early-returning chum salmon and giggled at the five mallards skid-landing nearby like off-balance seaplanes as the tide turned and began to pull us out.

Half-submerged logs, blackberry bushes and random shrubs followed us, as did two empty canoes ghosting along the far shoreline and a green kayak that the tide was stealing too. I saw a long narrow flash near the surface that reminded me of my oarfish obsession. It turned out to be an innocent reflection, another trickery of light, but believe me when I tell you that a real oarfish did show up two weeks later in the newspaper. It measured out at thirteen feet three inches, and took three oystermen to hold it for the photo, above which loomed an unflattering picture of Judge

Stegner and an article about an investigation into some favor he gave an old roommate.

Angie stopped paddling and asked if my mother had told me when she was coming back home.

"'In a while,' is all she said. Dad keeps saying she'll be back any day, but I doubt it."

Angie didn't try to talk me out of that, probably because she knew I was right, but maybe because she could tell that in the space of a summer I'd learned that everything was changing, including me. I grew six inches during the next ten months, then my voice dropped and tiny Miles O'Malley slipped away.

Angie turned halfway around in the bow so that she could look at me when she asked how the hell I knew the tide would come up so high. "Florence," I said.

"How'd she know?"

Over the next few weeks, we all learned a lot about what caused our crazy flood. Oceanographers admitted the original tidal prediction could have been off by a foot or two. Maybe the moon swung closer than 216,000 miles from the earth. Who knows? Plus, the tide tables couldn't take weather into consideration, and in our case, low pressure raised the sea, as did six inches of rain. Seismologists also pointed out that the same earthquake Phelps felt through his toilet seat likely squeezed even more rainwater from the soil that spilled into streams and rivers that lifted our bays too. Then, of course, the guilty wind played its part. And climatologists were quick to warn that the Sound was rising an inch a year anyway, and that Olympia would eventually struggle to fend off the sea without pumps and dikes. But even if you bought all that, it still didn't add up to water as high as we experienced, or make it any less remarkable.

What also followed was a complicated scientific explanation for all the strange sea life and debris that showed up that summer. El Niño had warmed the Pacific more than people realized, which pushed black dolphins, oarfish, Mola molas and other sea life farther north. We also learned that the huge north Pacific whirlpool, which often traps trash for decades, got ripped wide open by some timely westerlies that blew garbage and sea life into the Strait of Juan de Fuca. And the timing was perfect yet again for brisk northerlies and the strongest currents of the year to blow and suck glass floats, a Japanese street sign, a lost cargo load of hockey gloves and perhaps an ailing ragfish and an enormous squid down the Sound's narrow plumbing into our shallow harbors.

Humans were likely responsible for the rest of it. The killer algae probably got its foothold when a careless aquarium owner dumped it into the bay. And the Australian jelly and the Chinese crabs most likely hitched rides as babies in ballast water that Korean freighters sucked up in foreign ports and spat out in South Sound.

People lost interest once the explanations rolled in. Some even got angry, as if scientists were determined to squeeze the magic out of everything. But I saw gaps between what the scientists said and what actually happened, and I heard the astonishment behind their words. But by then, most of the people seeking miracles had stopped coming around anyway, especially after that bald crowd-pleaser who'd claimed to have spontaneously regained his hearing was written up as a serial hoaxer with a fake doctor and perfectly fine ears.

Yet none of that answers Angie's question.

How had Florence known the tidal predications would fall so short on this one freaky day? My guess is the old lady who was ultimately called the flood's lone casualty *didn't* know. It would take quite a while to recount all the predictions Florence told me that turned out dead wrong. My answer to Angie was that I had no idea how Florence knew.

The sun had only been gone for two days, but it already felt like a friendly stranger on my back as we paddled past Chatham Cove. Amazingly, I felt the way you feel after you've had a head cold for so long you forget how terrific it is to just feel *normal*.

"You realize that they had eleven hotshot scientists study that squid I found?" I asked Angie. "Well, they still didn't learn a dang thing from it—not even what it eats or how fast it swims or what its natural color is. Isn't that awesome? People seem to think we already know everything, that science is about what's already known. It isn't!" I watched the back of her head nod, but could tell I was losing her. "I mean we're just now getting around to dropping tiny, one-man submarines into the deepest ocean trenches. And they're finding all kinds of things we didn't know existed, including all these deepwater freaks that hang out next to hot vents." I shared some explorer's descriptions I'd read of six-foot tube worms, orange frogfish, viper sharks and colorful unnamed creatures that looked like hand puppets.

She kept nodding, but when she turned to sweep bangs off her face I could see her eyes were closed.

"Even a few years ago they didn't expect to find any life way down there," I continued. "And now all this crazy stuff is showing up. It's as if we'd finally got to the top of Everest and found blue owls and winged leopards enjoying the thin air. I mean they're discovering hundreds of new fish species *every year* now, which is terrific, but I kinda hope the ocean doesn't give up all of its secrets before I can maybe help discover some of them. I know that sounds selfish, but do you know what I mean?"

The more I talked the stronger I felt. Or maybe I talked out of a fear of being cornered with my thoughts. Regardless, I overflowed with words and I eventually—big surprise—rattled on about Rachel Carson. "Her brothers and sisters were so much older than her that she was basically an only child like me. But get this: She grew up near *Pittsburgh* and didn't even see the ocean or a tidal pool until she was twenty-two. Can you believe that? The lady who became the voice of the ocean didn't even see salt water until she was older than you. And you know one of the coolest things about her? She wasn't intimidated by time. Most people's imagination doesn't extend beyond a hundred years. Rachel Carson could imagine billions of years without blinking. At the end of *The Sea Around Us,* she summed up the entire history and role of the ocean in two sentences: 'In its mysterious past it encompasses all the dim origins of life and receives in the end, after, it may be, many transmutations, the dead husks of that same life. For all at last return to the sea—to Oceanus, the ocean river, like the ever-flowing stream of time, the beginning and the end.'"

Angie's head sagged and bobbed, then she stiffened and carefully turned in her seat and put her dreamy eyes on me. "I need to stretch out."

"You want to head back?" I dragged my paddle to begin a U-turn, and realized the current was already too strong to fight.

"I just want to stretch my legs," she said.

I shrugged. "Where?"

She braced herself on the rails and crawled toward me on her knees. There aren't many stupider things you can do in a canoe, but I didn't try to talk her out of it. When she got all the way up to me, the canoe wobbling on its stern, she pulled my knees apart and gracefully turned yet again, then leaned back against my seat and extended dark, mosquito-bitten legs. Her naked shoulders pressed against my knees as we drifted swiftly past Whiskey Point, our bow riding high.

I relaxed my legs to help her get comfortable, and eventually she settled, then lolled her head into my lap so that I could inhale the leafy smell of her hair and examine her whole face up close. I tried not to stare because I was pretty sure she was the sort of person who could see through eyelids, but I felt her body slacken, and when it was obvious she was sleeping I counted her freckles until I couldn't resist touching her eyebrow ring or running two careful fingers through her bangs.

"The ocean will wait for you, Miles," she whispered. "And so will I."

Maybe I didn't hear her right. It was just the faintest of whispers. She might have been babbling in her sleep. But I didn't let any of that stop me from taking her words exactly the way I wanted to take them.

After her breathing slowed and her lips parted, I tried to paddle without thinking about Florence, without moving below my waist, without flipping the canoe or waking the magnificent Angie Stegner. That all worked fine until my paddle plowed into rubbery water, and I glanced down at hundreds of pulsing moon jellies to the right, then thousands more to the left, an endless gaggle of fringed, see-through flowers packed so tightly together they changed the texture and color of the bay in the silvery glare of the forgotten sun. The more I looked the more there were, galaxies upon galaxies of brainless jellies, riding the powerful current, pressing up against the canoe, carrying us out to sea.

ACKNOWLEDGMENTS

Thanks to everyone who helped make *The Highest Tide* happen.

Kim Witherspoon and Karen Rinaldi embraced the story and provided vision and support. Alan Rammer shared his knowledge and love of tidal life. Panio Gianopoulos offered deft editing. Jess Walter inspired me in countless ways. Alexis Hurley kept me sane.

Others who helped in various ways include Delia Whitehead, Andy Parker, Steve Kroeger, Reid Phelps, Matt Willkens and Craig Welch. Thanks also to my parents, Levin and Janet, sister Jennie and daughter Grace.

But without Denise's daily gift of patience, wisdom and laughter this novel would not have been possible, nor so fun to write.

A NOTE ON THE TYPE

The text of this book is set in Adobe Caslon, named after the English punch-cutter and type founder William Caslon I (1692–1766). Caslon's rather old-fashioned types were modeled on seventeenth-century Dutch designs, but found wide acceptance throughout the English-speaking world for much of the eighteenth century until being replaced by newer types toward the end of the century. Used in 1776 to print the Declaration of Independence, they were revived in the nineteenth century, and have been popular ever since, particularly among fine printers. There are several digital versions, of which Carol Twombly's Adobe Caslon is one.